SHORTY IS IN *Love* WITH A REAL *One* 4

A NOVEL BY

SHVONNE LATRICE

© 2020
Published by First Class
Publishing Group
www.TheShvonneLatrice.com

ALL RIGHTS RESERVED

Any unauthorized reprint or use of the material is prohibited. No part of this book may be reproduced or transmitted in any form or by any means, electronic, or mechanical, including photocopying, recording, or by any information storage without express permission by the publisher.

This is an original work of fiction. Names, characters, places and incidents are either products of the author's imagination or are used fictitiously and any resemblance to actual persons, living or dead is entirely coincidental.

Contains explicit language & adult themes suitable for ages 16+

$19.99
ISBN 978-1-966375-20-3

CHAPTER ONE

Oden Bishop

I got home about an hour later, and found Khyle watching TV on the couch. She had on a thin nightshirt that clung to her small stomach lightly. The living room was dark, but the TV beamed on her, showing all of the beauty that she possessed.

"What you watching?" I asked, about to make my way over to her.

"*Facts of Life,*" she responded, with the last word trailing off at the sound of the door.

Someone had knocked, so I stopped and turned around to look through the peephole. I saw my father standing there looking like he'd been locked away, smoking nonstop. When Khyle was about to speak, I put my hand up to stop her. I watched my dad through the peephole, resisting the urge to snatch the door open and whoop his ass for how he'd done me as a kid all the way up until now. But I didn't because I needed to let that part of my life go.

He knocked three more times before he finally gave up and walked away. I kept my eyes on him through the door until he disappeared into the dark. When I couldn't see him anymore, I went to the back to change clothes, and then joined Khyle on the couch to watch TV with her.

"Who was that, Oden?"

"Nobody, trust me."

She looked at me for a little while, and then cupped my face to kiss my lips a few times. She then draped her arms around my neck, so I hugged her body as tightly as I could with my eyes closed.

"I love you, Oden, and I will always be here for you," she whispered as we sat there, embracing.

I quickly wiped the lone tear that was waiting to fall from my eyes before saying, "I know baby, and I love you too. You and my son."

It was crazy that she knew exactly who was on the other side of that door.

"Are you hungry? I can make you something to eat." She pulled away.

"This late?"

"I can be fast. You love pasta and it doesn't take me that long to make," she giggled, getting up from the couch. "I got it." She looked at me when I tried to help her.

As I sat there scrolling through my lineup of text messages in my iPhone, I heard another knock at the door. Knowing it was that deadbeat ass nigga again, I shot up off the couch ready to tear into his ass. He had me fucked up. I tried to let him go, but since he obviously wanted this tongue-lashing and possible fade, I was gonna give it to him.

I darted to the door, but when I snatched it open, I saw two policemen standing there. Confused, I said nothing for a little bit as we all stared at one another.

"Can I help you, officers?"

I glanced over to my left to see Khyle watching me from the kitchen with a worried expression on her face.

"You Oden Bishop?" one asked.

"Yeah."

"Mr. Bishop, you're under arrest for the murder of Huelo Kaiwi," he replied, going on to read me my Miranda rights as the other one snatched me out of the door and slammed me up against the wall.

"Oden!" Khyle shrieked when she came out of my townhouse.

"Get back, young lady!" the officer barked. "I said get back!"

"Don't be fucking yelling at her, muthafucka!" I hissed, ready to duke it out with that nigga. Handcuffed or not, wasn't nobody about to be disrespectful to my girl.

"Shut up!" the initial officer gritted, as they yanked me off the wall and towards the patrol car.

"Baby, it's gonna be fine! I promise, aight?" I shouted to Khyle as they placed me in the car. "My lawyer's number is in my phone! You know the cod—" I was cut off when they slammed the backdoor in my face.

Khyle stood in the doorway, wearing that same look she wore the night I caught Huelo trying to rape her. It just reminded me that what I'd done to him was all worth it.

But what I needed right now was to figure out who the fuck dropped the dime on me. And once I did, they were gonna be just as dead as Huelo's ass.

***

Three hours later...

As soon as we got to the precinct, two detectives questioned me for fucking hours about Huelo; how I knew him, and all that bullshit. They were getting nowhere because they had nothing connecting me to him. No one had ever seen the two of us talking, we had no classes together, and he wasn't connected to anybody I knew; well, he was but they obviously didn't know that. Somehow, somewhere, they hadn't figured out that he knew Khyle, and luckily, my lawyer showed up before they could.

"I'd like to talk to my client alone, please," my lawyer Lawrence came in.

He was an older gentleman, and very good at what he did. My mentor, Akachi, told me as soon as I took the reigns on his business, to get a lawyer and a prestigious one with a high win rate. I did my research for months, and finally decided on Lawrence Merry. He was expensive, and I'd never needed him in the past, but boy was I glad I listened to Akachi.

Once the two detectives left, Lawrence sat down at the cold steel table across from me. He was smiling, but I didn't quite see a reason why just yet.

"I'm gonna have you free in about a 15 minutes, I just wanted to let you know," he cleared his throat, as he looked through some files.

"How? They claim they have hard evidence against me."

"Look son, they're trying to charge you for a murder, yet they have no weapon and most importantly, no body. Right now, Huelo is simply a missing person's case and nothing more. For all we know, he could still be out there somewhere… right?" He gave me this look telling me to agree.

"Shit, probably. How would I know? I don't even know the nigga."

"My point exactly," he nodded.

Although I completely understood what Lawrence was saying, the fact that these niggas assumed it was me bothered the fuck out of me. Someone had to have said something in order for them to bring it this way. The only people that knew I killed him were Anton, Truman, Roone, Lloyd… and of course Khyle, but she wouldn't dare snitch. I knew the homies wouldn't tell because they'd go to jail too, for keeping that shit a secret. Not only that, but Lloyd and Roone were the ones who kidnapped Huelo from a party for me, which was a crime in itself, so why would they tell?

I kept pondering as Lawrence left the room. He came back pretty quickly, and waved for me to come out. I mean mugged everybody in that bitch, and couldn't help but notice this older guy watching me like a hawk. He was dressed up in a Brooks Brothers suit, so I knew he had to be somebody important. But the way he stared intently into my eyes let me know that he knew me, well knew of me, and that he had some personal shit against me. I had a feeling that whoever dropped the dime, knew this nigga very well, or was at least in cahoots with him. This shit was blowing me right now.

"How did they even connect me?" I asked Lawrence once we were in his Mercedes and on the road. His car smelled like cigarettes and cologne.

"That, I don't quite know. It's pretty puzzling. What I would recommend, Mr. Bishop, is paying close attention to those around you. And maybe just come right out and ask."

I was gonna do exactly that. I was good at sensing someone's energy, and if anybody I thought I could trust acted strangely, I was gonna have to put a bullet in their head. I just prayed that somehow this shit leaked and someone else told, because I would hate to have to off one of my niggas.

CHAPTER ONE

Khyle Luke

My eyes darted open when I felt someone getting into the bed with me. Clutching my stomach, I looked over my shoulder to see Oden smiling, so I turned my body to face him. His hair appeared to be damp, and I could smell his Old Spice body wash so I knew he'd just taken a shower. As good as he looked and smelled, I couldn't help but wonder why he was smiling, considering the fact that he'd just been arrested some hours ago.

"Oden, what happened?" I asked what I'd been dying to know, and what had been keeping me up while he was gone.

"Nothing," he kissed me deeply, but I yanked away.

"Oden—"

"Khyle, it has nothing to do with you," he frowned, obviously irritated by my questioning, but I didn't give a fuck.

"You think my child's father getting arrested in the middle of the night has nothing to do with me? Please tell me you're not that stupid," I fussed. I was ready to clock his ass.

Falling back onto his pillow, he ran his hand over his wild hair with his eyes closed. He looked to me as I sat up a little, waiting for an answer. Nobody was going to sleep tonight if I didn't get a fucking explanation.

"They arrested me for what happened to Huelo."

"I thought you said that it was taken care of and that no one would ever find out he'd even died. You said years from now he'd be declared dead from absentia or something." By this time I was sitting up straight, looking down into his handsome distressed face.

"I know baby, and they *don't* have a body. They won't get it. But it just means that someone close to me told."

"Someone like your friends?"

"Yeah, man. I just can't imagine any of them doing that, but how else would the cops find out I was connected in any way? I mean, I know you didn't tell so who does that leave?"

"Oden, I umm… I didn't tell the cops, but I told my friends."

"You what?" he shot up, staring deeply into my eyes with so much fury that I wished I hadn't said anything. Knowing what he was capable of had me slightly afraid; no, *very* afraid. "What the fuck possessed you to go around broadcasting that I bodied somebody, Khyle? Are you fucking stupid?" He got out of the bed.

"I didn't broadcast it, Oden, I just told them in secrecy!"

"Oh my gosh, man," he paced the bedroom floor. I understood his anger because I was angry with myself. I just felt comfortable telling them because I was confident that no one would find Huelo's body.

And I mean… they didn't.

"Oden…" I had nothing else to say really.

"So you told your damn friends, and ain't no fucking telling who heard that shit! Didn't you learn your fucking lesson when your abortion secret got out!"

"Don't yell at me!"

"No, you be happy that all I'm doing is yelling because right now I want to put the paws on you! I only told you about Huelo so you'd know that the shit was taken care of and because you are my woman! Not for you to go bragging! You know how many muthafuckas get caught because they brag too fucking much?" He bent down in my face as tears streamed my cheeks. He was so mad, and I was frightened. The way he looked at me, it was almost like he wanted to kill me.

"Oden, I wasn't bragging. We were talking about what he did and I told them that you'd taken care of it already."

"Cool," he nodded. "And now, the people who live next to your dorm probably recorded it and told on my ass."

"We weren't in the dorm when I told them," I whispered so lowly that I thought he didn't hear me. That was until he fixated his eyes on me, and I swear they were all black like a demon's.

"You spoke about this in public?"

"No one was around!"

"Khyle," he scoffed. "If I didn't love you, and you didn't have my baby in your stomach right now, I would murk yo' ass. On God I would," he gritted before leaving the bedroom.

I felt so stupid, but I also felt angry. Someone I told had to have mentioned it, which meant I was in the same predicament as Oden; one of my friends couldn't be trusted. I was gonna find out who though, and hope that it was one of them, and not some bystander that I didn't see listening in. Now that I think about it, both outcomes would be bad. Either I would lose a friend, or someone random out there knew about Huelo's murder.

Climbing out of the bed, I went into the guest bedroom to see Oden lying down. I pulled my nightgown over my head, and then pushed my underwear past my feet before walking to him. His eyes stayed on me the whole time as I peeled the covers back and straddled him. Removing his dick from his boxers, I licked the tip of it, getting my mouth wet. He began hardening in no time, so I started easing him into my mouth.

"Mmm," he moaned very subtly as I bobbed my head up and down.

My saliva was flowing freely as I took him into my mouth, all the way, almost. Massaging his balls, I kept switching it up going slow and then fast. His moans got a little louder, so I slurped a bit faster, keeping my throat open and my mouth tight, just the way he liked. His dick got stiff as hell, so I knew he was about to cum; but, to my surprise, he yanked me off. He tugged me so that I could sit on it, and I did just that. His big hands palmed my belly as I moved up and down his long, thick rod. He slowly toyed with my clit while staring between my legs, not being to rough at all.

"Baby," I whimpered, already feeling my orgasm on the horizon.

His hands traveled up my frame, and cupped my breasts. His eyes were filled with so much lust as they danced all over my body. It felt good to see him look at me the same, regardless of the fact that I had this stomach and had possibly let the cat out of the bag.

"So beautiful," he commented, tucking his bottom lip into his mouth as he groped the sides of my thighs. "Let it go, Khyle."

As soon as he said that, I released. He sat up, hugged my body as tightly as he could, and plowed upward into me. I was so wet, that I knew my juices were getting everywhere. To make matters worse, I came again, drenching my center even more.

"Odeeenn," I cried as he sucked and kissed on my collarbone.

"I love making you cum that hard. You always cum so hard for daddy," he said before pulling back a little and sucking on my nipples.

Once he'd gotten his fix, he put me on my back and pounded into me with deep ass strokes, until he was filling me up with his seeds. Our lips met before we could catch our breaths, as he sat inside of me.

"I'm gonna fix it, Oden," I said and he kind of laughed.

"I got it. Just know that anything you and I discuss should not be told to your friends, unless you're at a safe location, which doesn't include your dorm or public places. But even then, just don't say shit."

"Can I tell them about the arrest to find out if they told anybody?" I questioned.

"Yes, but here, nowhere else. Make that the last thing you tell them, aight?"

"Okay," I nodded.

He was hard again, so he just started thrusting into me slowly, getting me wet instantly.

I couldn't wait to find out what my friends had to say. And even though Perry wasn't around when I mentioned what Oden had done, she was the prime suspect.

CHAPTER ONE

Bella Bacigalupi

The next evening…

After class, Khyle rallied up Tasmine and I, and drove us to Oden's home. She said she needed to talk to us, and that it couldn't be on school grounds or anywhere public. She was already pregnant, so I racked my brain trying to figure out what she had to talk to us about that was this damn important.

The ride was quiet so I guess Tasmine was doing the same thing, trying to figure it all out. We finally made it there, and once we got inside, she gave us cold bottles of water. The three of us sat at the dining room table, looking at one another in silence. It was so awkward that we had to laugh eventually.

"Okay, so here's the thing; Oden was arrested last night because he was accused of killing Huelo. The reason I asked for you to come today is because I want to know if either of you said anything to anyone."

I suddenly felt like my heart was palpitating as I thought back to the day I'd told Santino what Oden had done. He promised me he'd leave it alone though. Maybe he went behind my back. If so, it was on.

"No, I never repeated it or talked about it with anyone," Tasmine shook her head before gulping down some of the water.

"Bella?"

"I— no, never said anything."

I contemplated telling her the truth, but what would that do? Get Santino and I killed? No way I was going down for this, and no way was I gonna get my nigga killed for it either.

"What about Perry? I hope you didn't tell her. I mean I understand we're back cool with her, but she's proved that she's a fucking snake," Tasmine hissed.

"True," I nodded, trying to get the attention off of me.

"Trust me, I feel like she had something to do with this. The only thing holding me back from that is how would she have found out? I mean with the abortion thing she saw it firsthand and was present during many conversations. This one, she would have to have been undercover or something."

"Perry is sneaky, Khyle," Tasmine chimed in.

Even though I felt like Santino had betrayed my trust and told, I also felt like Perry did have something to do with all of this. She wasn't this meek, confused person that everyone thought she was. She was conniving, mischievous, and very intelligent. I mean the way she set Khyle up would have been admirable if it wasn't so damn shady. The bitch was a for real snake when she wanted to be, and I bet she used that quiet shy shit to cover it all up.

"I know she's sneaky. If anyone knows I know. I'm gonna get at her," Khyle nodded.

After talking for a little longer about other stuff in our lives, and sharing stories from our Christmas break, Khyle cooked some spicy hamburgers for us. I wasn't sure if I was just starved, or if my appetite had increased due to me being scared as fuck over this Oden and Huelo situation, but I ate *two* burgers. I tell you, that nigga Huelo was still causing problems from his damn grave… or wherever the fuck he was.

Around 8pm, the three of us left Oden's. Khyle was gonna spend the night in the dorms since Oden would be working late. I think she was still scared to be alone after almost being raped, and I would be too, honestly.

"I'm gonna wait for Santino," I told them before they hopped onto the elevator inside of our dorm building.

Me: Where the fuck are you? I'm waiting.

Sanz: Coming down now baby, relax.

As I waited for him, I toyed with my engagement ring. It was so beautiful, and reminded me how badly I wanted things between Santino and I to work. But if he'd opened his big mouth about Oden killing Huelo, I wasn't too sure we'd make it down the aisle.

Oden was smart and very well connected. People liked to say that Billz ran Las Vegas before he got killed somehow, but everyone knew it was Oden Bishop. By saying that, I didn't need to open my mouth for him to find out Santino snitched; he would figure it out on his own soon enough.

"What's up?" Santino hugged my body tightly from behind. I must have been so lost in my thoughts that I didn't realize he'd come down.

"Can we talk in your car?"

With his eyes bucked and his lips slightly parted, he nodded his head. Hand in hand, we left the dorm building and went out to sit in his car. Thankfully, Tasmine and Khyle's room window was on the opposite side of this parking lot, so I didn't have to worry about them seeing me in the car just sitting. Nothing was suspicious about me being with Santino, but sitting in a car talking and not moving… yeah. Or maybe I was just paranoid.

"You good, baby? What's wrong?" Santino gripped my thigh, turning me on a little bit despite my stomach being in knots.

"Santino, remember you promised me that you wouldn't say anything about what I told you about your *friend*?"

"What? Bella— oh yeah, I do. And I kept that promise, baby."

"Swear to God you did, Sanz. Because if you opened your mouth about this to anyone, we could be in big trouble."

"You told me that already, and I promised you that I wouldn't say a word. What happened? Why are you all of sudden on my head about this? It's been months."

"Because somehow Oden got arrested for the murder of Huelo."

I looked into his eyes to try and see if I could sense that he was lying. Thankfully, he looked just as surprised as I did when I heard what happened to Oden.

"Bella, I swear to you I didn't say shit. I admit that I thought about it, and even went up to the dealership to get at him on the subject, but I changed my mind."

"You what!" I shrieked, turning to face him completely in my seat.

"I went to the dealership to approach him, but I didn't! I didn't even mention Huelo! We talked about other shit and then went our separate ways."

"Oh my fucking gosh. Why would you do that?" I turned my lip up.

He was so stupid. I wasn't sure what changed his mind about mentioning Huelo, but the fact that he went down there with the intention to, annoyed me. I specifically told his ass that he needed to keep this shit under wraps. It was almost like he just didn't give a fuck. He could have gotten us both killed.

"Don't be mad, Bella," he touched my leg.

"Don't fucking touch me, nigga! I explained to you that Oden was dangerous, and only told you what happened to ease your mind. You were constantly talking about Huelo, so being the nice trusting girlfriend that I am, I let you in on a secret. Fuck, I wish I hadn't. You could have gotten us murdered, but you don't care, do you?"

"Oden wouldn't have—"

"Are you crazy! He killed Huelo, what the fuck makes you think he won't kill us?"

Turning away from me, Santino stared out the window, shaking his head. He always did that when I was right and he wasn't. He hated to be wrong, so instead of saying anything, he'd always just shake his head.

"Does he think I'm the one that dropped the dime?"

"No, I don't know. I guess if he did you'd be swimming with the fishes already."

"I'm not afraid of him, Bella."

"I know, and that's what scares me Santino." I took his hand into mine. "I'm not asking you to be afraid, and it's actually a turn on that you're not, but I'm asking that you be smart about this. Stay out of it from now on, okay? Oden is psycho."

I was trying to butter him up some, because I knew he wasn't scared of Oden. Santino was that guy who would fight eight niggas by himself, and not think twice about it. I loved that about him usually, but right now I needed him to tone it down. I just wanted to be a regular girl in a loving relationship, not on the run from crazy ass Oden, especially when it wasn't necessary.

"I understand," he finally replied. "I didn't snitch, so you and I have nothing to worry about," he kissed me.

I admit I felt a little bit better after talking to Santino, but I would still be on edge until the actual culprit was found.

CHAPTER ONE

Shayne Luke

I was lying back on the examination table, staring at the small screen that had my baby plastered across it. It didn't look like much, but it still made me smile. Just knowing someone was inside of me that I would have to love and watch grow up made me feel all warm inside. I loved this baby so much, and I finally understood why women cried so hard from miscarrying. I used to think it was so stupid to be attached to someone you'd never seen, especially with it being so early in a pregnancy, but at this moment, it all made sense. I wouldn't know what to do with myself if this little thing was suddenly gone.

"Perfect health, Ms. Luke. The baby is in perfect shape. I'd like to ask what you eat and if you do exercise, what do you do?"

"I don't eat too many greasy foods or heavy foods which has been really hard for me because I love Mexican cuisine."

"Yes she does," Lloyd commented, making me roll my eyes playfully. "She slips up though. We had quesadillas last night."

Damn, he couldn't hold water!

"Lloyd!"

"It's fine, Ms. Luke. It's not good to completely deprive yourself of foods that you crave because what happens is you will go on a binge after a while. So when you crave Mexican food, have a little of it. You want to enjoy your pregnancy." She wrote something down, and then looked back up at me. "Now exercise?"

"We have a treadmill in the home so I get on it for 10 minutes, twice a day."

"Perfect." She scribbled something down. "Well, I think on your visit next month we should be able to determine the sex since you will be about 16 weeks."

"Can't wait, I smiled."

We talked with my doctor for a little longer, mainly because Lloyd had questions about sex. He liked to do too many positions, and lately that shit was uncomfortable as hell. I was happy that my doctor told him to only do it in ways that I was comfortable with, because he swore something was wrong with me.

"Missionary sex for the win!" I joked as Lloyd and I walked through the parking lot hand in hand. He just chuckled before kissing me a couple times.

"Nah, we gon' figure some shit out. However, as good as your pussy is, you could ride my dick from the back and it'd still be good as fuck."

"Ugh, I got a visual." We laughed in unison before he opened the car door for me.

"Hungry?" He got in on the driver's side.

"Yes, I'm craving a big wet burrito right now from Taco's Mexico." I licked my lips just thinking about it. I knew I was gonna have to keep in shape while pregnant if I didn't want to completely blow up once I delivered, but I'd cross that bridge when I got to it.

"Aight, let me stop for gas first."

When he pulled into the gas station, I let my seat back a little so that I could lie back. Although only three months pregnant, I felt like a whale and like my stomach was huge as fuck. I knew I was being extra, but hey.

As I laid there, enjoying the little bit of sun beaming through Lloyd's windows, my phone rang. I picked it up to see who it was, and saw it was the same Atlanta number that had been calling me for the past two weeks now. I answered the first three times, and it would just be someone breathing, so I stopped for a while. But right now I was irritated, so I tapped the green button.

"Hello?"

"Stupid bitch!"

Click.

Looking at my phone as if it were the person, I dialed the number back, only for it to say it had been disconnected. Now I was scared because who in the Sam hell could disconnect a number that quickly? And why have they been calling me?

I sat there thinking about who would possibly have some shit with me over in Georgia. Then again, the muthafucka probably was just using a Georgia number.

"Hand me those wipes, babe," Lloyd got back into the car.

I handed them over, and watched as he cleaned his hands. He was such a clean freak, always sanitizing shit like he was a doctor or a serial killer.

"What bitch did you fuck in Atlanta?" I sneered, ready to knock his ass the fuck out. The only time bitches played on your phone was when a nigga was involved.

"What? Shayne, I don't even know anybody in Atlanta," he frowned his sexy chocolate face.

"You're from Birmingham, nigga! You know muthafuckas in Georgia!"

"Shayne, that's like me saying because you're from California, you know people up in Oregon, or Arizona."

"And I do, nigga! And it's more like you saying I know people in Nevada, which I do. Now who did you fuck in Georgia?!" My fists were balled and my mouth was twisted up.

Laughing, he threw his head back and covered his mouth with his fist. I slapped his hard ass chest, which ended up hurting my fucking knuckles, so now I was even more infuriated.

"Shawty, you crazy, I swear. Aight, I know people in Georgia, but the bitches I did fuck were years before you. Why are you asking me this?"

"Because some hoe from Atlanta has been calling my damn phone, and she called me a stupid bitch before hanging up."

"Call the number back." He waved for me to give him my phone but I declined. "Give me the damn phone, shawty."

"I already called, Lloyd, and the number is shut off. Let me get one more damn call and watch me leave your ass."

"While pregnant?"

"Yep, me and my baby will be perfectly fine without you." I folded my arms, staring out the window. "I'm not one of these dumb bitches that you're used to, nigga. If I find out some shit, whoooo Lord! You can't play a player, nigga!" I fussed, leg bouncing rapidly. "I will knock the shit out of you."

"Baby, calm your little nerves. I have not cheated on you, and I have not cheated on you with anyone from Atlanta, Georgia. If they call you again, let me know okay?"

"Yeah."

He leaned over the center and kissed my cheek softly. He kept doing that, and I tried to hide the smile that wanted to burst through. I couldn't help it after a while, so I was grinning from ear to fucking ear before he pressed his soft lips against mine.

"I'm not playing with you, Lloyd."

"I know that, and I swear I've been on my best behavior. It's probably nothing anyway, but we'll figure it out if it is."

I just nodded as he pulled out of the gas station.

A part of me agreed that maybe this was nothing, but the other side of me felt otherwise. Why had this all of a sudden started, and why were they so persistent? Something deep down in my gut was telling me that the person calling me knew who I was, and had plans for me, or that my nigga was lying his ass off.

CHAPTER TWO

Oden

$\mathcal{I}$ walked into my office inside of Palace, hoping I could complete whatever was on my schedule today. I'd called a meeting with my close niggas only, because I needed to look each of them niggas in the eye and see if I could tell who was lying.

I low-key ain't even want to do this shit because I was scared of what I would find out. Anton, Truman, Roone, and Lloyd were like my brothers damn near, and if I found out they'd snitched, that would hurt deep. There would be no discussing shit or apologies though, because I'd dead whoever it turned out to be. I couldn't go on having snakes in my camp.

Sitting down, I powered on my computer so I could take a look at my schedule. I saw I had interviews all damn day basically. I texted Cara to come into my office because I needed to know what the hell she was doing without talking to me.

KNOCK! KNOCK!

"Come in, Cara!" I called out, taking a sip of this natural juice that Khyle made me. Shit was strong as fuck, but she was about to cry when I told her I didn't want the shit so I took it.

"Hey, Oden, what's up?" Cara walked in, caressing her belly.

"Cara, why are all these damn interviews on here? We're not hiring, we're fully staffed."

"I'm not sure if you forgot, but I'm eight months pregnant, Oden, and you said you were gonna get someone to work here temporarily while I was on leave. Chiina helped me a lot, but she's on maternity leave as well. I can't be wobbling around this huge club."

"Oh yeah, I guess it slipped my mind with all this shit going on. I apologize. So you've screened these people and made sure that they're qualified?"

"Yeah, Truman helped me sort through them, and now we're down to those seven you're gonna meet today."

"Okay, cool. You can go for the day, actually, I don't want you on your feet."

"Awww, thank you," she smiled. "But I can stay, Oden. I'm actually doing okay right now. Plus, I don't want to miss out on money."

"I will pay you for the day, just go. My girl is pregnant and she makes me rub her feet faithfully, so I know yours are in pain as well."

"Oh yes, Khyle *is* pregnant." She looked into my eyes, saying nothing. "Well, thank you for letting me go. Ebony can handle my job for the day."

"You don't think she could be in your place while you're gone then?" I frowned.

"Hell no!"

We laughed in unison before we said our goodbyes.

A good two hours had passed, and I'd interviewed four damn candidates. I had three more over the course of two hours, and I prayed that shit flew by. I was tired of asking the same shit over and over. I sent Ebony a message to one of the business iPhones I'd given my staff, to let her know that I was ready for the next candidate; Winter Cannon.

Ebony: Bringing her up now.

A few minutes passed before Ebony was knocking and walking in with Winter behind her. My eyes traveled from the top of Winter's head, all the way down to her toes; she was beautiful. She was wearing a tight black dress that hugged her body tightly, and had a little cleavage on display. It didn't seem unprofessional though, but maybe that was because I was looking and thinking with the wrong head right now. Clearing my throat, I closed my eyes so I could get in my right mind. I had no room for mistakes in my relationship, but even if I did, I would never start with her.

"Good afternoon, Mr. Bishop," Winter smiled as Ebony left my office.

"Afternoon, have a seat." I gestured for her to have a seat across from my desk.

She kept her eyes on me for a little bit, and then finally sat down but very slowly, giving me full view of her cleavage. That dress was definitely unprofessional now that I was thinking more clearly and with my actual brain. She was also very much on the flirty tip.

I chuckled at her behavior lowly, before pulling out the resume

I'd gotten from Cara.

"Something funny?" Winter asked, grinning.

"Nope. So have you ever worked with upscale clientele before? I just see that you've been a manager at a couple bars. Cara is more than a manager, she handles our VIP guests and booths."

"I have worked with high profile people but that was when I was in the retail business. The places I managed were nothing like this,"she waved her hand around.

"So what makes you think you're qualified to work the job?"

"Well, I'm very hardworking and a perfectionist. I have experience catering to customers who are very entitled. I make sure the task is done right the first time, because I don't believe in cutting corners whatsoever. Also, I've always had perfect attendance at every job I've worked. I think another plus is how sexy I am."

"I'm sorry, what does that have to do with anything?" I squinted my eyes, clasping my hands under my chin.

Chuckling, she said, "I'm sure most of your VIP guests are men, and with me managing that, I'm positive I could boost a lot of sales."

"Look, Winter, I'm not looking to hire an escort. I want someone to come in here, be professional, and get the job done. For starters, that outfit would not be appropriate for a club manager; it would better suit a VIP hostess. However, despite you coming on a little strong, your resume has been the most impressive today as far as you dealing with upscale people in retail. I will have someone call you if you get the job, okay?" She had annoyed me and I was ready for her to go.

"And how much is the pay? Well, how much would it be if I were to get hired?"

"Sorry, I assumed they'd already gone over that with you. The job pays $30 an hour, with benefits and paid vacation. But since this is temporary, the additional details outside of the hourly pay don't apply."

"I see."

"Have a good day." I rose to my feet and gestured for her to leave.

"Please, Mr. Bishop, I really want this. I guess I thought that I needed to portray myself in a certain light in order to get hired. I do apologize for my behavior, and if you hire me it won't happen again."

"Someone will call," I repeated, ready for her to go.

She just stared at me for a few moments, and turned to leave.

Once the door closed behind her, I ran my hands over my face. I hated that she appeared to be the most qualified, because I didn't like her vibe. She was doing too much and I ain't have time for any bullshit when it came to my business. I was just happy that there were two more people after her.

"Fuck," I mumbled before texting Ebony.

I met with the last two candidates, and then headed straight to the warehouse to meet with my niggas. On the way there, I kept trying to think of ways that the Huelo shit could have leaked, but not through them. I tried to tell myself that maybe someone overheard Khyle while she was running her mouth about it in public, but something in my heart was telling me that unfortunately, that wasn't even the case. The thought of some random overhearing Khyle and being bold enough to run off and tell just didn't track for me. Shit, you could barely get eye witnesses to a murder to come forward at times.

When I pulled up to the warehouse, I saw everyone's car was already parked. That was a good sign because the first red flag would have been on the muthafucka who either didn't show up or was late. Getting out, I said a quick prayer and then went inside. When I walked into the back room, Lloyd, Anton, Roone, and Truman were seated at the table, waiting for me.

"Sup fellas?" I greeted the room, and went around to dap everyone up. As I did, I made eye contact with each one of them, attempting to sense something early on.

"You good, man?" Truman squinted, trying to read me.

"Nah, I'm not. So, I haven't told y'all about this yet, but I was arrested a couple of days ago for the murder of Huelo," I came right out with it, and then scanned the four of them.

"How?" Anton cocked his head, looking thoroughly confused. I guess Khyle hadn't talked to Tasmine about it yet. Either that or Tasmine wasn't the type to run her mouth.

"Don't they need evidence to do some shit like that?" Truman added with a twisted face as well. "I mean I'm not understanding right now."

"Same thing I said when I was getting them cuffs placed on me."

"Did they present anything to you?" Roone inquired. "Like did they tell you how they were able to point the finger?"

"Nope, all they did was ask me questions. My reason for calling you all here was because there is no evidence, not even a body, yet somehow I was fingered for this shit. What that means is one of you ran down there on some bitch nigga shit and told."

As soon as I said that, Truman and Anton looked at Lloyd and Roone.

"Aye, I swear to God I ain't do no shit like that. I'll fuck around and break out in hives if I even get close to a police station," Lloyd held his hands up in mock surrender.

"I ain't no snitch," Roone shook his head repeatedly.

I looked to Anton and Truman to see if they had anything to say.

"Nigga, the fuck you looking at me for? You know I wouldn't do no shit like that!" Anton hissed.

"Me either! All the shit I know about you, why I would wait until now and use something like that? If anything, I would go for the gusto my nigga, you know me," Truman added, shaking his head.

"Right now I don't know what the fuck to think!" I boomed. "All I fucking know, is that one of you who I have trusted this whole time, went behind my back and snitched. And I swear to God, bruh, when I find out which one of you it was, I'm icing you with no questions asked. I don't know why one of you would do this shit to me, but just know this, you've made a big ass mistake."

"Oden!" I heard Truman call after me but I was done, and I'd said what I had to say, so I kept it pushing until I was outside and in my car.

What pissed me off the most was that all of them appeared to be telling the truth. What if I fucked around and murked the wrong person? I ain't want to let the muthafucka who dropped the dime on me live another day, but I also didn't want to end someone's life by mistake, especially not a friend. Today was just not my fucking day; shit, this wasn't my fucking week.

After pulling off, I went back to the club and got high as fuck in my office. I was gonna stay and chill, but I knew Khyle would be complaining and moaning about how I needed to change now that I was gonna be a father. So once I was high enough, I bounced and headed to my crib.

"Shit," I mumbled, getting out of the car after swooping into my designated parking spot. I was high as hell and hungry as hell.

As I walked up to my condo, I spotted Truman and Anton standing in the front, waiting on me. I just laughed angrily, before glancing off to the side for a little bit.

"Aye man, it has to be one of them niggas," Anton spoke up, stopping me from bypassing them and going inside.

"How can you be so sure?" my brows dipped.

"Because Anton and I are not stupid enough to try and throw you under the bus. Doing that to you would be putting us out in the fire too. It has to be one of them," Truman explained.

"We'll just see. Goodnight." I slipped past them and went inside of my condo.

Leaning my body up against the inside of the door, I slid down it and just dropped my head. It seemed like bullshit just kept falling into my fucking lap, and I was tired of it. A nigga was about to be on some savage shit.

CHAPTER TWO

Roone Rollis

"What the hell is wrong with you?" Marie asked, lying on my chest.

We'd just gotten done fucking, and to be honest, I was surprised that I was even able to get my shit up will all the stuff on my mind.

Suddenly, I was regretting snitching on Oden, because I felt like none of this was worth it. At the beginning, it seemed like the smart thing to do so I could get ahead, but now I was scared for my fucking life. Oden was *that* nigga, and he was trustworthy as fuck. He looked out for his people, as long as you didn't cross him. I would give anything to go back in fucking time, because now I was surrounded by muthafuckas like me: snakes that did whatever it took to get ahead.

"He's gonna kill my ass," I finally responded to Marie, staring up at the ceiling.

"Who?" she questioned dumbly, as if me telling on Oden wasn't her damn idea. Shit, she was just as deep in this shit as I was.

"Oden, Marie. Who the fuck else?" I moved from under her and sat up on the edge of the bed, dropping my face into my hands. I wasn't even this type of nigga, but greed and a little jealousy turned me into a muthafucka I didn't recognize.

"He has no idea who it was, baby." Her soft hands rubbed up my back as she planted soft gentle kisses on it.

Marie and I started fucking around a little after Truman killed her husband Billz. She basically had his empire in her lap because his right-hand man had gotten murdered shortly before that; I'm sure by Oden, Truman, or Anton. Anyway, we met at a club, which I think she low-key followed me to, and she told me she would be willing to let me run her husband's shit since she knew nothing about the drug game. Me on the other hand, I came from this drug shit, and it was what I knew best. Shit was *all* I knew growing up in Brooklyn. I wasn't like Lloyd who was suddenly familiar with the car business, so I felt like a fish out of water sometimes, unless Oden was right there directing me.

I tried to get Oden to do the drug thing in conjunction with his vehicle theft business, but he basically told me to fuck myself. So when Marie dangled a whole empire in my face, of course I bit. She only had one stipulation, take Oden down. I would have thought she would have wanted Truman since he actually pulled the trigger on her man, but she'd cut a deal with some lieutenant that wanted Oden.

I didn't want to put the police onto his vehicle shit because I felt like it would be too hard to detect. Like I said, I didn't know much, and only took care of tasks that Oden directed me to take care of. However, what I did know was that he had Lloyd and I kidnapped that Tongan nigga so he could murder his ass. It was a stretch trying to get Oden in trouble for that, because we burned the body and the clean-up crew scoured the blood out of the warehouse, but it was worth a shot since it was all I really had on him.

Now, I was shitting bricks because I knew he was getting closer to finding out who it was. The fact that he'd figured out it was someone within his upper crew so quickly, had me shaking in my Giuseppe sneakers.

"You hear me, Roone? I said he has no way of finding out," Marie repeated.

"Marie, shorty, he called a meeting yesterday to let us know that he knew it was someone from his immediate camp. Fuck, I didn't think this shit through." I shot up off the bed.

"I told you to think of something that multiple people in his crew knew about! Not just his close friends!"

"I know, and I fucked up but the damage is done now. The only people that knew about Huelo or whatever the fuck his name is, were me, Lloyd, Truman, and Anton."

Running her fingers through her long hair, she sighed dejectedly.

"Well let's just hope that he lands in jail—"

"How? There is no fucking body! There is no weapon! There is nothing! This shit was stupid as fuck from day one, but I let you convince me otherwise!"

"Relax, Roone. Maybe you can pin it on someone else. Tell him something that will make him believe it was anyone but you." I nodded my head as I thought about what she was saying. "And if push comes to shove, he'll just be an enemy. You will have the same power Billz once had."

"Same power Billz once had," I repeated laughing. "And how well did that work out for him against Oden, huh? Marie, I witnessed him firsthand murk that boy, and he is not nice. I'm just not ready for this shit."

"Oh yes you are. And if you think about backing out, I will make sure Oden finds out exactly who it was that snitched on him. So you need to grow a bigger ball sac and get the fucking job done or else. Truman would do it, even though he's a fucking loser ass nigga."

I ain't know if Marie was doing this to avenge her husband's death and seal the deal with the lieutenant like she claimed, or if she was mad that Truman wasn't fucking with her anymore. Whatever the case was, I was clearly in too deep to back off now. I was definitely gonna attempt to get Oden's attention on someone else.

***

The next morning…

"Hey! Oden, man, let me talk to you!" I caught him walking out of his dealership, on the way to his car. I could tell by the look on his face that he wasn't in a good mood, and for obvious reasons.

"What?" he stopped, slipping his hands into his pants pockets.

I was sweating bullets, praying that my plan didn't fail miserably. Me trying to point the finger may backfire, and I didn't need that so this shit had to go over smoothly.

"I wanted to talk to you about that Huelo shi—"

"We can't talk out here. Get in my car."

He cut me off and started towards his Porsche. Once we got inside, he locked the doors, which had me on edge.

Calm the fuck down my nigga.

"So I umm, I wanted to say to you that one day I saw Lloyd talking to some guys that looked like detectives, outside of my apartment."

He turned his head slowly to look at me.

"When?" He was calm, not angry like I'd expected.

I ain't wanna throw Lloyd under the bus, but I felt like picking Truman or Anton wasn't a good idea. He'd known them too long so he probably wouldn't have gone for that shit at all. I needed to be safe with how I went about this. And honestly, when it came down to me or Lloyd, I would always pick me.

"Like a couple weeks ago. He said they were nobody, but it didn't seem that way to me. They were driving in an all-black car like detectives do, B. Shit was mad suspect."

Tucking his lips in, he nodded his head up and down as he stared out of his front window. His eyes were squinted, almost like he was thinking about the shit I'd just told him.

"Thanks. I have to go."

"Ye-yeah, no problem. And aye, don't worry about me telling him anything. You know I didn't say nothing before because that's my boy, and I didn't think it was anything until our meeting, you know?"

"I understand and I appreciate you bringing this information to me. Now please," he gestured for me to get out of his car, and since I was still alive I did.

I watched as he sped out of the parking lot with Young Jeezy blasting, and once he was a little ways down, a smile spread across my face.

Mission accomplished, I thought.

As soon as I got in my car, my phone started ringing off the hook. I saw it was that same un-stored number that constantly called me up. Blowing out hot air, I answered the phone, wondering what the fuck I was gonna say.

"I need something, Rollis," Lieutenant Gaines barked into the phone.

He was the one Marie had me give the information to on Oden killing Huelo. They had no evidence as of right now, but he needed me to bring in something so they could arrest Oden again. I ain't have shit before, and it was highly unlikely that I'd get something now. All that I did have was my own witness testimony, and that would just be my word against Oden's, which would get me killed. We needed a body, but that shit was long gone, Lloyd and I made sure of it. At the moment, I wish I hadn't covered Oden's tracks so well.

"Just give me some time, aight?"

"How much time? I need to take this kid down, and you're fucking it up! You told me you had something and if you don't deliver, I'm arresting both you and Marie for drug trafficking. And believe me, that will be a heavy sentence because I have plenty of *evidence* against you both."

"I hear you, man."

"Good," he hung up.

I had never regretted something so much in my life. This hole I'd dug just seemed to get deeper and deeper.

CHAPTER TWO

Truman Morrison

A few days later...

"Just one more push, Ms. Barnes," the doctor urged Chiina. She clenched her teeth together, and squeezed the fuck out of my hand, before doing what she was told.

She was currently delivering our son, and I hated to see her in so much pain, but I was beyond anxious to meet the little nigga. I was excited to start my family with Chiina, believe it or not.

I'd been really working on myself, and keeping away from the hoes no matter how hard that shit was. I couldn't even look at the strip club level of Palace nightclub, or else I would be bringing bitches to my office to smash. I shook my head at myself as I thought about it. None of them were worth what I had with Chiina, is what I had to tell myself in order to stay on the good foot.

"Mr. Morrison," the doctor nodded for me to come over.

I went over to him, and he assisted me in cutting the umbilical chord. My baby boy was still screaming at the top of his lungs as they handed him off to the nurse. And Chiina was still breathing heavily with her head pressed deeply into the pillow.

"Just gonna clean him, okay?" the nurse glanced from Chiina to me, and we both nodded, giving her the go.

Once everyone was gone, except a nurse that was cleaning Chiina, I leaned down to kiss Chiina's lips and just admired her beauty for a second. She offered me a soft smile before I kissed her again.

"Are you finally happy?" she asked.

"Finally? I've been happy for a long time; well, ever since I got with you."

"You sure?"

"Yes, baby, I'm sure. I don't need you to ask me that all the time. I'm old enough to make decisions for myself, and if I didn't want to be here with you, I wouldn't be."

"Good."

I kissed her lips again, and then we waited for the nurse to return with our son, Truman Jr. Leaning my head back and closing my eyes, my mind began to wonder about who it could have been that told on Oden. I mean I knew it wasn't Anton, or myself, but I was trying to figure out who seemed the most disloyal out of Lloyd and Roone.

My thoughts were interrupted when the nurse walked into the room with my son wrapped up in some blanket with a cap on his head. She handed him to Chiina after I helped her sit up, and then we both just looked down at him. He didn't really look like either of us yet, but

I guess that would come in down the line.

"He's adorable," Chiina cooed.

Sitting on the edge of Chiina's hospital bed I thought, *I can really do this family shit.*

***

I was going over some bullshit paperwork in my office when my phone buzzed. I looked down to see it was Chiina asking me to pick up some things for our son, along with a picture of him. I smiled, taking him in, and chuckling at how she stayed taking pictures of my kid. I didn't like it because I felt like the flash would blind him, but as we all know, Chiina did what the fuck she wanted, when she wanted to, and how she wanted to do it.

Me: Okay I should be home in like an hour.

I started back doing my work, when my phone buzzed again. Picking it up, I was surprised to see an Instagram DM from Pilar since I hadn't talked to her in months. She appeared to be doing well, according to Instagram, and honestly, I didn't think about her like that anymore. Shit, I felt like Chiina would know if I were simply thinking about another bitch.

Pilar: Hey we need to talk.

Me: Nah we have nothing to talk about.

Pilar: Fine, I will just talk to Chiina about the baby I'm carrying.

I stared down at the message for ages it seemed, before hitting her back with my number and telling her to call me. She had to be joking right now.

"Hello?" I answered before the first ring could even complete itself. "Pilar, what the fuck is you talking about right now?"

"I'm talking about the baby of yours inside of me."

"I haven't fucked you in months, shorty! What are you talking about?" I couldn't help but repeat myself because she had me flabbergasted.

"Just know that I'm due any day now, and if you don't meet up with me, I will have to meet up with your girlfriend. The baby may be here by then so she can see him in the flesh."

"Okay, shit. Alright. When are you free?"

"Tonight."

"I can't tonight, I have somewhere to—"

"I'm only free tonight. Either you come by, or I can stop by your place in the morning with my bundle of joy."

Laughing, I ran my hand down my face because I wanted to wrap it around her damn neck. Pilar had seen the super crazy side of me, and she was begging for me to bring the shit out. Why every time a nigga try to live right, some shit pops up?

"Aight, I will be there in 30 minutes."

"Good, don't be late."

She hung up the phone and I just sat there staring at the wall for a little bit before standing up. As soon as I did, there was a knock at my door.

"Come in!"

What walked through that door immediately had my dick hard,

and by the smile she wore on her face I bet she knew that. I watched her switch her wide hips towards me, pouting her sexy lips and tossing her hair behind her back.

"I don't think we've met, I'm Winter." She stuck her hand out and I shook it.

"Nice to meet you, Winter, I'm Truman."

"Yeah, Cara told me that you were one of the owners of the club." She nodded with a smile as she looked me up and down. "Well umm, I came to see if I could get set up with a company phone. Ebony said you guys message one another throughout the day to prevent having to do the extra leg work."

"Right, I have to order you one so it won't be in until tomorrow morning. But if Cara is here, get hers and tell her she can go home with pay for the day. Just let everyone know they can message Cara to get to you since you have her device."

"Great! Thank you, Truman."

We stared at one another for a little bit, and when I felt my dick rising yet again, I walked to my office door and opened it for her. *Not today satan, not today.*

"Good luck tonight," I told her, locking the door behind myself, and walking the opposite way of her. I could feel her eyes on my back, prompting me to let out a deep breath.

I hurried to my whip and sped to Pilar's condo before her ass did something dumb and made me kill her ass. I said a prayer before getting out of the car, because I was hoping that she was lying, and fucking with me just to get me over here.

"Hey," she answered the door, wearing a crop top and jean shorts. Her stomach was flat as hell, making me happy yet pissing me off at the same time.

"Pilar, are you serious?"

"I knew if I told you that shit you would bring your ass over here," she laughed, sighing afterward like her plan was genius.

I walked in and she closed the door behind me.

"What was all this for?" I was only giving her this time because we had history and I cared for her… just a teeny bit. If any other bitch had done this shit, I would have done an about face at the door.

"Because I miss you," she rushed me into the wall. "And I know you miss me."

"I'm fine where I am."

"Are you?" she dropped to her knees, trying to unbutton my pants.

"Yeah I am, P. Chill out." I moved her hands away from my crotch area. "I don't wanna do this, especially with you. I love Chiina, and I care enough about you not to have you as my side chick."

"No if you cared about me you wouldn't be trying to make a family with that young bitch! I spent years with you, Truman! How are you that deep in love with that hoe already?"

"Watch your tone and your language when speaking on my baby mama. Pilar, whatever you have in your head about us, kill it. I've already asked Chiina to be my wife and she's going to. I mean what happened with that nerdy cat you were fucking on?"

"He's not a nerd just because he makes legal money. And I told him I was conflicted with my feelings and that I needed space."

"Wait, you're conflicted? I thought you just said you missed me," I laughed at her ass trying to be a player. "Pilar, you ain't meant for the pimp life, shorty, trust me. Go be with your Steve Urkel, and be happy."

"So you wanna leave all of this." She moved her hands up and down her body with an eyebrow raised.

Baby Jesus, take me now.

"Already left it."

With that said, I yanked the door open and went out to my car. When I got inside, I felt like I needed a damn inhaler. Turning down that sex just now took every damn muscle in my body, but I was proud of myself. I just prayed that shit got at least a little bit easier for me.

CHAPTER TWO

*C*lass was finally over for the day, and I'd told Perry to meet me in the back parking lot of our dorm. She'd been hard to get in touch with ever since she started dating that Austin guy. She was barely in her room, and if she was, she was sleeping or doing work. The four of us didn't hang out much and honestly, that was perfectly fine with me. I forgave her for telling Oden about my abortion but I hadn't forgot it. I couldn't trust her like that anymore, and that was why I wanted to talk to her.

I spotted her BMW parked, so I shot her a text to make sure she was inside of it. Once she let me know that she was, I made my way over. I heard her hit the unlock button, and when I pulled open the passenger side door, a cloud of smoke slapped me in the face. Looking down at her with a frown, I saw she was smoking a blunt bigger than her. I swear this bitch surprised me every damn day.

"Perry, can you come to my car? I'm not trying to inhale all of this smoke while pregnant."

"I have to—"

"Would you just bring your ass!" I slammed the door and started off towards my own BMW.

I didn't care how new her personality was, I would still clock her skinny ass dead in the face. And I guess she knew that shit because she was right behind me like she should have been. New Perry or old Perry, she could still get that work.

"Sorry about the smoke," she apologized once we got into my car.

"No problem," I replied, trying to think of a way to ask her about the Huelo situation without actually telling her anything. Because if she didn't do it, that meant I would be giving her information that I no longer wanted to give out.

"You said you needed to talk?"

"Yeah, I wanted to know if you umm, if you've talked to the police lately?" I turned to face her and looked deeply into her eyes like Oden always did people to see if they were lying. I didn't know if I was doing it right though.

"About what?"

"Anything! Have you been down to the police station running your mouth!"

"No! Why would I do that?"

"Hmm, maybe because you decided to tell some bitches I don't like about my abortion, because you knew they'd tell my man. So, let's just say you have a bit of a habit of snitching, Perry."

"I haven't talked to any police and I don't have any information to tell them. Why though? What did you do?"

"I didn't do anything. I'm just randomly checking on you because I know how sneaky you are now. It'd be nothing for you to lie."

"The abortion wasn't a lie."

"Perry," I sighed, trying to stop myself from knocking the shit out of her. "Get out of my car."

"Sorry, I didn't mean it like that. I was just trying to show you that I wouldn't make anything up, just to be able to tell on you. Khyle, I want to be friends and I thought you forgave me."

I glanced over at her to see her push her new pair of glasses up. She'd been wearing those lately and not her contacts. I have never met anyone as weird as her.

"I did forgive you, Perry, I'm just a little stressed out right now so I do apologize for being so rude at times, okay?"

She nodded.

"You know, Austin is having a birthday party, and I want you, Bella, and Tasmine to come. It will be a lot of fun."

"I'm not really in a partying condition, Perry—"

"Aren't you due later this month? His birthday isn't until months after that, you should have recovered by then. I looked it up to be sure. I will drop off official invitations for you guys. Can't wait to see you there." She leaned over and kissed my cheek before hopping out of the car.

How did she know when I was due? And why the fuck did she think it was okay to kiss me? I had a feeling that Perry wasn't done making our jaws drop.

Once she got out of my car, I drove to Oden's house because he and I were gonna go shopping for some more baby stuff. The baby room in his townhouse was coming together so nicely, and Oden spared no expense when it came to his son. At the moment, we were just gonna get some small things that I may need while taking care of my baby at home.

"You think after you give birth your butt will stay like this?" Oden asked, grabbing my ass as we walked through the baby section of Target. Lately, Target had been getting a lot of damn money from us.

"That would be nice, but if not oh well. You didn't like it before?"

"I loved it before." He hugged me from behind and started kissing on my neck, making me giggle.

We were so into what we were doing, that I didn't even notice someone standing there in front of us. When Oden and I noticed her, he jumped back from me, almost like she was his girlfriend and he'd gotten caught with me. I looked back up at him for a second to see his face, and he was surprised by what he saw.

"Naomi, I thought you moved back to Colorado," he finally spoke.

Turning my head slowly to look at her, I scanned her body from head to toe. So this was the infamous Naomi. She was cuter in person, nothing special, but her body was to die for. Yes I said in person, meaning my friends and I had already scrolled through her weak ass Instagram page.

She smirked before throwing her hair behind her back, and placing her hand on her hip.

"Why would you think that, Oden? I told you I'd moved back

here when went out for lunch."

I knew what she was trying to do, but little did her ass know, I was well aware of that lunch. Bitch.

"Right. Naomi, this is my girlfriend, Khyle."

"Yes, I remember her. You're a very lucky girl, Khyle." She stuck her hand out to me but I ignored it because that wasn't a fucking compliment she was giving me.

"Oden, let's go," I demanded, switching off. I looked out the corner of my eye to see if he was behind me and he was. Naomi was watching like a hawk, too, with a mischievous smirk.

"Hey," he turned me around once we hit the corner, and then pressed me into the wall using his body. "Why you acting like that?"

"Like what?" I didn't mean to frown but I could feel that my face was all twisted up.

"Like you're jealous of her or something. Don't be acting like that, making her think you're worried or some shit. Ain't I your nigga?"

"Yeah," I grinned.

"Alright then. When another woman steps to you, you make sure she knows that shit and that you don't care if she talks to me."

"I'm a jealous lover."

"I know, and I like that about you because it lets me know you care. But in that case, keep your head held high, aight?"

I nodded before he pressed his full lips against mine. We were literally up against the wall, kissing heavily like we were about to fuck in a minute. When we finally pulled away, I saw an older lady walk by shaking her head and mumbling. Maybe because I was already pregnant, and we were doing the most, but I didn't give a fuck.

After shopping, we stopped to have dinner, and then went home to take a hot shower together. Afterwards, like always, Oden laid a towel across the bed, and I lied on my back so he could rub me down with oil. This had become one of my favorite things that we did because he was so good with his hands.

"Oden, I talked to my friends and they didn't have anything to do with snitching on you, not even Perry," I assured him.

"I know who it is already, baby." He kept his eyes focused on my thighs as he massaged them, rubbing the oil in.

"You do?"

"I do."

"Were you right about it being someone close to you, or was it because of me talking about it in public?"

"No, wasn't you, shorty. And unfortunately, I was right about it being someone close to me. Just goes to show you that you can't trust everybody that calls themselves your friend." He finally looked deeply into my eyes as he massaged my thighs.

"I know. Would you have hated me if it was my fault?"

"Could never hate you."

"I'm sorry, I won't tell anything ever again. I don't care who you kill."

Chuckling lightly as he focused his attention on my other thigh, he said, "I appreciate that and I know. Being my woman is a learning process and you're getting there. You're getting there."

Whomever it was that told, I felt really bad for what they were about to endure. I knew Oden like the back of my hand, and the calmer he was, the angrier he was. That's why I liked when he fussed at me because that meant he'd be over it soon. But when he was silent, that meant he'd been pushed to the limit.

God have mercy on the person that was gonna feel my baby's wrath. But then again… snitches always get stitches.

CHAPTER THREE

Tasmine Randall

Khyle, Bella, and I were having lunch at the Hexx Kitchen, a restaurant on Las Vegas Boulevard. It was Thursday, which was our Friday, so we always went to have lunch together to kind of celebrate getting to the weekend. Now that I was a sophomore, my classes were harder, and I didn't get many passes on shit like I did when I was a freshman. I guess they felt sorry for me then.

"You are about to burst, Khyle," Bella smiled at her as I nodded.

I agreed. Her belly had grown tremendously, and she was due any day now. Her tummy seemed to be the only thing that grew though, because her body appeared to be the same size, minus a few minute changes.

"I know and I can't wait. My parents wanted me to have the baby in Los Angeles, but Oden said no. We're gonna be living here so the baby's records and stuff should be here."

"Makes sense. Are they gonna come out and see the birth?" I quizzed.

"They're gonna try. The only way they'll miss it is if the birth is a surprise."

"That's good that they support you like that now," Bella said, and Khyle and I nodded in agreement as the waitress set down our food.

"I finally saw Oden's ex girlfriend in person," Khyle blurted, glancing from me to Bella to catch our reactions.

"Really? Does she look as trashy as she looked on Instagram?" I asked.

"Yep, and I could tell by the look in her eyes that she still wants to be with Oden. He told me she's over it, but that smirk she gave told otherwise."

"Want me to fuck her up?" Bella questioned, always ready to fight some damn body. She was just like Santino, but if you told her that she'd deny it.

"No, I will. I may have to wait until the baby gets here, but it will be worth it. I just hope she doesn't act on her feelings for my man, because it won't end well for her."

"Please let one of us record so we can put that shit on World Star," I chimed in, making all of us laugh heartily.

"That would be fucking hilarious," Bella agreed.

"Did Perry tell you guys about the party she's having for her boyfriend, Austin in some months?" Khyle inquired.

Hearing that Perry had a boyfriend still surprised me, even though they'd been together for a while. It was just weird seeing her in a relationship, or imagining her even having sex. Not to mention

I expected her to end up with some science nerd, yet she was with a damn dope dealer.

"No, and I'm kind of scared to go. This new Perry is a little off," Bella sipped her drink.

"Well I wanna go and be nosey," I admitted as we chuckled.

We continued our lunch, and then did a little bit of shopping in the mall across the way. We couldn't do too much because Khyle was getting tired, and funny enough, so was I. I usually could walk around this whole mall damn near, but lately I'd been feeling very tired all of the time, and very hungry.

"You going back to the dorm?" Khyle questioned me as we piled into her fresh ass BMW.

"No, take me to Anton's please."

"And I will go with you to Oden's," Bella said to Khyle.

Khyle nodded and pulled out, turning up her music, so the whole way to Anton's townhouse, we jammed to it. It made me miss the parties we used to stay up in, but I knew once Khyle had her baby and recouped some, we'd be back at it.

"I think I'm pregnant," I sighed just as Khyle slowed down in front of Anton's condo. My body jerked when she slammed on the brakes, and I could also hear Bella gasp.

"Bitch, what?" Bella shrieked.

"Yeah, I mean I think so but I'm not sure. Like, I'm always hungry, I feel tired a lot, and yesterday I tried to put on my jean shorts and they were tighter than usual."

"Pregnant," Khyle said.

"We need to confirm though," Bella said. "Let's go to the store right now and get some tests."

Khyle turned back out of the complex and drove to the nearest Walgreens we could find. We picked out three different kinds of tests, and hurriedly purchased them so we could get back to Anton's townhouse before he did.

Khyle barely even parked straight, before we were falling out of the car and rushing inside. I downed a bottle of water even though I already had to pee, and then squatted over the first stick. Only 10 minutes later, I had to pee again so I went for the second one. I felt like that was enough, so I washed my hands and let Bella and Khyle into the bathroom.

"Okay, you got your timer on right?" Bella asked.

"Yeah."

"Wait, what did the first one say?" Khyle inquired, since it had been well over the time for that one to come through with an answer.

"It said negative," I smiled.

Khyle walked over to the sink where it was, squinted her eyes and cocked her head. She then turned to me shaking her head.

"Bitch, there are two lines here, one is just faint as fuck which means it's really early," she said, pointing to it with her long acrylic nail.

"No, I looked at it good!" I rushed over to inspect.

"Oooh, chica, Khyle is right. Your daddy is gonna kill yo' ass," Bella pointed to the second test that came through.

I slowly walked to it, and just stared hard at the word pregnant.

Because this test was the kind that just showed you the word and not some stupid ass lines, it was more obvious. I blinked repeatedly, feeling like I wasn't even in the right body. I never saw myself being pregnant before I got married, or shit, before I graduated college, but here I was. And like Bella said, my father was going to murder my ass.

"I can't be," I mumbled. "My dad is gonna have a heart attack."

"That's the same thing I thought too, Tas. And my dad did go crazy but he eventually got over it. Your dad will too," Khyle rubbed my back.

"No, Khyle, my dad is nothing like yours. He is going to do the most when he finds out." I wiped the lone tear that traveled down my cheek.

"I promise it won't be as bad as you think, Tasmine. My dad was upset at first, but eventually he got over it."

"You're gonna keep it, right?" Bella looked to me.

"Of course, I don't believe in getting abortions. It's just not right. No offense to you guys," I sighed, staring at the test as if that would make it change somehow.

"None taken," they spoke simultaneously.

We hung out for about an hour longer, trying to help me forget about the situation at hand, but it was too hard. About 30 minutes after they left, Anton came home seemingly in a chipper mood. It was different from the mood he'd been in lately, so I guess that whole situation with Oden had been resolved already.

"You look nice." He slid onto the couch next to me and kissed my face. When his hand ran up my thigh, I gently took it into mine, prompting him to sit up and look at me. "You aight?"

"No, I'm not," I shook my head and like clockwork, the tears began running down my cheeks.

I felt bad for more reasons than one. First off, I knew my father would be angry and disappointed in me, and so would my mother. Secondly, I thought I was more responsible than I was, which disappointed me as well.

I didn't know if I was as strong as Khyle. My schoolwork was already too much as it is, so I couldn't imagine having a baby to care for while attempting to write a paper I could barely write before I had a kid.

"Tas, baby, what's wrong?" Anton hooked my chin and kissed me very gently. I covered my face out of embarrassment, and then turned away to dry off the tears.

"I hadn't been feeling too well lately, so I took a test, a pregnancy test, and it said I was pregnant, Tony."

He nodded coolly, before pulling me into a hug. Inhaling his cologne, I broke down yet again.

"It's gonna be okay, Tas. Your people are gonna be angry, but they'll get over it eventually, don't you think?"

"How did you know that, that was the reason I was sad?"

"Because I know you're not sad about you and I having a baby together, right? That's a great thing."

"Yeah."

"And also, I know how much your parents' approval mean to you, and from being around them, I can tell that this isn't something they're gonna be too happy about."

"Right."

"But they love you, and you have your sister and your cousin who are gonna be rooting for you, so relax, babe."

"Okay," I smiled at him, caressing his chin hairs and admiring his deep dark skin. "You always know how to make me feel better, Anton."

"That's my job," he palmed his chest, grinning. "I love you, shorty, and making you happy or feel good is what I'm all about."

"I love you too," I whispered before slipping my hand behind his head to kiss him passionately.

I didn't know if he was right about what he was saying, but it sure as hell felt good to hear him say it.

64

CHAPTER THREE

Shayne

"Well?" I leaned in the doorway, staring at Lloyd as he brushed his teeth.

His towel was around his waist, exposing his chiseled chocolate chest. His facial hair was growing out some more, complementing his beautiful and luminous curly hair. If there was a more beautiful man in Las Vegas, I had yet to see him. However, despite him being so damn fine, I didn't let that deter me from what I came to speak to him about.

"Well what?" he frowned as he began to floss.

"Who the fuck called me from Atlanta, nigga?"

"Shayne, I told you I would figure it out, and to tell me if they called again. Have they?" he looked to me with his bushy brows dipped in the middle. Damn he was fine.

"No, but I'd still like to know. What if they call back, what can you actually do over the phone, nigga? Or what if they're out in Nevada now and don't feel the need to hit me up anymore?"

"I think the baby has turned you into a paranoid person." He gulped down some mouthwash, swished it for a minute and spit it out. "I think it was some bored person that was fucking with you, and you fell for the shit. I mean think about it, how would someone I know in Georgia get your number when I haven't been there since before we linked up?"

I shrugged because I now felt like I was being extra. Maybe it was because I had too much time on my hands now that I was on paid leave from my job. I wasn't even showing yet, but because all of the moving around made me nauseas, I had to go on leave. My manager said I could come back once I hit four months if my nausea slowed up and if I wasn't showing. And if I was carrying like my sister, I wouldn't be.

"Maybe my mind is just too idle." I fidgeted with the doorway as Lloyd approached, towering over me and giving me a good whiff of his body wash.

"Yeah, I believe so."

"Ah!" I shrieked when he picked me up and pinned me against the wall.

Dropping his towel, he reached between my legs and pushed my panties to the side as he sucked on my neck. I felt his head at my opening before he pushed himself inside, filling me up and prompting my pussy to gush all over his rod.

"Damn," he grumbled at the feeling.

Being pregnant seemed to keep my middle wet all damn day. All I had to do was feel something rub against my clit and I was leaking.

"Mmmm, shit, Lloyd!" I cried out as he slammed into me, while gripping my ass.

I was sure the neighbors could hear him pounding into me because one of our picture frames fell, and I was just that drenched down there. Before I knew it, I was releasing on him as he continued to beat it up mercilessly.

"Cum on it again, Shayne," he whispered into my ear before licking it.

I locked my legs around his waist, while he slammed into me, enjoying how sopping wet I was. Our lips met, but because he was pulverizing my shit, I could barely kiss him without hollering.

"Oh fuck, fuck," he groaned against my lips.

Our skin smacking together in combination with his dick slamming into me could be heard around the fucking world. A few more pumps later, and he was filling me up. We stood there, panting heavily while kissing, as my pussy throbbed around his thick dick. He finally pulled out, placing me to my feet, before we resumed kissing.

KNOCK! KNOCK!

Someone knocking at the door jarred us from the position we were in, so Lloyd rushed to the bedroom to clean up and get dressed, and I darted into the bathroom. After getting myself together, I took Lloyd a warm, wet towel to the bedroom and then went to answer the door.

"Damn bitch, you good?" Marisol walked in, dressed to the nines like always. You'd never catch her in a hoodie and sweats. I don't even think she owned a pair of either.

"Yeah… yeah, I am, sorry about that." I swallowed hard because I was still out of breath.

I closed the front door behind her, and then cut the light on in the living room. Marisol had never been over to Lloyd's newest condo, so as she walked to the couch, she took in her surroundings with her mouth open.

"I mean other than the fact that Lloyd looks 10 times better than Pierce, you won because he's definitely more caked up."

"I told you, bitch," I chuckled, looking at how nice Lloyd's place was. He liked for me to call it ours, but I wouldn't do that until we both picked out a big beautiful house.

"And you got his baby? Jackpot!"

"Shhhh!" I put my finger up to my lips.

I didn't want Lloyd thinking I was only with him for his money. I mean, yes, I loved the fact that he was paid, bought me whatever I wanted, and took care of home like a real nigga was supposed to, but I was truly in love with him. I didn't need anything jeopardizing what we had.

"Oh shit, he's here?" she pointed to the back and I nodded.

Just as we sat down, Lloyd came walking from the back smelling good as hell, and looking even better. He wasn't doing too much with his attire, but in my eyes he stayed fitted.

"Sup, Marisol. See you tonight, baby," he leaned down to kiss me.

"Where are you going?"

"To meet up with Oden, Tony, Tru, and Roone."

"Oh, so Oden's not tripping anymore about the situation you refused to tell me about?" I smiled, even though I was a little bothered by him keeping secrets.

"Nope, he's good."

"What situation?" Marisol's nosey ass piped in as soon as Lloyd closed the front door behind himself.

"Girl, I wish I knew. He just said Oden was hot as fish grease, and that someone within their little shit was a snake."

"Damn, whomever it is must not like living."

"Same thing I said. But as long as it's not my baby that Oden is coming for, I couldn't care less about the soon to be victim."

She nodded slowly.

Marisol and I chatted for a little longer before going into the kitchen to start making lunch. My little sister was coming over, and something we always loved to do these days was eat.

"Oh, that must be Khyle," I said once I heard someone knock on the door.

Wiping my hands off, I made my way to the front door to answer it. When I pulled it open, my mood immediately shifted upon seeing Alanna's shady ass standing there like she had an issue. I was pregnant and I wasn't in the mood to tussle with her, so I hoped she wasn't here on any bullshit.

"I need to talk to you," she barged in, making me stumble back some. "Oh wow, new best friend," she scoffed, seeing Marisol in the kitchen seasoning the chicken for the nachos we were gonna make.

"Talk to me about what, Alanna?" I closed the door. "You and I are no longer cool, so I really don't see what the hell we have to talk about."

"Can we get some privacy, please?" she looked to me with pleading eyes as she sat down on my couch.

"No, we ain't close like that no more, so whatever you have to say, you can say that shit in front of Marisol."

Oooh, it was so hard for me not to call her a bitch. Of course I didn't want Pierce anymore; shit, I haven't wanted his ass for a long time, but it just irked me that she would go behind my back like that. It had me wondering if she was only helping me move on so she could be with him.

"Fine," she inhaled and exhaled sharply, while cupping her knees on the couch. "I need you to help me break things off with Pierce."

"Excuse me? Why the hell would I help you with that?"

I turned my lip up at the sight of my old engagement ring sitting on her finger. Didn't even come close to the little 'just because' gifts I got from Lloyd.

"Why do you need help? Just tell the nigga you're not fucking with the relationship no more and it's a wrap," Marisol chimed in, shaking her head at Alanna's ass.

"Anyway, *Shayne*, I need your help because you know him better than me. I don't want to upset him too much, and I do care for him. I just want you to help me let him down easy."

Because I was slightly interested, I asked, "Why don't you wanna be with him anymore?"

"I don't really want to tell you because I'm not in the mood to hear you go off on me at the moment."

"Tell me or I'm not helping you."

I heard the oven close, and when I looked over my shoulder at Marisol, she was tuned in as well, munching on some of the bagged kettle corn we'd been snacking on while cooking.

"Earl Jr.—" Alanna stopped talking once Marisol and I groaned loudly. "He's gonna leave his wife, and he said I needed to break off my engagement if I expected him to let his wife go."

"You honestly think that man is gonna leave a woman he just married some months back? Not to mention the entire time he was with you, he never let her go, yet all of sudden he's ready?"

"Yes, I do honestly think he's gonna leave her! Don't you see that he can't leave me alone? That means something!"

"All that means is that he doesn't want anyone else to have you! He's forcing you to break up with Pierce, and only making you think he will leave his wife so that you will do it! Alanna, get a fucking clue, please!"

I was honestly begging her. I couldn't stand her, but for some reason I loved her and seeing her be so stupid broke my heart. She was gonna end up alone, and with 100 cats if she kept waiting around for Earl Jr.

"For real," Marisol chimed in.

"Bitch, fuck you! I came here to talk to my best friend, not you!" Alanna barked back, moving in Marisol's direction a little bit.

"Best friend? How the fuck is she your best friend when you're currently engaged to and smashing her ex nigga, huh?" Marisol came out of the kitchen, looking just as ready to fight as Alanna.

"I was here long before you! She used to talk shit about you and you think she likes you? Girl, bye! Like I said, stay out of my damn business before I fuck you up!"

My eyes were bucked because I'd never seen Alanna with so much damn spine. I was… speechless, which was crazy for me because my ass always had something to say. My eyes continued to dart back and forth between them as they argued over me like I was some prize, and well, I guess I was.

"Fuck me up? Bitch, I wish you would! You can barely stop a nigga from dogging you out, and you think I'm gonna be scared of you? Please try me so Shayne can see that she needs a bitch with a backbone and a crazy left hook as her best friend."

"Okay! Wait!" I finally piped in when I saw Alanna about to charge Marisol. I knew Alanna would get fucked up, and I didn't want them fighting in the house with all these nice things around. Lloyd would put a bullet in them no problem. "Y'all need to chill. Marisol, go back to the food because my sister will be here any minute and she's gonna want to eat." Once Marisol was in the kitchen, I turned back to Alanna. "Lana, just sit Pierce down, compliment him a little and tell him that you need some time alone because you don't feel right dating my ex."

Alanna glared at Marisol for a few more moments, and then finally turned to me and nodded her head.

"Okay, I will do that." Looking back over to Marisol she said,

"And I will see you, bitch."

"Can't waaaaiit," Marisol sang as she chopped up some jalapeños for the salsa.

"Alanna, leave, please."

"You're really gonna be cool and hanging out with her instead of me?"

"Yeah, me and you… we… we can't be cool anymore. The damage has been done. Be glad I gave you the advice I did."

Scowling, Alanna shook her head and walked out of the door. Not but five minutes passed before Khyle showed up, and boy was I happy that she missed all of that hoopla.

"So how is everything coming along?" Khyle asked as she sat at the bar, watching Marisol and I cook.

"Perfect, Khyle. Perfect."

I had for real just prevented a murder scene.

CHAPTER THREE

Santino D'Stefano

"Congratulations, D'Stefano," my coach brought me into a hug and patted my back.

He'd just had me announce the fact that I was choosing to go with the Los Angeles Rams, so we were about to sip a little champagne since our workout was over. Half of my teammates and I weren't 21 yet, so the coach forced us to finish it off while we were in the locker room.

"Congrats, bro," another one of my teammates, Gerald, slapped hands with me. He, too, had gotten drafted, but to the Steelers in Pittsburgh.

"Thanks, man."

"Huelo would be happy for you if he were here."

"Yep," I nodded and then we parted ways.

Him bringing up Huelo had me paranoid yet again. I felt like Oden was watching me or something, because he thought I told the cops on him.

For one, I wouldn't do that shit because I liked Khyle and they had a baby coming. I wouldn't want her to be alone and having to raise that child. I mean, yes, it was wrong to keep Huelo's murder and murderer a secret, but he brought that shit on himself when he tried to rape the man's girlfriend. I had to put myself in his shoes to really understand that shit. I couldn't imagine walking in on some nigga trying to fuck Bella, especially against her will. I might have killed his ass on school grounds. Not to mention, Oden had saved my life by putting that bullet in Leena's ass.

Truthfully, I ain't want her ass to die, but after seeing she had come to kill me, I was all for murking that bitch. I just wished it didn't have to come to that. It's like no matter how clear you make yourself to these hoes, they still be on some other shit at the end of the day. But hey, at the moment, I was good and my relationship was good. But I knew all would be better once I got word that Oden had found that bad apple.

"Aye man, why you ain't stay for champagne?" I spoke to Trevor since I saw him sitting up in the bleachers of the football field, looking all sad.

"Wasn't in the mood."

"What? Big T not in the mood for no champagne? Crazy," I laughed but he didn't. He just sniffled and looked off like he was in deep thought. Walking up into the stands, I took a seat next to him hoping to find out what was on his mind. "I was just telling everybody about the Rams."

"Lucky you."

"Okay, what's going on with you my nigga?"

"Ain't like you care."

"If I didn't care I wouldn't be asking yo' ass. Now what the fuck got you over here damn near about to cry and skipping out on free champagne?"

"I feel like everybody is getting drafted, except me."

"What happened with the Chargers? Didn't you meet with the coach? I mean he came over for dinner, didn't he?"

"Yeah, and I thought the deal was sealed, but he ended up only being able to draft three players, and three other guys had better stats than me."

"Not here in Vegas, right?"

"Nah, two were in Idaho, another in Utah."

The Chargers were looking at me too, but once I told the scout that it was between the Rams and the 49ers, they left me alone. I wasn't gonna tell Trevor that though, because I felt like it would rain on his already cloudy parade.

"Damn. Well man, there is always next year."

"Really, Sanz? You know damn well that's fucking terrible. We used to always say during freshman year that after sophomore year, if we weren't drafted, we'd move on to something else."

"Yeah, but that's because we said we didn't want to ruin our bodies and shit, but Trevor, you're good, man. Just give it your all in the upcoming fall year, and you—"

"Give it my all?" he turned to me with a deep frown. "Nigga, I busted my ass on that fucking field all last semester, and look where that got me! No muthafucking where! I don't even know why I came to work out today." He shot up to his feet.

"Well, if you're ready to give up so quickly then maybe you don't deserve to be on a team my nigga! This is something you have to work for, and sometimes it may feel like you have to work harder than others."

"Says the nigga who has a contract dangling in his face for millions of dollars."

"Aight," I chuckled angrily, rising to my feet as well. I ain't have time for this shit. I wasn't in the business of coddling grown ass men. "Hopefully, this is just a mood you're in and about to be out of."

I walked off and just glanced over my shoulder to see him still scowling with his jaw clenched tightly. I mean, I understood why he was upset, but I couldn't imagine giving up on football like that. Trevor was a great player, and I felt he should just keep at it.

As I left the area, I made a detour to my car because I wanted to get some snacks from CVS down the street. Bella and I were gonna watch some movies together tonight in the lobby, and she always wanted to have a gang of shit around for us to snack on.

When I got closer to my car, I saw Crystal leaning up against it, wearing a devious smile. I smiled back, and she blushed, making my dick hard. Her body was looking right in that short ass skirt and barely-there top she was rocking, which only made my little man down below, perk up even more. I could smell her sweet perfume the closer I got to her, and when I arrived, she licked her glossy lips seductively, and twirled her ponytail around her finger.

"What you doing out here in Nevada?" I quizzed, adjusting my bag on my shoulder and looking down into her pretty ass face.

"I came to see you."

"For what, Crys?" I was grinning widely even though I shouldn't have been. I checked over my shoulder and around, just to scan the parking lot and make sure that no one was there; no one meaning Bella, Khyle, Tasmine, or even weird ass Perry.

"Because I want to have some fun, and I was hoping that I could finally get a taste of that dick I've been craving for years now. And baby, I know you've thought about fucking me."

You damn right!

"Crystal, I told you I was in a relationship."

"Well, I don't care. I tried being respectful these past few months, but then I thought fuck it. I want you and you want me."

"No, I want my girlfriend."

"Bella is it?"

Taken back a bit, I nodded slowly with squinted eyes. "How do you know my girlfriend's name, Crys?"

"In the age of social media, it's easy to find anything. You guys are sickening on Instagram, my love. It's hard to even ignore the fact that you two are dating."

"Oh well. Anyway, I love my girl and since you follow my social media, you should know that we're engaged already."

"But uh, see, I don't care about any of that."

"But I do. Excuse me, Crystal." I tried to move her to the side but she wouldn't budge.

Before, this was all fun and games, but seeing that she was serious about fucking was irritating me a little bit. It was obvious that no matter what you told these bitches, they still wanted to hop on your dick.

"Remember I told you my dad was the lieutenant of the police department out here in Las Vegas?"

"Never told me that," I sighed.

"Oh, well I'm letting you know now. I'm staying with him for the weekend, and it would be nothing for me to have him look into what happened to Leena."

"What does that have to do with me?" On the inside I was sweating and panicking like crazy.

"A lot considering the fact that she told me she was going to meet you one night, and ever since then, I haven't seen her and her family has been going crazy back in Scottsdale. By saying that, I could give that information to my father and he would definitely start asking you some questions."

"Why are you doing this?" I asked calmly, keeping my hands occupied because they wanted to snap her damn neck.

"I'm doing this because I want you, and I want you to want me. Wait, you already do. I want you to fuck me, Santino." She moved closer to me and rubbed her hand down my chest.

"Crystal, come on man, don't do this shit. I thought we were cool."

"We are cool, but we can be even cooler if you stop being stingy with that dick. Either you fuck me, or you start answering to my father on Leena's whereabouts."

Did I have a sign that said 'Blackmail Me' on it, pinned to my back? It seemed like every time I looked up, some bitch was trying to fuck me over to get some dick. But this one seemed to be the worst blackmail of all.

"Just once?" I finally asked after weighing my options.

There was no way out of this. I mean technically I didn't kill Leena, but I saw who did and I didn't say shit. I could easily run off and tell on Oden, but then I'm sure his people would get my ass. Oden wasn't the type of nigga you could put a stop to just by throwing him behind bars. He could have shit done to you while he sat in his living room watching the football game.

"No, I will see how good you do the first time. If you make me cum good enough, the number will be low."

"Crystal, come on, man. I am engaged! I have no room to mess up with Bella, and I cannot do this shit to her," I pleaded with Crystal, hoping the woman inside of her would surface and understand how this would hurt Bella. And shit, even though I would most likely enjoy the sex, I would feel super fucked up afterwards.

"She won't find out, Sanz. Just think, you get to fuck me on the low, while still being in a relationship with her. But hey, you may realize you wanna be with me instead."

"And how do I know you won't still tell your Dad after I fuck?"

"Because I don't wanna do this to you, Santino. I like you and I'm just trying to show you that we would be good together."

"I'm not spending time with you, Crys. When I come through, I'm gonna fuck you and then bounce. And I'm not eating your pussy."

"Oooh, aggressive. Fine, I just want the dick anyways. And plus, when you see how pretty my pussy is, you're gonna want to eat it."

"Whatever."

The only pussy my mouth had ever touched was Bella's, and it was gonna stay that way.

"So be at my father's house tomorrow night around 9pm. Text me when you arrive, and I will come out and get you. We can do it in the pool house," she whispered the last part, running her tongue over her teeth. "See you tomorrow, baby, and don't even think about trying to play me or the Rams will never have you on their team."

I watched her walk away, before getting into my car and hollering at the top of my lungs. This bitch had me by the fucking balls, and sadly enough, I feared losing my woman more than I feared going to jail. I wanted to just tell her fuck it and allow her to sic her father on me, but that would ruin my life. Because not only would I still lose Bella, but I would lose my football contract. I was just gonna have to do as I was told until I could figure some shit out.

CHAPTER THREE

Anton Nickerson

"He's getting big," I smiled at Athen as I scooped him up.

He was much chunkier now, and looked exactly like Violet. She'd found out who the father was, but he wasn't feeling the idea of being a dad so he told her to kick rocks basically. I enjoyed helping her and being there for little man, but I didn't know how I would be able to keep this up once Tasmine had our baby. I didn't just want to leave Violet's son in the dust or anything, but I also knew if I missed one minute of my kid's life with Tasmine, Tasmine would go berserk.

"I know. I can't get enough of kissing those cheeks," Violet replied, watching her son giggle as I bounced him in my lap.

"Stupid," her sister Vanessa mumbled, shaking her head and inspecting her tired ass ghetto nails.

She lived about 30 minutes away in Arden, so she didn't come up much, but when she did, I tried to stay away. Usually, Violet would tell me when her sister was in town, but I guess it somehow slipped her mind.

"Say something, Vanessa." I looked to her, ready to hear what was on her damn mind. "You've been mumbling and shit this whole time."

"Don't worry about me mumbling, nigga. If I have something to say to you I will say it, aight?"

Chuckling, I shook my head and turned my attention back to Athen. I'd been here for two hours now, and felt like it was time for me to go.

"Aight, well I will see you later, Violet. You need anything?" I looked down at her as I rose from the couch.

"Nope, we're good. Thanks for coming by," she glanced at her sister angrily before looking back up at me with a warm smile.

"No problem."

I hugged Violet, and then continued to the door, ignoring Vanessa's mumbling. I laughed because as soon as I closed the front door behind me, she started going in on my ass to Violet. I was beginning to think she wanted this dick, because she was doing way too much, and cared way too damn deeply about a nigga she barely knew. Yeah, it was obvious what she wanted.

After texting and finding out what Tasmine wanted to eat, I pulled out of Violet's complex and headed towards UNLV. I had only one class this semester before I would graduate, and it was online. Business had been booming and I had less time for class than expected. It was easier for Oden because he'd graduated last fall and had all the time in the world to devote to the liquor line, Palace nightclub, and the vehicle business. I was currently trying to get on his level, therefore I needed to finish strong with this class and get that diploma.

I went to drop off the check for my cap and gown, and as soon as I got back to my car I saw some guy dressed in a cheap looking suit, approaching me. When he saw me about to get into my car, he started jogging which prompted me to be still and place my hand on my burner.

"Anton Nickerson?" he questioned and I nodded.

"You've been served." He handed me a brown manila folder, which I damn near ripped open once I got into my car.

"What the hell?" my brows dipped.

Scanning the document sitting on top, I realized Selinda had filed a paternity suit. I couldn't believe this bitch was coming back with this shit. She saw the damn DNA results just like I did, but she still wanted to take it there. I did not have time for this bullshit. I barely had time to do stuff I cared about, and I damn sure wasn't trying to add these shenanigans into the mix.

Pulling my phone out, I dialed Selinda's ass, praying she answered. I was gonna attempt to talk her out of this shit since killing her wasn't an option right now. I didn't know what all she'd told to her lawyers and whomever else she had involved, and I didn't want them knocking on my door and arresting me for murdering her while I was chilling, like they did Oden. On top of that, she had a son that needed her.

"What!" she barked into the phone.

"A paternity suit, Sel? Really? Why are you doing this to yourself?"

"I'm not doing anything to myself, I'm doing it to you! I was not aware that you were testing my baby, and therefore I want it done over by someone who is not biased."

"No matter who does the test, it's gonna come back the same, saying that I'm not Antonio's father and you know it."

"No, nigga, what I know is that you're gonna pay up once it's clear that you're his daddy. I don't know about these other bitches, but I'm not about to take your medical peoples' word for it."

Laughing angrily, I just shook my head with the phone still plastered to the side of my face.

"Selinda, you're wasting time *and* money, I'm telling you. You fucked my homies and God knows who else, yet *I'm* the father?" I pointed into my chest and frowned as if she were right in front of me.

"Yep!"

"Okay."

"And if you're so sure you're not the dad, then this shouldn't be a damn problem. Only reason you're calling me is because you know the truth is gonna come out, and I'm gonna be deep in them pockets when it does."

"No, I'm calling you because I'm tired of dealing with you. I'm tired of hearing your name, seeing your face, and listening to you accuse me of impregnating you, when you know you're a hoe!"

"A hoe? Nigga, you got me fucked up!" she hung up abruptly as if she were so damn offended.

She smashed the homies and now she's mad because I called her a hoe? You damn right she's a fucking hoe. Hoes do hoe shit like let the homies fuck. I don't know what it was about me that made her point the finger, but I was bored with the shit. I thought having that test done would fix everything, but clearly that wasn't gonna be the damn case with Selinda.

I went and picked some Chinese food up for Tasmine and I, and then headed home. I planned to keep this shit under wraps, but I knew I was gonna tell the homies, and if the homies got to know then so should Tasmine. After all, I learned a hard lesson by keeping secrets from her. I shook my head as I parked at my crib and cut the car off.

"Damn, you already have the plates out?" I laughed, walking through the door and into my kitchen.

Tasmine was sitting down with our plates already on the dining table. I don't know how I didn't recognize the change in her eating habits and behavior before, because it was so obvious. She kind of wasn't herself.

"Yes, I know, but when you called, I couldn't stop thinking about my food order."

"How are you feeling?" I asked, placing the containers down, and then getting some sparkling water for her from the fridge.

"Horrible. I didn't even want to take a shower today, but since your bathroom is so nice, I decided to. But after showering and brushing my teeth, all I did was eat, throw up, and lie down, looking at the TV."

"I don't know if that's normal or not, but we will find out when you go to the doctor. When is the appointment so I can let Oden know ahead of time?"

"You have to let him know? Like a real job?" she chuckled lowly. She hadn't smiled that much in the past two weeks.

"Yeah, just so he knows if I won't be able to make a certain meeting, and usually he will try to reschedule if it's something both Truman and I need to be around for. And fuck you mean, *like* a real job? It is a real job."

"I know, I didn't mean it like that. I meant like a nine to five. I just thought you guys kind of did what you wanted." She reached for my hand as I sat down at the table so we could say a prayer over our food.

Once we were done, it was slightly quiet, due to me trying to get my thoughts together, and her greasing down on her food.

"Baby, Selinda filed a paternity suit."

"What? Why now? You proved that you weren't the father ages ago."

"I don't know why all of a sudden she's doing this, but I have to go to court I guess and take another DNA test."

"But why?"

"She feels like I paid the person to make the results come back the way they did."

"Oh yeah, I remember her saying that the day I saw her in Victoria's Secret. She's like a fucking gnat."

"Don't stress over this right now, you have enough going on. I tried to talk her out of it, but she's adamant that I'm the father, that the court will prove it, and that I'm gonna have to pay up for child support."

"Well, I guess, if that's what she wants. You know it's not yours, and that you didn't convince Phoebe to fuck with the results so all should be well," she shrugged.

"I mean she had sex with Truman, Oden, and who knows who else, so why choose me?"

"Ewe, she did? Wait until I tell Khyle—"

"No, baby, Khyle doesn't need to know about anyone else that Oden fucked," I touched her wrist and we laughed.

It was quiet for a few moments before she asked, "So was it like a train?"

"Tasmine! The fuck man?"

"I just want to know! Like, did she lie there on the pool table with her legs cocked open, waiting for you guys to penetrate?"

"That's nasty, for one. I'm not fucking a bitch in a room full of niggas."

"So you've never ran a train on a girl before?" she raised her brow. I could see in her face how amusing this shit was, and because I hadn't seen her this happy for the past few weeks, I decided to answer.

"Yes, baby, I have done a train before, but I was 14 and a freshman in high school. The girl was some senior cheerleader with a fat ass and nice tits, so hell yeah I got some of that shit."

"So, you lost your virginity to some school hoe, and during a train?" she was smiling while looking disgusted at the same time, which made me laugh.

"Yes, and it wasn't that great. It felt weird being in a room full of people while fucking."

"Oh, okay," she nodded, chuckling. She ate some of her chicken and then asked, "Did you go first or last? Or somewhere in the middle?"

her lip turned up.

"Shorty, eat your fucking food!"

We chuckled in unison.

Just like Tasmine to help get that Selinda shit off of my mind for the night. That's what I loved about her.

CHAPTER FOUR

Oden

$\mathcal{I}$ stood in the background of the underground strip club, just peeping the scene like I'd done in the regular club upstairs about 30 minutes ago. I smiled, watching people have a good time, spending money on drinks, food, and of course the ladies.

Currently on stage was this chick named Brown. She had the sexiest shade of brown skin that I'd ever witnessed, and I guess she knew that. It reminded me of some kind of milk chocolate candy and there was not a blemish in sight. When she first got hired, I thought her name choice was strange until I saw her alluring ass skin tone. And even better was the fact that she brought in a lot of cash, so after only a week, she didn't have to share the stage anymore. She was a great addition after losing Amethyst's crazy ass, and after, Truman decided to impregnate and wife Chiina, taking her away from the dancing department as well. So right now, Brown, unfortunately Ice aka Keesha, and this girl named Caliente, were our top performers.

I knew I should have fired Keesha after she fought my girl and lied to her, but at the end of the day it was my fault, and money needed to be made. I shouldn't have had Keesha at the hoe crib with me, and in a bedroom. It was obvious she thought something was gonna go down so I couldn't put all the blame on her. Plus, Keesha had quite a following here at Palace. Some niggas came here just to watch her, drop loads of bread on her, and then bounce. Khyle already whooped her ass anyway so I felt like she suffered some sort of consequences anyway.

"Hey, boss," Winter walked up to me, smelling very good.

"Hey, what's up?"

"There is a girl here. She says she knows you and she wants to talk to you in private about a job perhaps."

"I mean, I don't really handle that. You're supposed to handle that, and then send them to me for a final interview, Winter. You know that."

"I do, and I explained that to her, but she said she's a friend of your baby mama Khyle, and she didn't want to deal with me. She was kind of rude."

"Aight, umm, tell her to come sit with me. And don't refer to Khyle as my baby mama, that's my girlfriend."

"Got it."

I sat down at the nearby table, which was deep in the back and in the dark. I didn't want to be seen by thirsty ass bitches, and I definitely didn't want to listen to some weak ass nigga tell me how he was just tryna eat and be a part of my team. Shit, I already had a snake within.

As I waited for this *friend,* I sent a text message letting Roone know I wanted to talk to him about helping me take Lloyd out. When I placed my iPhone down, I almost burst into laughter upon seeing that little skinny bitch Khyle hung with occasionally.

"Paris?" I said, pulling a chair out for her.

"It's Perry," she sat down, nose damn near in the air. She seemed to be different than before. Usually she'd be stuttering if I even said 'hello', but now she had… confidence.

"Perry, I'm sorry. Uh," I laughed. "What can I do for you?"

"I'd like a job. My parents have decided that they will only pay for my school fees, residential fees, my on-campus food, and my car note. Anything else I may need like clothes, shoes, extensions, etc., I have to pay on my own."

"Par—Perry, I don't think I have a job for you. I mean our clerical jobs are filled, and even then, you'd need a bachelors degree or four years of experience."

"I don't want a clerical job, I want to be on stage."

"On what stage?" my brow raised.

She couldn't have been talking about becoming a stripper. I mean she ain't really have shit to look at. I don't know about other niggas, but I liked to see ass and titties, and she had neither.

"That one," she turned around and pointed, "over there. I wanna dance. I know I don't have much experience, but I took a couple classes last summer and I think I've gotten it down."

Not wanting to hurt her feelings by mentioning that her physique was the problem, I said, "Perry we don't have any openings for dancers right now."

"Well what do you have?"

"We have two recent openings for VIP and table waitresses, but you can't serve alcohol. I mean the only thing you could do is food delivery and orders."

"Then it's settled," she grinned, moving her hair from her face. I admit she had improved on her looks over time.

"No, it's not settled. Have you ever worked in food service?"

"Yes, see," she handed me her resume. "I worked for Coffee Bean during my junior and senior years of high school. Please Oden, I need the money. If I don't have money I can't buy clothes and that means I'm gonna go back to being that same nerd I used to be, with friends that don't really like me. I may even lose my boyfriend—"

"Aight! Chill! Damn! Fuck did you eat, gunpowder?" I frowned and she giggled nervously. "I have to talk to my girl, and if she's okay with you working here then I will give you a trial run."

"Oh, so she told you."

"Told me what?"

"Nothing. My number and email are at the top of my resume. I will be waiting for your call, Oden. And thank you again."

"Have a good night, Perry."

I shook my head as I looked over her resume some more. We did need separate girls to bring food to the tables since we were becoming more crowded now that it was getting closer to spring. But damn, Perry was weird and quiet, and this job required personality. I'd just have to talk to Khyle.

I messaged Winter to come get Perry's resume and file it. I also told her to put it in my calendar to call her in case Khyle approved.

After scoping the scene for a little longer, and personally checking in on the VIP guests of the club and strip club, I went home so that I could change out of my Gucci slacks and button up.

"Are you gonna be back in time for dinner?" Khyle sat on the bed with her back against the headboard, rubbing her exposed belly.

"Yes." I came to her and bent down to kiss her stomach.

I couldn't wait to meet my son, and it had me thinking about buying a house now. I never thought I needed one, but now that I was becoming a family man, I felt like I did. We needed more room for when we eventually expanded even more, and I wasn't trying to be moving around with *two* babies.

"Where are you going?" Khyle questioned, caressing my hair.

"To a meeting." I pulled my shirt over my head, and then grabbed a pair of black joggers. "Perry came by the club looking for a job. I told her she could be a food service girl, but only if you approved."

"I don't know, Oden, she's sneaky."

"Perry? Baby, I'm talking about the little skinny one y'all use to hang with heavily," I smiled, realizing she didn't know who I was talking about obviously.

"Yes, I know. I had to punch her ass around because she told Raquel about my abortion. How do you think Raquel really found out?"

"I thought she overheard like she said."

"No, Perry told her because she was jealous of the bond I'd built with Bella and Tasmine." She moved around, frowning to show how uncomfortable she was. "But I think it was because she wanted to sleep with me."

I burst into a fit of laughter.

"Wow, I don't mean to laugh, baby, I'm just surprised by that. So I can't hire her?" I placed her cooling back pillow behind her. "She said she needs the money and I low-key feel bad for her."

"Yeah, that's what she does. She uses the sympathy shit to make you do what she wants you to do. But I guess she can't do too much harm working in the club; at least not to me and my friends."

"Exactly. Well, I will give her a trial run and see it how it goes." I kissed her full lips a couple times. "I will be back shortly."

***

Pulling up to the warehouse, I spotted Roone's car. I threw mine into park, and then got out to go inside and meet him. When I got into the room we usually met in as a team, I saw him sitting at the table tapping his fingers against the top. He rose to his feet as I neared him, and we dapped one another up.

"So what's the best way to do this?" I quizzed.

"I mean, I say we get Lloyd down here and just let him know we found out he's a snake, and then blow his head off."

"Yeah, but are you sure? I just can't see Lloyd trying to snitch on me like that."

"I'm 100 percent sure. I mean, who else could it be? Truman and Anton wouldn't do you like that, and neither would I. I love what we have going on here. But Lloyd, I think he's still hot about you smashing his baby mama," he nodded as if he were sure.

"So run it down for me again."

"We umm, were chilling one day outside of his condo, and umm, he was talking to some police officers about something."

"The police was chilling on the porch with y'all?"

"Nah," he laughed. "They came up, I guess when I went to the bathroom. So when I came back out, he was already talking to them about something like in the little parking area surrounding his complex."

"And when you asked him about it, what he say?"

"He just said it was nothing, and he like didn't want to tell me shit else, you know? And honestly, I let it go because I ain't think he'd do you dirty like that, B." He pushed his dreads back nervously.

"You nervous?"

"Nervous? Nah, why would I be?"

"Don't know, that's why I'm asking. You seem a little bit on edge. I hope you ain't been doing lines or some shit because it seems like it."

"You know I don't fuck with that shit, man."

"Good, good," I spoke lowly, keeping intense eye contact with him. His eyes constantly darted away, but I kept staring. "So I'm having trouble with believing Lloyd would do that."

"You are? Why? I mean hey, maybe he didn't. I ain't actually hear nothing, I just saw him conversing with some detectives."

"Well, because your story has changed a lot. I mean one minute it was detectives, the next it's police officers. Then at first you said it was in front of your house, but tonight it happened in front of his," I smiled widely, enjoying the fear I saw in his eyes. "I suggest you drop it." I rose to my feet with my gun drawn. I already saw him trying to low-key whip his out once he'd realized I'd caught on to his ass.

"Oden, man, let me explain to you why I had to do it."

"Okay."

"I'd been telling you that I wanted to get into selling drugs, but you were tripping about it. And man, I felt like I couldn't do this shit right, and I-I-I—"

"I see your mouth moving but I don't hear shit you're saying, Roone." I grimaced down at his drenched face. "And you crying ain't gon' do shit my nigga. The least you could do is go out like a real nigga. Since when does a nigga crying do anything for me?"

POP!

I shot him in his shoulder when I saw he tried to reach for his heat again.

"Ahh! Come on! No! Okay, I'll do whatever I need to do to fix it!"

"Now see, at first I thought you were doing better by trying to kill me just now, but you're back to begging and shit. Damn."

"I can fix it!" he hollered, rocking back and forth and cradling his gushing wound.

Leaning down closer to his face, I gritted, "I don't need it to be fixed, stupid. See, what you failed to realize is that Huelo is nowhere to be found, thanks to you, so it'd be pretty hard to get me thrown in jail for his murder. He's not even declared dead. You get an F for effort my nigga. Maybe Huelo will let you suck his dick for trying to avenge his death."

"Ode—"

POP! POP!

He fell out of the chair as soon as both bullets penetrated his forehead. I shot his ass one more time, and then dialed my clean-up crew to come get his ass out and scrub the area.

Hopefully that was the last snake slithering through my grass, but if I found more, best believe they'd meet the same fate.

I sped home after dealing with that shit, because I couldn't wait to take a nice warm shower, eat, and climb into bed with my lady. Just the thought of feeling her soft skin in our big ass bed had my dick hard.

I pulled into my parking space, and someone pulled up right next to me only seconds later. After pocketing my phone, I got out and the other person and I were face to face.

"Naomi, what are you doing at my crib, shorty?"

"Don't worry, I'm not here to see you. This place had some vacancies, so I decided to move in. I've always loved your home, so," she shrugged, smiling giddily.

"Tell me your joking." I closed my car door and hit the alarm.

"No, I'm not. And don't flatter yourself. I honestly moved into this complex because it's beautiful and spacious. My new job pays well so I was able to treat myself. Maybe you and Khyle can come over for dinner some time."

She pranced off, and hit the corner. I didn't know which condo she was in, but if she parked here it must have been close to mine.

Would I ever catch a damn break?

CHAPTER FOUR

Perry Washington

A week and a half later...

I stood in front of the mirror in my dorm room, putting makeup on as I danced to the Yo Gotti Pandora station. I couldn't believe I listened to this stuff now, but it seemed to be the only thing that helped me get dressed after doing that with my friends and then Austin. I really didn't care too much for the lyrics still, but it was easier to listen to now that I understood many more of the sexual references.

As I put on my mascara the same way I'd seen Bella do it hundreds of times, my phone rang for the tenth time tonight. Austin had been blowing me up because he knew tonight was my first night working at Oden's club. He didn't want me doing it, but I was my own person and no man was gonna tell me what to do. I needed money, and I wasn't gonna depend on him to give it to me; okay, maybe I didn't need money, but I wanted to work at Palace to meet new people. Not to mention I was kind of over Austin's and my relationship. Austin was small potatoes compared to guys like Oden, Anton, and Truman, and

I definitely felt like it was time for me to upgrade.

"Yes," I answered my phone, rolling my eyes.

"You better not fucking go down there tonight, Perry."

"Austin, you're not my father. I do what I want when I want, and until I see a ring on my finger and a marriage certificate, then things are not gonna change," I repeated what Tasmine told me to say.

"You don't wanna see the bad side of me, Perry."

"Why can't you just understand that I'm trying to make money on my own? It's not like I'm stripping, I'm just serving food."

"Yeah, in a tiny ass outfit, and to niggas who are gonna be expecting the works from you! I've been to strip clubs and them niggas expect pussy from every bitch up in there, not just the dancers."

"I'm gonna be late if this conversation goes on any longer, Austin. And regardless of what they expect from me, I'm not gonna do anything. I just wanna get paid."

"Perry, if you—"

I hit the end button and as soon as I did, my music came back through so I swayed my hips, or lack thereof, to the beat. When I was finally ready to go, Bella walked in with sexy Santino who gave me that same look he always did. I knew he didn't like me, and I didn't blame him, but I also didn't care. Plus, I wasn't trying to make amends with him and get my ass beat by Bella in the process.

"Hey, wow, where are you going?" Bella asked as she slid into Santino's lap. He was now sitting at her desk, texting on his phone.

"To work. Khyle didn't tell you Oden hired me at the club? Well the strip club."

"Oh yeah, she did. But what are you doing at the club?" she chuckled almost along with Santino, which irritated me a little bit. I hated that people thought I couldn't be sexy.

"I'm basically a waitress but only for the food. I can't touch the alcohol for obvious reasons. So how do I look?"

"Like a new person, but then again, I've been seeing your style progress a lot lately," Bella replied before turning her attention back to Santino and kissing his lips. I saw their tongues connect, so I quickly grabbed my purse and phone before leaving.

By the time I made it to Palace nightclub, it was 7:55pm, and my work shift was from 8pm to midnight. Oden said he wanted to start me with small shifts as an opener, and then we would go from there depending on how I did. I was getting $16 an hour, which was much more than I expected anyway, so I was fine with such a short shift at the moment. I wasn't sure if everyone got paid that much, or if Oden gave me that much because I'd lied about my parents cutting me off.

Oden was a pretty professional guy when it came to his business, and honestly, I didn't expect such. I thought this would have been handled sloppily, and not as traditional as it had been.

Getting out of my car, I switched through the parking lot in my short black booty shorts, black crop top, and black ankle boots. My makeup was flawless which was due to me watching countless YouTube makeup tutorials during Christmas break, and Bella. My hair extensions were brand new, and my real hair was washed and freshly styled so it had that bounciness to it. To say I looked bomb was an understatement. There wasn't a better-looking red head on the premises at the moment.

"Aye, baby," some guy with a mouth full of gold nodded his head up to me as I approached the front. I simply ignored him.

The place wouldn't be open for five more minutes, and the line was already on its way to being wrapped around the corner.

"I work here," I looked up at the big bouncer when he blocked me from going in.

He just stared at me, so I pulled my new work ID out and showed it to him. He coolly nodded his head, moved to the side, and opened the door for me. As it closed, I heard him yelling at people in the line to get back.

The music from the club upstairs was already thumping, so I guess they were getting ready to open up too. I went to the back locker room, which was next to the stripper one, and put my things up before clocking in. As soon as I did, rap music blasted through the speakers as if it were on some sort of timer set at 8:00pm. I left the back in search of the wide hipped woman they called Winter, and found her talking to that skinny friend of Oden's, Truman.

"Hi, Winter."

"Oh hi, Perry. Are you ready for your first day?" she smiled, pushing her hair behind her ears.

The scent of her lotion was sickening, and you could tell she was the type that bought the whole set at Bath and Body Works, and used every bit of it. That would be fine if the scent was better.

"I'm Truman, one of the owners here," he stuck his hand out to me, as people began to pile into the club, some getting escorted to their tables and VIP booths.

"Nice to meet you, Truman."

"Likewise. You ladies have a goodnight." He walked off, and when he moved past me, I smelled his very nice but subtle cologne. You could tell he was a very clean guy.

"So," I said to Winter who was watching Truman walk away with enough lust in her eyes to get an orgy popping.

"Oh yes. Okay, so earlier this week was all training. Do you remember what you are to do?"

"I believe so."

"Okay, well for starters, here is your iPhone. Now remember what I told you about this phone. It is only for work, and it only works inside of the establishment. It's hooked up to Palace Wi-Fi, and cannot be attached to any other service or it will brick, so don't try to steal it. Do not message your boyfriend, your friends, your baby daddy, the babysitter, or anyone else. The other owner, Anton does periodically check the texts being sent using his system upstairs, and people have gotten fired for using the phone for leisure purposes."

"Got it." I inspected the iPhone 6, which was in pretty pristine condition.

"Now, you're working the same booths and tables as Monica, so that means you handle the food for those booths and tables, and she will handle the drinks. Even if the glasses are empty, do not clean them up. You are not allowed to deal with alcoholic drinks, or even glasses that once contained them. Only clean up the plates, and take orders for food. If the patron is the entitled type and doesn't want to wait for you to get Monica, go ahead and take the drink order down on a napkin, not in your tablet, then pass it off to her."

"Okay."

"Alright, perfect. You're already logged into that phone, so any messages received are for you. Any messages for the whole floor will come to the Palace group conversation here," she pointed with her long fingernail. "Let me know if you need me. The bouncer right there will keep an eye on the place just to make sure the guys don't disrespect you or the strippers." She sauntered off. Her huge butt made her look like a bumble bee.

I slipped the phone in my pocket, and swayed to the music while watching Monica. No one was at her booths or table yet, so she was just making sure they were clean.

"Alright, y'all ready for our opener?" the DJ yelled over the club, and the guys roared loudly, scaring the shit out of me. "Coming to the stage, Kandy and Kokoooooo!!!!!"

Last time we fucked like it was all night. Now you got me thinkin' 'bout you all night. Me and you, seemed like it'd be alright. Long as we can keep it all night…

Kandy and Koko came out to some song by Jeremih, and began swaying their thick bodies. And every time they touched one another, the crowd of men went crazy. I bobbed my head to the music, and scanned the floor to see Oden leaning up against the wall adjacent to the one I was on. Some girl dressed in barely anything, was standing in front of him talking, and they were laughing and stuff.

I wonder what Khyle would think about that.

"Hey!" I heard someone yell, so I looked to see Monica's sections was now packed.

"Sorry," I said even though she couldn't hear me, as I rushed over to her.

"You have to stay on it honey, because it's gonna get crazier tonight, aight?" Monica said once I reached her. I just nodded in response, and got the tablet ready to take the order.

At first I was messing up a little bit, but thank God Monica was nice. She helped me every time, and after a while, when we had to split up due to it being busy, I had it down pat.

"You fellas hungry?" I asked, scanning the crew of guys. The smell of expensive cologne, weed, and the strippers' perfume was in the air.

"Yeah, I want some wings, what flavors y'all got?" one dude spoke up, snapping at the stripper in his lap so that she'd move. He blew smoke out of his sexy mouth as he waited for my response.

"Umm, well we have barbecue, honey barbecue, hot honey, teriyaki, buffalo, and spicy lemon." Why was I so nervous?

I couldn't help but admire his fresh haircut, his crisp quarter sleeved button up in blue, with the heavy gold chain hanging from his neck with a dollar sign attached. Every time he moved, his wrist blinded me. He was so fine that when the disco lights shined on his face, I felt myself getting turned on by just the sight of him.

"Aight, what y'all niggas want? Fuck it, just bring the regular barbecue, baby," he licked his lips and stared at me. I was staring back until he said, "Ain't you gonna write that shit down?" Then he flashed me his beautiful smile.

"Oh, of course. Anything else?"

"A side of fries!" his friend chimed in, looking around the stripper that was straddling and grinding in his lap.

I processed the order right into the tablet, and then turned to leave, but the cutie grabbed me.

"What's your name?" the sexy one asked.

"Perry," I nodded as if I needed to do so for him to believe me.

"That's beautiful." He gazed into my eyes intently again, making me nervous as hell.

I felt like I'd started my period, but I knew exactly what it was… I was horny. The way he licked his full brown lips, and the way his lids sat low over his pretty hazel eyes. His brown skin had not a spot or scar in sight, but I could tell that he was rogue as hell. He was like Austin, but sexier and more rugged; the perfect upgrade like I'd been talking about earlier.

"What's your na—"

"Aye Cash, y'all doing good up in here?" Oden interrupted me unintentionally, as he greeted the sexy man. When he rose to his feet, I almost fainted Disney princess style. You know, all dramatic and stuff.

"Yeah man, thanks for setting shit out for me."

"Only way to do it," Oden grinned. "You doing alright?" Oden looked to me, smiling, and I realized he had a deep dimple in his cheek.

Lord, why do you have me around so many sexy, tall, good smelling men? I'm finally in a relationship!

"Ye-yes, thanks, boss."

Oden just nodded, dapped Cash's friends up, and then left the booth.

"Nice to meet you, Perry. I hope I see you here again soon," Cash said as I tried to walk down the three small steps. I was surprised because I thought he'd forgotten about me that quickly.

"I hope so too."

I was gonna love working here, but I had a feeling Austin was gonna continue to hate it.

CHAPTER FOUR

Bella

"Mmm," I moaned with my face in the pillow as Santino slammed into my sopping wet middle from behind.

He was gripping my hips tightly as his thick rod rammed me with precision. I tried to muffle my moans as the orgasm ripped through my body, sending a tingling sensation throughout my lower half.

"Fuck, you're so wet," he grumbled, slowing down his strokes and winding his hips into me. "You hear that?" he asked, thrusting into me so I could hear how wet I was.

Pulling out slowly, he dipped down and started to suck my clit from the back. He held my butt cheeks apart as he feasted, pressing his face deep in it. My nails scraped the pillowcase I was currently biting down on, as his tongue flicked over my clit. His lips collapsed around it, sucking for dear life, as he slipped his fingers inside of me to hit my G spot.

"Baby, I'm cumming, fuck!" I hollered as he continued to suck on my pussy like a baby did a bottle. Slamming my hand onto the bed, I released and he just lapped all my juices up before sliding back inside of me.

"Shit!" Santino groaned as humped into me, smacking my ass here and there which only made me wetter. "Here it comes… oh fuck, Bella," he spoke, obviously almost out of breath. "Pussy stay tight."

"Ahh! Ahh!" I cried out, feeling his big dick pound my G spot at the perfect pace.

I came so hard my body trembled, and he was right after me, filling me up with his seeds. We sat there in the same position, not caring if someone walked in, before he finally slid out of me. I fell flat onto my bed, because my legs were still shaking wildly, and I was sweating profusely. After a few moments, I finally turned over.

"Hey you wanna— where are you going?" I asked when I saw him slipping his clothes on after wiping his dick down with a wet towel.

"I have a meeting to go to. The scout from the Rams wants me to come and have an early dinner so we can talk."

"Really? Why didn't you mention it before?"

"I just got the text, babe. But do you think Perry is coming back tonight? Because if not, I can spend the night with you."

"She may come, but you can sleep here even if she does. You have before."

I was still lying in my bed, completely naked, and a little caught off guard. I thought we were gonna chill tonight, watch some movies, eat junk food, and fuck some more.

"Aye, calm down, you know I'm not doing no fucking dirt. I

finally got you to be my fiancée, you think I'm gonna fuck that up?" he got close in my face, allowing me to admire his perfectly chiseled features and full lips.

"I know; I'm not thinking anything like that, baby. I just thought you were in for the night."

"Me too until I saw the text. But I have to go shower and brush my teeth so that I can meet this cat. It won't take long at all, so don't start the movies without me." He kissed me a couple times, pulled away to look into my eyes, and then pecked me again but with parted lips. "I love you so fucking much, Bella, don't you ever forget that shit."

"I love you too, baby."

I watched him leave my room, and then grabbed my robe to put on. I paced the room for a second, wondering if I should let my jealousy take over, or just trust my man. He'd never fucked me and left right after like that, so something just wasn't right.

Grabbing my iPhone, I dialed Khyle.

"Hello?" she answered sighing.

"Would you and Tasmine be willing to go on a mission with me?" I asked, still pacing the same spot in front of my bed. I wanted to be ready before Santino left so I could follow him.

"Shit, I'm down," Khyle said.

"What kind of mission?" I heard Tasmine in the background.

"I will tell you guys once you come across the way. Give me like 15 minutes though because I have to take a shower."

"Ugh, you nasty!" they sang in unison.

"Bye!" I laughed, grabbing what I needed for the shower, and darting to the bathroom before them hyenas next door got in there.

I quickly cleaned up, washing my whole body with my favorite soap, and when I got out, I brushed my teeth. I slipped into some tights, a tube top, and a zip up hoodie just as I heard Tasmine and Khyle making beats like some fools on my door.

"Okay, so do we need eggs again?" Khyle rubbed her big belly with a smile. She had no business trying to throw eggs at anybody in her state.

"No, not any eggs, but can we use your car?"

"Yep!" she nodded, dangling the keys to her BMW in the air.

"Okay, I will tell you once we get in the car. Hold up." I rushed to my side of the room, jumped on my bed, and looked down out of the window. I almost squealed when I saw Santino's car still parked down there. "Aight, come on!"

The three of us tread down the hallway, got onto the elevator, and then rode it down and left. We hurriedly climbed into Khyle's car, and she cut the heat on so I could explain.

"Aight, this nigga dicked me down and claimed he had to meet with his coach right after. It's going on 8:30pm right now, so I have no idea why his coach would be texting him this late."

"Not unless he's trying to smash," Tasmine joked, making us laugh heartily as fuck.

"Exactly. So Khyle, I want you to follow his car so we can see where he's going exactly."

"These are my favorite types of missions. Catch a nigga doing dirt missions," Khyle hi-fived me as we laughed.

I was chuckling but deep down I prayed that Santino wasn't lying. I loved him so much and I didn't think I would be able to handle it if he was cheating on me.

"I think he's being honest," Tasmine's optimistic ass chimed in. She was always optimistic with other people's lives, but when it came to hers, you'd bet not come to her with that glass half full mentality.

"I hope so," I sighed.

"There he is! He's jogging to his car!" Khyle tapped me, and we all put our seat belts on.

As soon as he cranked up and pulled out, Khyle started following behind him slowly. She let one car get in between us just in case. I didn't know if Santino knew what Khyle's car looked like, but I wouldn't be surprised if he did. She and I hung together all the time if I wasn't with him, so it wouldn't be odd for him to have seen her vehicle a time or two.

"Damn, where is this nigga going?" Tasmine frowned. "That coach must have a nice little spot."

"I know, right," Khyle agreed.

Right now, I was too in the zone to have conversation. My heart was beating out of my chest, hoping to God that Santino wasn't fucking around. What would I even do if he were going to see a girl? I didn't bring my bat with me, so I guess I would have to just whoop her ass without fucking up her car if she had one. I felt my eyes getting glossy, so I knew I had to change my tune. I needed to have faith in Santino and not believe the worst about him.

"I think we're here, well almost," Khyle snapped me from my thoughts as we followed Santino onto Millhaven Trace Lane.

The whole street was lined with beautiful newly built homes, but not somewhere that I would expect a scout for the Rams to live. Wouldn't he be doing it bigger? Not to mention, wouldn't he live in Los Angeles and *not* Las Vegas? Everything about this sounded fishy, but I still wanted to believe Santino.

Finally, Santino pulled over, so Khyle did the same, but a few houses down. She shut her engine off, and quickly killed her headlights so that he wouldn't be suspicious. All three of us sat there in silence; I couldn't even hear anyone breathing. I think we were all nervous as if Santino were all of our boyfriend. Reaching across the beautiful gearshift in Khyle's BMW, I gripped her hand into mine. I felt her look at me, but my eyes were fixated on Santino's car.

"Oh shit," I whispered as if he'd hear me.

He'd gotten out of the vehicle and closed his door. He stood there for a minute, and then leaned on his whip, dropping his face into his hands as if whatever he was about to do, he didn't want to.

"What is he doing?" Tasmine asked what I'm sure we were all wondering.

After a couple minutes of looking up and down the street, running his hand over his face, and seemingly blowing out hot air due to frustration, he hopped back into his car and closed the door. A few more minutes passed, before I saw his backlights come on and him peel off down the street.

"Go!" I hollered to Khyle who quickly cranked her car up and followed behind Santino but not too closely.

He appeared to be heading back to the school, but instead, kept driving down Maryland Parkway, hooking a right onto Flamingo. He kept going before pulling into a shopping center parking lot. By this time, I didn't want to follow him anymore, and actually felt kind of bad for doing so. His coach story sounded fishy still, but I'd just have to ask him about that tonight.

"Let's just go back to school," I sighed, plopping my head back onto the headrest.

"You sure?" Khyle looked to me and I nodded.

"Told y'all it wasn't that bad," Tasmine sucked her teeth.

"Bitch, it's still up in the air," I laughed, as Khyle whipped it out of the shopping center parking lot and back onto the street.

When we made it back to school, we decided we'd watch movies together in the lobby until Santino came back for me. Khyle went up to her room to get some blankets, Tasmine decided to stay so no one would try to take the living area, and I opted to go get my snacks from my room.

"Damn, can I have some?" Trevor, Santino's teammate grinned at me as I made my way down the hall to the elevator, carrying the snacks.

"No you may not. This shit is for me and my friends, and possibly Santino if he makes it back in time."

"Back? Where is he? It's 8:50 at night."

"He umm, he had to meet with the Rams scout for something."

"Is that what he told you?" Trevor laughed loudly, covering his mouth with his fist. "I guess."

"Why, do you know something different?"

"Nah, I just know the scout for the Rams, Martin Foster, is in New Orleans."

"Like in Louisiana?"

"Well, it ain't here in Nevada, beautiful."

Nodding, I said, "Goodnight, Trevor."

"Same to you."

I didn't want him to see me sweating even though I was already embarrassed as fuck that I'd been duped, and he knew it. Looking over my shoulder, I saw him watching me. When we made eye contact, he gave me a cocky smirk.

As soon as I got back downstairs and sat with my friends, I Googled Martin Foster on the sly. The first thing that came up was a news article saying he'd just signed some guy from Xavier University.

"You okay, Bella?" Khyle looked to me.

"Perfect."

CHAPTER FOUR

Truman

I walked into my son TJ's room to see Chiina placing him in his crib. She was wearing a short white night gown that, in combination with her gleaming golden complexion, made her look like an angel. Coming up behind her, I snaked my arms around her waist and hugged her body tightly while looking down at my kid. He was about to be a month old already, and it seemed like it was just yesterday that he'd gotten here.

"He's so adorable, huh?" Chiina looked over her shoulder at me and I nodded before kissing her soft lips.

Scooping her up, I carried her to our bedroom because I had marked on my calendar when the doctor said she'd be good for sex. I hadn't touched anyone or anything in forever it seemed, so I hoped I was able to get my dick out of my boxers before I came.

"I love you, Truman," Chiina whispered as I released her beautiful curly hair from her bun. I loved to pull on that shit so tying it up was not an option. And while she gave me head, I liked to hold it back for her.

"I love you more, baby," I responded lowly, kissing her collarbone, which smelled like heaven in a damn bottle.

Lifting her silk gown over her head, I let my eyes wander all over her frame. Her body was getting back to normal fairly quickly. The only difference I saw was that she had more hips, and her stomach didn't have that little four pack she liked to rock; it was just flat.

Pushing her back onto the bed lightly, I dropped down, cupping her breasts and devouring her nipples. I had my eyes closed, while making sure to be gentle enough to where I wouldn't hurt her. As I got my fix, flicking my tongue over her hard nipples and latching onto them every now and again, I touched between her legs to see how wet she was. She could give water a run for its money at this point, so I trailed my lips down her stomach until I was face to face with her pussy. Spreading the lips, I saw she was glistening, so I swiped my whole tongue from the bottom to the top, very slowly.

"Mmm," her voice trembled, as she caressed the top of my head.

Placing her legs onto my shoulders, I began feasting on her pussy like it was my last requested meal before the electric chair. I never loved eating pussy the way I did now, because it was something about Chiina's that had me craving that shit. Her pussy stayed wet, it was pretty as fuck, and her nectar had the perfect taste.

"Fuck, Tru," she cried as I sucked her clit like my favorite Jolly Rancher.

I caressed her thighs as she pressed her pussy more into my mouth, winding her hips a little bit. I was slurping, flicking my tongue, sucking, and just going ham on the pussy. Her cries got louder and louder before her body stiffened and then trembled from cumming. She tried to pull away, but I yanked her closer by her ass and continued eating until her juices were covering the whole bottom of my face.

Rising to my feet, I pushed down my boxers and stroked my dick, so she scooted to the edge of the bed to start sucking the tip. She let her tongue play with my head, before easing her mouth down. As she bobbed, her mouth got wetter, and in typical Chiina fashion, she didn't stop it.

"Damn," I threw my head back as I pumped her face.

My hands were all in her voluminous curly hair as she slurped me up like a damn porn star. I was about to bite a damn hole in my lip as I watched her fine ass suck me up like a damn freak.

"Ahh, aww damn, baby," I groaned in a higher pitch than I'd intended to just before busting all in her mouth. She took it down like a champ, and flashed me that smile I fell in love with. "Lay back."

She laid on her back, and opened her legs so I could see my pussy. I climbed in between her legs, and kissed her very softly as my head poked around at her hole. I put her legs over my forearms, and pushed my thick tip into her snug ass hole. I swear she could snap my shit off with how tight she was.

"You okay?" I asked when I saw her frown. She nodded, gripping my biceps with her small delicate hands.

I paused for a second because with just the tip in, I felt myself about to nut. I already got my first one out the way, so the fact that my second one was trying to be quick, lets you know just how good Chiina's pussy was. My second nut usually took a nice little minute.

Once I gained *some* composure, I pushed all the way in, letting out a throaty moan against her neck once she hit the base of my dick.

"Ahhh, ahhh, uuuh," she whimpered softly as I began to thrust in and out of her slowly.

I wanted to savor the feeling, and stop myself from busting too early. I'd been without pussy for so long, and on top of that, Chiina had some fire.

Once I felt her walls start to accept me more, I leaned up off of her in the push up position, and started beating it up. We were singing our praises in unison as I pounded her tight, wet hole. My teeth clenched together when she gushed on my rod, getting even wetter and somehow tighter. She had a straight slippery chokehold on my shit, and it was too damn good.

"Fuck, Chiina, I'm about to nut."

Locking her ankles around my waist, she said, "Give it to me daddy."

That was all it took. A few more slams into her middle and I was shooting up the damn club. Raw sex was the business.

Falling down onto her, I sucked on her full lips as her little hands rubbed up and down my back. I moved my mouth down to her neck, and then back to her lips.

"Shower?" I asked, just as my son started wailing.

"Bath. Get it started and I will be in there, okay?" she smiled as I rolled off of her.

"You notice how he didn't cry until after we were done? That's a good sign. That means my little nigga ain't gonna be a cock-blocker when he grows up!" I hollered after her and she just giggled, grabbing her robe.

***

A few days later...

"How long are you gonna be here tonight?" Oden asked me as I sat behind my desk.

I wanted to just go home and have sex with my girl, but I had too much shit to do. I tell you, I was not used to being so damn backed up. I knew I was killing Chiina, but she'd been taking it like a G for the past few days.

"I'm probably gonna stay until like 1am, just so I can get caught up on the scheduling and have a list prepared of stuff we need to improve on for the employees tomorrow."

"Cool, well I'm gonna go now. Khyle's water is gonna break at any minute and I don't like being away from her for too long."

"Aight, let me know if shit pops off, literally," we laughed in unison, as he reached over my cherry wood desk to dap me up.

"Will do. See you later." He walked out, closing my door behind him.

For the next three hours, I worked, trying to keep my mind on my job and not on getting some pussy. When it was a quarter 'til 11pm, someone knocked on my door. The club was in full effect, because I could faintly hear the music, and when I checked the night's sales, the numbers had spiked within 30 minutes.

"Come in!" I shouted.

"Hey, I brought you a drink," Winter closed the door behind her, holding a glass of something dark. "I know you like bourbon, namely your own brand," she grinned.

I watched her in silence as she switched over to me in her black tight pants and black dress top. Even though her outfit wasn't provocative, her body shape made it appear that way.

"Thank you," I took the drink and set it down. I didn't know her like that, and I had to watch people make my drink before I would actually sip it.

"You're welcome. I thought you needed a break since you've been in here all night." She licked her big lips, and tossed her long brown hair behind her back.

"A lot of work to do. Is there something I can help you with, Winter?" I turned from my computer to fully face her, adjusting my hat slightly so I could see better.

Running her tongue over her teeth she asked, "How long are we gonna do this?"

"Do what?"

"Pretend like we're not sexually attracted to each other."

"I'm not pretending anything with you, Winter. I don't even know what attraction you speak of," I lied through my teeth.

Damn, she was making this hard for me.

"So you've never watched me walk by and thought about bending me over your desk? And you've never imagined my lips wrapped around your dick every time I spoke?" Her brow raised. She had this look on her face as if she just knew I had those thoughts.

"No, I haven't. And I want you to leave my office right now so I can finish my work."

"I don't think you do." She stood to her feet, and leaned on my desk, putting her cleavage on blast.

"Winter, this is a job which means you need to carry yourself professionally at all times. Throwing yourself at your boss is unacceptable. Not to mention you know I have a girlfriend whom just had a baby. I'm giving you one more chance to get the fuck up outta here and still have a job."

She got up off of my desk with a stunned expression. I knew she was surprised by my reaction, and shit, so was I.

"Sorry about that, boss, it won't happen again. I won't be here tomorrow since it's my day off, but if you need me, just call Treasure Island hotel. I'm in room 1214."

She wasn't slick at all. She gave me that information because she wanted me to stop by tonight. Shaking my head at her and at my hard dick, I went back to work.

When the clock hit 1:10am, I was finally done, so I shut down my shit and left the club. When I got home, I checked the oven and saw Chiina had a plate for me in there. Uncovering the fried chicken, macaroni and cheese, sweet potatoes, and string beans, I did a little dance at the smell. I got some water from the fridge, and then killed that plate before going to the bedroom.

Once I did though, I stripped down out of my clothes, and

climbed into the bed with Chiina.

"Baby, wake up." I kissed the nape of her neck, and started trailing down while lifting her nightgown. Her thighs felt so smooth as I groped and caressed them.

"Not tonight, Truman. I'm still sore from this morning," she whispered, moving my hands from her petite frame.

Falling onto my back, I let out an exasperated sigh. My dick was rock hard, and I wasn't in the mood to jack off. Glancing over at the clock, I saw it was 2:15 am and I knew Winter got off at 2:30 am. I contemplated for a minute, before rolling out of bed quietly and slipping my clothes back on. I crept out of the house, got into my car, and sped off to Treasure Island hotel.

When I got there, I gave my car to valet, and just sat outside. I didn't want to go into the lobby because I was sure some people who knew me would see me. This secluded seat outside was perfect, especially because I had a large hood over my head.

By the time I spotted Winter taking a ticket from valet, it was 2:55 am. I was about to leave since I'd changed my mind, but she called after me. Pausing for a second, I turned on my heels to face her. She switched towards me with her purse hanging from her forearm, smiling widely.

"I see you came."

"How'd you know it was me?" I quizzed, looking down at her.

"I know how you walk. No one is as bowlegged as you, baby," she winked. "Ready to go up and have some fun?" she cocked her head and licked her lips, awaiting my answer.

As I stared down at her, it was like I had finally realized what the fuck I was doing. I loved Chiina, and I had no business bringing my ass over here in the middle of the damn night. I was just gonna take my ass home and see if a cold shower would help.

"Nah, shorty, I don't even know why I ca—"

"Truman!" I heard a very familiar voice bark. "Truman Morrison!" she yelled again, but with more bass in her voice. I was scared to turn to her, but I knew if I didn't she might shoot my ass.

"Is that your baby mama?" Winter asked, eyes bucked. I still hadn't looked over yet.

Ignoring Winter, I turned to see Chiina in the driver seat of her Lexus with the passenger window rolled down. Her glare was hard, and I was beyond scared to get in the car even though I was bigger than her.

"Chiina—"

"Get in the fucking car, nigga!"

"I drove here, I can't just leave my fucking whip!" I yelled back, trying not to look like a complete bitch in front of Winter.

"Get in this car, before I get out and beat you and that bitch's ass," she gritted.

"Go," Winter nudged me with her scary ass.

Before the door even closed good, Chiina peeled out of the roundabout driveway, going about four hundred miles per hour. All I was thinking about is if I was gonna live tonight, and when I was gonna get my damn car from valet. I looked in the back seat to see my son's carrier, but the blanket was covering him.

"Why you got him out here at this time of night?"

"Because his daddy decided that he wanted to go back to his hoe ass ways and creep out!" she screamed as she dipped through traffic.

"Stop yelling with him in the car."

"Nigga, fuck you! You thought I was playing with you when I said I wasn't taking any more of your shit, Truman? Nigga, I'm ready to stab you." She plopped back in her seat since we were at a red light. She looked good as fuck in her cloth shorts and top with no straps. Her curly hair was wild, but it looked nice. "Hello?" she barked, smacking me across the head so hard I almost hit her ass back.

"Baby, I'm sorry, but it wasn't even like that. She works for me and—"

WHAM!

"Lie again!" she sped off at the green light, periodically looking from the road to me and vice versa. If I got another hit, I may slip into a coma. She was strong as fuck.

"Baby, I'm sorry, what you want me to do?"

"Nothing. Don't do a damn thing. I don't wanna be with you anymore anyway. You're nothing but a little ass boy who can't control his dick. I will get me a man and be just fine."

"I am a man."

"You're really not," she chuckled as if she honestly believed her words. "Men know how to be faithful. Then again, the woman has to make you want that and clearly I'm not it for you." She quickly wiped the one tear that had dripped from her eye before swooping into the park at our townhouse.

"Chi, don't cry, baby. You are it for me. I just had a slip up. I've been doing good this whole time, but I almost relapsed. I need time to change completely."

"Yeah you do, but I won't be your fiancée while you do it. Go back to Pilar, she's used to your little boy bullshit." She took her ring off and reached it out to me.

"Not gonna take it."

"Fine." She threw it in my lap and got out of the car.

"Chiina, for real?" I smacked my lips as soon as I got out the car too, rounding the back as she got our son from the back seat. "This is one mistake! It's been months since I've done anything! And technically I didn't do nothing! I was telling her that I was leaving when you pulled up!"

"I've given you enough chances, Truman."

"Baby, please, what you want me to do, beg? I will beg you." I followed her to our front door.

"Don't, it won't help you." She walked in the house with me following her.

I continued trailing her as she laid our son back into his crib. She then went to the bedroom to change and climb into bed. I stripped down to my boxers and got in with her.

"TJ and I will go stay with my aunt until I find a place since I was stupid and let you convince me to give up my new condo."

"Chiina, please."

"It's done, Truman. Accept it now."

I sat up on the edge of the bed, and just dropped my face into my hands. I felt so stupid and disappointed in myself.

CHAPTER FIVE

$\mathcal{I}$ woke up feeling excruciating pains every other minute or so, which made me yell out. They were horrible and something I'd never felt before. Before one groan finished, another burst through since a new sharp pain took over my body. As tears came out of my eyes, I hit Oden on the back repeatedly. I didn't know what the hell was going on, but I didn't want any more of it. He needed to clock my ass with the lamp and then call the ambulance.

"What? What, Khyle?" he turned to look at me. I could tell he was really tired, but I would give my left leg to end these pains so I didn't care. "Baby, why are you crying?"

"I'm in pain! Call the hospital! Something is wrong with the baby!" I whined loudly.

"Okay, okay. I'm gonna call Dr. Parrish."

He jumped up quickly and grabbed his phone from the dresser. As he spoke to my doctor, he stared down at me in horror. I was sure the doctor could hear my screams in pain because I couldn't even hear anything else once I opened my mouth.

"Aight, baby, come on. He said it's probably labor pains. Just do that breathing shit you learned for a quick second." Oden rushed out the bedroom.

He brushed his teeth and then slipped on some sweats, a wife beater, socks, a hoodie, and some sneakers, while swishing mouthwash. He came to my side of the bed and peeled the covers back to help me once he came back from spitting it out.

"I can't do it tonight. I'm not ready," I whined.

"Maybe tomorrow. He said this can last for hours."

"Hours!" I began crying as Oden sat me up.

Right when I got to my feet, liquid gushed from between my legs. I was happy but I wanted to sob because I knew I was gonna have my baby soon. I was so scared of the pain. The way my mother explained it had me biting my nails down to the white meat. She went all natural with Shayne, but got the shot with me. I was definitely getting medicine because these labor pains alone were about to have me six feet under.

"Shit, come on," Oden gripped my body.

He helped me out of the house, grabbing the bag we had packed that was sitting on the table by the door. Once we got into the car, he sped out of the complex, allowing the cool night air to hit me. It seemed to help distract me from the pains so I didn't complain about my hair getting in my face like I usually did.

When we arrived, Oden had them bring a wheelchair out, and then they helped me into it. Rolling me to the back, they got me out of my nightshirt and hooked me up to all of these machines that were giving me a headache because of the beeping. And worst of all, while I laid there in pain, Oden was just chilling, feeling all good.

"We're not having anymore bab— ah!" I cried out at the sharp unbearable pain, letting tears fall down.

"Uh huh, shut yo' ass up talking mess," Oden laughed as I laid there crying. He got up from his chair and smoothed my hair back before kissing my wet cheek. "It'll be over soon, baby."

"When! It's been hours!"

"It's only been an hour and a half shorty, relax. Just do your breathing—"

"It doesn't work!" I growled, making him buck his eyes and smile like this was amusing. If someone gave me a gun, I just might shoot his ass then myself.

"Hold my hand while I call your parents. Just squeeze it when you feel a pain, okay?"

I nodded as he dialed my mother and father's house. I didn't know if they'd answer since it was so late, but we did tell them that this might happen. My dad said he had a friend at the airport that could get him on the next flight to Vegas whenever. I just prayed the next flight wasn't hours away.

I listened to Oden call my parents, and squeezed his hand hard as hell whenever I felt the pain. I looked over at his face to see if I was hurting him because it seemed like I was, but he was unbothered.

He finally got off of the phone and said, "They will be here as soon as they can."

"Did you call Shayne like I asked? I asked you to call Shayne."

"I will, baby, but I need your phone. You made me delete her number, remember?" he frowned in confusion.

"Don't look at me like I'm crazy," I sniffled. "Get my phone." I pointed to the baby bag we brought in, so he went to retrieve it.

As he talked on the phone with Shayne, a nurse came in to check me.

"It's time, honey," she said after looking at me.

"For the shot? I've been asking for the shot for the longest."

"I know, and we were scheduled to give it to you in the next 10 minutes but right now, it is too late." Her mouth seemed to be moving in slow motion when that last part of the sentence came out.

"Too late? Too late? What does that mean? I said I needed the medicine earlier!" I cried, just thinking about all those natural births I watched on TV.

"I understand, and we didn't expect you to be ready for birth so soon. You jumped from five to 10 centimeters so quickly. Again, I'm sorry. Daddy, please follow me so you can get cleaned up and changed." She rushed out for the doctor with Oden on her heels as I began to wail like my life was over. It was over. I couldn't survive this.

The doctor, two nurses, and Oden returned, and by that time I was sweating profusely.

Lord, when I see you today, please let me into those pearly gates.

"Alright Ms. Luke, let's get a good first push," the doctor spoke from between my legs after everyone got in position.

"Ahhh!" I yowled.

*****

A couple days later...

Oden opened the front door of our townhouse for me, while holding our son, Oden Jr. in his carrier. I felt so sore still, and was surprised I could even walk. My parents and sister had been up to the hospital every day since I had him, and it felt good to have my family there. On one day in particular, my family was there, and so were Bella and Tasmine; that was really cool to me.

"Okay, honey, I prepared a dinner for you guys that should be good for tonight and tomorrow night," my mom said as soon as I sat down gently on the plush couch. Oden placed the baby's carrier next to me, and Shayne sat on the other side so she could look at him.

"Thanks, Mom."

"You need anything else honey?" my dad looked at me. I knew this situation still had him feeling some type of way, but he was doing great at not saying anything about it.

"No, I'm good."

"Did you guys need a ride to the airport? It's on the way to the club. I have to get some work in anyway," Oden offered.

"Yeah, thanks, son," my dad nodded. Both of my parents came over to kiss and hug Shayne and I, before leaving with their bags.

Oden pecked my lips a couple times, and then followed after them so he could drop them off at the airport.

"Wow, so you're a mom now," Shayne grinned. "He is just the cutest little thing. I have never seen such fat cheeks on a newborn," she chuckled.

"Yes, I know. I thought he had something in his mouth when they first brought him to me. And what do you mean *I'm* a mom? You'll be a mom soon too."

"Yeah, but I'm not yet," she giggled and so did I. "So how does this work with school? I mean, do you get time off?"

"Yeah, I told my teachers he'd be coming some time this week, so they just asked that I show proof, and then they will send me my assignments through email. Oden is gonna take them the letter from my doctor."

"I see you got everything handled."

"Yep. So how are things with Lloyd?"

"Great as usual. But someone has been playing on my phone from Atlanta, and I think it's because of him. They'd been doing it for like two weeks, and then when I finally called back the number was disconnected and they stopped for a bit. Now they're back at it again."

"What'd Lloyd say?"

"I told him about it, and he said if they started back to let him know but I didn't. I'm clearly gonna have to take care of this shit myself."

"Shayne, you're almost five months pregnant, what are you gonna do?" I laughed at her as she tousled her hair and sucked her teeth.

"I don't know, put a hit out on the bitch? I just want to find out who the fuck is playing games on my phone. Lloyd just better hope it doesn't have anything to do with his ass."

"I hope so too, for his sake," I chuckled. Shayne was just as crazy as me. My mom always said we got that from our father because she was never as feisty.

"Want me to warm your food or go get you anything? My appointment is in a little bit, and I have to go home to meet Lloyd."

"Could you just make me a banana smoothie, and warm whatever mom made for me tonight. I'm sure she has it labeled."

"Okay."

Shayne made me a smoothie as requested, and put it into my reusable cup I'd gotten from Starbucks. She then warmed up the chicken quesadilla my mother made, and put some chips with the homemade salsa in a bowl for me. She laid out a couple bottles of water on the coffee table, and a few of my favorite snacks my mother purchased from somewhere.

"Thank yoooou," I sang, eating my food.

Shayne leaned down to kiss my cheek and said, "You're welcome." Turning to Oden Jr.'s carrier she beamed, "Auntie will be back to see you soon."

When she left, I continued to eat and as soon as I was done, my baby began crying. Since I had all his stuff nearby, I quickly changed him and then breastfed him. I didn't want to breastfeed, but when the doctor told me it'd help me lose my stomach and it was better for the baby, I was all in.

Finally, he fell back to sleep, so I placed him in this little bed pallet that Tasmine bought for me, on the couch. I kissed his plump cheek, and then turned the TV on so I could catch up on some shows that I would usually miss while in class.

KNOCK! KNOCK!

I paused the Maury show, and then made my way to the door to peek outside. I saw that bitch Naomi standing there holding a big platter of some sort of food. What the fuck was she doing here?

"Yes?" I opened the door.

"Hi, Khyle. I heard you had your baby, and I just wanted to bring by some of my oatmeal frost cookies. They're homemade."

"Oh. Thanks, but I don't like oatmeal cookies," I lied.

"Really? Oden *loves* my cookies. I'm sure he wouldn't mind having them all to himself so here you go." She reached them out to me, and I just looked at the plate like it had shit on it.

"No, he only eats what I let him, and unfortunately oatmeal cookies are on the banned list," I fake smiled.

"You know, neighbor, we should try getting along."

Neighbor!

"Neighbor?" I turned my head slightly so that my ear was towards her face a little. I hoped I was hearing her incorrectly.

"Yes, neighbor. Oden didn't tell you I moved into this townhouse complex? It's so beautiful and nothing else compared, so when I saw there was a vacancy, I hopped on it. A bit pricey but it's worth it and I can afford it. I party plan for *Maxim* magazine."

"Thanks for that information. And no, he didn't tell me."

"Really? He must have felt the need to hide it."

"Or he forgot because it wasn't important."

After staring at me with the tip of her tongue sitting on her front teeth for a little bit, she finally said, "You know, Khyle, before you there was me. Oden was in love with me, and everything I did. Do you honestly think he's just somehow over that?"

"Yeah, I do," I half lied. I knew he loved me, but I wasn't sure if his feelings for her had vanished.

"Wow, I forget how young you are sometimes. Well, I'm just here to tell you that I'm very much in love with him, and I plan to rekindle the love we had. But don't worry, I will make sure he's a good father to your son or daughter."

"You couldn't pay him to leave me." I wanted to fight her so bad, but I had stitches down below, and my doctor specifically said no rough activities.

"I won't have to," she smirked before winking.

I chuckled lightly before flipping the plate of cookies up, making it hit her in the chest and the cookies fly everywhere. She yelped just as I slammed and locked the door.

I wasn't gonna lose a wink of sleep over that bitch's threats. And if by a miracle she did get Oden to leave me, I'd kill both of their asses.

CHAPTER FIVE

Tasmine

Some weeks later…

"You sure you don't want Anton to fly you out like he offered?" Khyle frowned.

She, Bella, and I were sitting in our dorm room, along with Baby Oden. He was such a cute well-mannered baby. He stayed quiet pretty much most of the time, and he had cheeks that looked like lollipops were stuck in them. Seeing him definitely gave me some excitement about the baby I was carrying, which was new for me.

"No. I was gonna wait two more months for when summer hits, but I will be a little too far along at that point. It's been long enough."

"And it's safer to tell your parents over the phone," Bella nodded and I definitely agreed.

Once I started dialing, the three of us took a deep breath as if we were all in the line of fire. But that's just how close we'd become. I never thought I would meet two of the greatest girls ever while being here in college, but I had. I couldn't ask for a better set of best friends. I was really blessed to have Bella and Khyle.

The line rang and rang as I held my breath, and finally when my mother answered I exhaled.

"Hi, Mom, is Daddy around?" I questioned, feeling Khyle and Bella's eyes on me.

"Yes, you'd like to speak to him without even talking to me?" she joked.

"No, I want to speak with both of you," I giggled to lighten the mood.

"Oh, I was gonna say. I know my baby didn't call here and not wanna speak to her mother. Hold on one second, honey." She pulled the phone away. "Myron!"

"Huh?"

"Come to the den, Tasmine wants to speak with us!" she hollered back. "Okay, he's coming. So how is school going? You're gonna be home for the summer in soon, and then on to junior year."

"I know, time is surely flying, Ma." I fidgeted with the ends of my sweater.

"It is. Okay, he's here darling, and you're on speakerphone now." She sounded slightly further away so I already knew that.

"Hey, Daddy."

"Hey, sweetheart, is everything okay?"

"Yes, it is." I glanced over at Khyle and Bella who were chuckling lowly while on Snapchat. "Actually, Daddy, no, everything isn't okay."

"What's wrong, baby?" my mom inquired.

"I umm, I'm pregnant by Anton," I finally blurted out. There was silence. It was so quiet I thought they might have hung up on me. "Hello?"

"Ye-yes, baby, we're here," my mother replied. "Are you sure?"

"Yes, I'm sure. I found out some time ago. I'm a week shy of being two months pregnant now, and—"

"Tasmine, you're coming home!" my dad barked. He must have taken it off speakerphone because he sounded much closer than before.

"Dad, I'm in the middle of the spring semester I can't—"

"And once it completes, you are coming back to Kentucky and you will attend University of Louisville for your studies."

"But Daddy, it's too late to transfer. I would have had to apply last year for that. You know that! And I don't want to leave! I can't. I have my friends here, Anton, and—"

"I do not care what you have! If you want to continue spending my money and living off of me, you will come home in May like I just advised you! I do not want you around that boy anymore!"

"He's the father, Daddy, I can't do that! I won't stop him from seeing his baby, and I love him!"

"You don't love him, you're just a confused little girl who's emotional right now. And believe me, that boy does not love you! No matter what he tells you, once that baby gets here he's gonna be a new man."

"Daddy, please," I cried, as Bella and Khyle neared me to rub my back. I knew he'd be mad but I didn't think he'd go this far.

"Tasmine, agree to come home or you'll have to figure out how to pay for your classes, dorm fees, dining, and anything else you need to finish school in Nevada. Don't forget you're an out-of-state student so it's a lot of money."

"I can't, Daddy. I'm sorry I made a mistake, why can't you see that and just forgive me? I will finish school, and I will still make you proud—"

"You can't make me proud now that you're gonna be some teenaged mother!"

"I will be 20 in June!"

"Here, Junie. Take this phone before I fly down there and kill her and that boy. She's either gonna come home, or she can pay her own way," I heard him tell my mother with the phone pulled from his mouth.

"Honey, just come home. What's wrong with going to school here?"

"A lot, Mama. I like it here, and my friends are here. Not to mention Anton lives here, and I have been set up with his doctor under his insurance."

"Your friends can visit; well Bella can. Khyle is a bad influence. You would have never gotten pregnant if you weren't friends with her. I knew she was fast the first time you showed me her picture."

"Ma, stop it, she has nothing to do with this. I'm gonna go, I will talk to you guys later. Tell Tasia and Mia I love them."

"Tasmine—"

I hung up in her face, which I would have never done, but she and my father had pissed me off. I understood that they were angry, but to try and force me to move back home knowing I'd made a life here was fucked up. Not to mention what my mom said about Khyle. Khyle had nothing to do with me letting Anton fuck, and raw at that. I didn't like hearing her get talked badly about.

"They will come around," Khyle said, ending the awkward silence in the room.

"No, I don't know if they will."

"What all did they say?" Bella quizzed.

"Just that I needed to come home and go to school at University of Louisville," I sniffled.

"No, you cannot leave Vegas for good," Khyle shook her head.

"Hell no, especially not now that Khyle and I are moving here. Well, that's if I still wanna be with Santino, but you get the point."

"Yeah," I chuckled. "I don't want to leave but they said I would have to. I mean if my dad stops paying for school they're gonna kick me out anyways."

"Ask Anton, shit," Khyle said before slapping hands with Bella. "It's his baby too, and I'm sure he would do anything to keep you from having to go back to Kentucky."

"I can't ask him."

"Why the fuck not?" Bella placed her hand on her hip.

"Okay, maybe I will."

"No, you will ask him and he will say okay. If not, I will let you borrow my bat so you can bust his ass over the head."

We all burst into laughter at Bella's violent ass. Bitch had a bat but never played softball or baseball in her life.

"Thanks, B. I will keep that in mind. Now can we go to Fridays?"

"Yeah, let me just text Perry because she wants to come," Bella said, typing on her iPhone.

Oh Lord.

***

The next night…

Standing up in Anton's huge Jacuzzi tub, I grabbed the big warm brown towel that I'd placed nearby to wrap around my body. Before drying off, I misted myself with scented oil, and then began patting myself dry.

I loved spending my nights here, especially when Khyle stayed with Oden. She was doing that every night now that she had a baby. It worked out though, because Oden and Anton lived in the same townhouse community, so I was still close to her. And even better was that Bella had convinced Santino to look at a place over here.

"Smells good in here," Anton came into the bathroom wearing just boxers, basketball shorts, and socks. His deep dark skin looked so beautiful, decorated with his many tattoos. His strong chest, arms, and chiseled abs only added to his sexiness. I could tell that he'd just gotten his hair cut and his beard lined up, turning me on like crazy. This pregnancy had me acting like an addict for the dick.

"Hey," I gave him a small smile as I began to brush my teeth.

He peed, flushed, and then began washing his hands as I handled my mouth. As I flossed and then rinsed, he planted soft kisses on my damp neck and back, before hugging my body from behind. I spit the mouthwash out, and then picked my head up to look at him through the mirror.

"You're so beautiful, Tasmine. Every time I look at you I'm in awe," he spoke lowly, before kissing my neck.

"Thanks, baby."

He removed my towel so that it dropped to the floor, and then started kissing from my shoulders all the way down to the small of my back. Spreading my cheeks a little, he began pecking my lower lips gently, making me so fucking wet. Clutching the sink, I let out soft moans as he devoured my middle like I was his favorite food—macaroni and cheese.

"Babyyyyy," I whined, feeling his tongue flick over my clit before he went back to sucking it.

I knew my juices were covering his mouth because I was sopping wet down there. My body shook subtly when I came, so Anton began sucking my button harder, and slurping my nectar like a thirsty animal. He lifted my left leg a little, and pressed his face further into my center, prompting me to cry out pretty loudly just before a powerful orgasm tore through my body.

"Tastes so good," he whispered to me on his way to standing up, sucking random areas of my back until he got to my shoulders.

He turned my face to the side so he could tongue me down, as he pushed his bottoms to the floor. He started teasing my clit with his thick head as we kissed, making me even hornier. He always knew just what to do to push me over the edge. He bent me over the sink gently, and then pushed himself inside of me, causing me to cry out.

He spanked me a couple times as he thrust into my pussy from behind with precision. I held onto the sink for dear life as he pummeled my center, making me cum so hard I felt it dripping down my inner thighs.

"Ahhh! Ahhh! Ahh!" I cried in sync with his pumps.

Gripping my hair, he pulled me up to suck on my neck while pounding into me from the back. I gushed on his pole once again, before he gripped my breasts and came inside of me. We both collapsed down onto the sink, breathing like we'd just ran a marathon. I figured this was the perfect time to ask for a favor.

"Baby?" I panted.

"What's up?" He gave me light kisses on my back as he slid out of me.

"My parents aren't gonna pay for me to go to school anymore because I won't come home for good. They were mad about the baby. I did my best to convince them—"

"I got you," he cut me off, turning me to face him and pecking me.

"You do?" I pulled away.

"Yeah, I do. I love you, Tasmine, and I told you I'm gonna marry you. Plus, it's about time I started taking care of you as your man."

"I'll have money one day too."

"I know, and at that time you can take care of me and my baby." He draped his strong arms over my shoulders. He smelled so good, even after a sweaty sex session.

"I may do so." I tilted my head back so he could kiss me. "Thank you, Tony."

"No, thank you. You've done a lot for me, baby, whether you realize it or not. So me paying for your schooling and shit ain't nothing. I think you need a car now too."

"I do! I love the new— I mean, get whatever you want me to have."

"Nah, tell me what you want."

"Okay, I love the S-Class Mercedes. It's a lot, so you don't have to get it but—"

"Stop with that fake modesty shit. I know you want me to buy it no matter what," he grinned, and I laughed because it was true. Khyle told me how much money they made *just* from the club alone, so he had it. He could buy hundreds of those Mercedes.

"Thanks, baby daddy." I started cleaning between my legs.

"You're welcome. And I think we should fly to Kentucky and talk to your people some time soon." He cleaned his dick off with a warm clean towel, and then tossed it into the hamper before cleaning his hands. I followed suit, tossing my towel and slipping my hands into his under the warm water. "But for now, let's go to sleep."

"Ah!" I shrieked and giggled when he scooped me up bridal style.

I knew he was right about going to work things out with my parents but… I just didn't want to right now. I was afraid.

CHAPTER FIVE

Shayne

Khyle, baby Oden, Marisol, Khyle's friend Bella, and I were out to lunch at this place named Eat. It was a very interesting spot, and when Marisol said this was where we were going, I hesitated. But the food turned out to be bomb as hell, so everyone was happy; or at least I was happy.

"Okay, I'm tired of waiting, Shayne. Am I having a niece or nephew?" Khyle smiled, munching on her salad. Now that she'd dropped my nephew, she was eating super healthy and working out. She was determined to get her body back, which never even really left in the first place.

"Fine, but I need a drum roll," I grinned, making her and Marisol roll their eyes. Bella started doing the drum roll, which was why I liked her ass. "It's a little boy," I poked my lip out.

"That's not what you wanted?" Marisol quizzed.

"I didn't care what I got too much, but I was hoping for a girl. I feel like he and Lloyd will be on a team and I will be by myself."

"Boys usually cling to their mommies at a young age," Bella said, sipping her drink.

"Really?"

"Yeah, and girls cling more to their dads," she added. "At least that's how it went with my brother and me."

I nodded, taking in what she'd said. I hoped she was right because I could already feel myself getting jealous just thinking about my baby crying because he wanted his dad and not me.

"Well then, I'm very happy that it's a little baby boy in here." I rubbed my small but still slightly noticeable bulge.

"Shady ass," Marisol joked. "Khyle, have you healed and stuff down there yet?"

"Umm, it's gotten better but not all the way. I still have two more weeks before any activity can take place."

"I know Oden is going crazy. He has a big sexual appetite," Marisol laughed, prompting Khyle to look at her.

Oh fuck.

"How would you know?" Khyle's eyes squinted at Marisol, as Bella and I sat there on the edge of our seats.

"How do you think I know? I fucked him before, on more than one occasion. Shayne and I did it together once," Marisol laughed, but it faded once she realized no one at the table was on that same tip.

"Can anybody at this table say they haven't fucked my boyfriend?" Khyle scanned the three of us, wearing that fake smile she always wore when she was heated. Bella slowly raised her hand with a shy smile.

"Thank God." Khyle went back to stabbing her salad. "And for the record, Marisol, if you're gonna be around me, I would appreciate it if you didn't bring up my man and what kind of appetite he has. I know everything about him so I don't need you dropping what you *think* are facts. Next time I won't be so nice."

"Well—"

"Apologize," I cut Marisol off.

I knew she wasn't a punk but neither was Khyle, and I didn't feel like witnessing a brawl. Not only that, Khyle was my baby sister and I wasn't gonna sit by and watch a bitch my age come at her foul. Khyle may not even get a chance to fuck her up because I would.

Staring at me for a few moments, Marisol turned her attention back to Khyle and said, "I'm sorry. I guess I'm just not used to having to hold my tongue with certain things. I wouldn't like someone talking about my man that way either, so it won't happen again."

I looked to Marisol shocked, because I'd never seen this bitch give such a heartfelt apology. The most she would do is say sorry, but then follow it with a low blow.

"I accept," Khyle nodded.

"Okay, now back to me and my baby. You know I don't like to be out of the spotlight for too long," I joked, and thankfully, everyone laughed.

After we finished lunch, Khyle and Bella wanted to go shopping but I was way too tired, especially after eating all that food, so Marisol and I retired to the home I shared with Lloyd. I said that as if I had any other home. It was just hard to call that place mine because I didn't pick anything out. Lloyd promised we would move somewhere we both liked, but I'd been too lazy to look or call a realtor.

"That food was good, huh?" Marisol smiled as we sat on my couch.

"Yes. I was worried at first, but after the first bite I was cool."

We chuckled in unison.

"I'm sorry about your sister. I honestly thought she knew I slept with him. I wasn't trying to upset her or anything honestly."

"But even if she did know, Marisol, why would she wanna hear you talk about her nigga like that? No woman wants other women knowing what her man's dick is like."

"True. Well on the bright side, neither of us knows what his head game is like so she has that. I always wanted to know because his lips were so nice." She checked her phone to make sure she hadn't butt dialed her man, since they'd just gotten off the phone when we first arrived.

I chuckled at her, "Girl, you better shut up talking that shit before Ivan's crazy ass hears you."

"You saw me checking my shit."

We chortled in unison.

Her nigga was crazy as fuck, but hella nice at the same time. He was a *super* blood from California, or Balifornia as he called it. That meant he banged on everything in his path. On the flipside though, he would give you the shirt off his back in a minute. I usually wouldn't approve of someone so violent, but Marisol needed a strong nigga to keep her in check, just like me.

"We should have stopped at Jamba Juice on the way home."

"I know," she nodded. "Is it true that Oden and his crew killed Roone? I mean, he usually would be bugging me for some pussy again by now. And people have been saying they ain't seen him."

"Girl, I don't know what Oden and *his crew* does. Lloyd doesn't tell me shit really, especially if it has something to do with murder."

As I sat there on the plush couch, fighting the urge to pass out, I kept hearing a chime sound. I knew it wasn't my phone because I didn't use that ringtone for anything, but it was definitely an Apple device.

"That's you?" Marisol asked.

"No, I was gonna ask you the same thing."

I rose to my feet, eyelids low, looking around the living room until I spotted Lloyd's iPad sitting on top of the speaker next to the Plasma. I picked it up, and removed the top part of the case to display the screen, which was covered with text messages from none other than Elodie. Opening the iPad, I went to the conversation and saw these muthafuckas had been texting for some time. I scrolled up until something caught my eye.

Lloyd: Stop playing on my girl's phone.

Elodie: I will when you talk to me.

He didn't respond to that. Some time had gone by, two weeks to be exact, before she texted him again.

Elodie: Thanks for the plane ticket, but you could have come to Birmingham.

Lloyd: Nah because Shayne would be on my head.

Elodie: That's why you need to leave her.

Again he didn't respond.

Blinking back tears, I scrolled some more to read the next message after the time stamp which was yesterday.

Elodie: I'm settled. Grand Luxe tomorrow?

Lloyd: Aight. 3pm. Make sure you get everything off yo' chest shawty because I'm done playing games with you.

Snapping my neck to look at the time, I saw it was 3:45pm, and I hoped they were still out to lunch together so I could come wreck that shit.

"Marisol! Get up! You have to leave, because I have to be somewhere." I shook her out of her sleep that she'd just fallen into.

"What? Who?" she quizzed, still somewhat out of it.

"Just get yo' ass up and go!"

She hopped up after sucking her teeth, and we both rushed out to our cars. Before she was even in her whip all the way, I peeled out of the parking lot, headed to the Grand Luxe cafe. After parking my car with Venetian valet, I rushed out my car and inside the hotel until I found Grand Luxe.

"May I help you, ma'am?" the hostess smiled.

"What table is a Lloyd Gardener at? I'm a little late for our dinner meeting."

She checked her list and then replied, "He has someone at the table already—"

"Because it's a three-person dinner meeting! Since when are meetings defined by consisting of only two people, huh?" I was ready to slap this bitch.

"Yes, okay, I apologize. Right this way…"

"Don't worry about my name."

She nodded and led me through the large upscale restaurant, and when I spotted Lloyd sitting across from some ugly ass pale light-skinned bitch, my blood started to boil. I mean I was light skinned too, but my shit had a glow, this hoe looked like she hadn't had a drink of water in six months. Saying Lloyd had upgraded was an understatement.

"I got it from here," I said to the hostess, snatching the little menu she'd grabbed for me. She quickly walked away as I continued to the table. "Did my invite get lost in the mail?" I spoke happily once I got to the table, and then whacked Lloyd with the menu before dropping it.

With his eyes bucked wide as saucers, Lloyd rose to his feet and tried to grab my waist. I already felt the tears coming, which reminded me not to get too wild because I was pregnant. Any other time I would not have been tearing up.

"Shayne, baby—"

"No, move! What are you doing here with this bitch!" I hollered loudly over the restaurant, not caring who looked at me.

"Don't call me a bitch," the *bitch* Elodie piped in like she was so damn bold.

"You clearly didn't tell this hoe your girlfriend was crazy," I looked up at Lloyd who was lightly holding my midsection so I wouldn't move.

"Shayne, calm down. I was just coming here to hear her out and—"

"Why are you flying bitches out here, nigga? And you knew this whole time that she was the one playing on my fucking phone!"

"I'm sorry, you guys are gonna have to quiet down or leave," the hostess came up.

"I'm leaving. Enjoy your lunch, and I will see you in court for child support," I sniffled, tears coming down in abundance. I felt like a crazy person.

"Baby, stop. Come here." Lloyd tried to hug and kiss me but I was nudging him off. I wasn't strong enough though, because he was finally able to pull me in and kiss my lips.

"Dramatic ass," I heard Elodie mumble.

CRASH!

I grabbed her wine glass, broke it on the table to turn it into a weapon, and shoved it towards her, prompting her to hop out of her chair. Her seat fell onto the floor, as people around mumbled all kinds of shit.

"What did you say, bitch?" I tried to get around Lloyd with my broken wine glass, but he was like a wall. Finally, he picked me up and started carrying me out, so I tossed the glass in her direction. It missed her by a damn inch, crashing onto the floor. "Next time I see you I'm fucking you up!" I screamed over Lloyd's shoulder as Elodie stared me down with wide eyes.

Lloyd carried me to my car, and sat me inside on the driver's side. He kneeled down so he could look up into my eyes, even though I was facing the steering wheel.

"Shayne, I only met her to talk to her because she was tripping. I flew her out because I knew if I went to Alabama you would wanna come. And if I said no, you'd be suspicious. I was simply trying to settle shit with her, give her some type of closure so she'd let us be."

"I don't believe you."

"Baby, I swear. I do not want her. Look who I'm with right now. If I wanted her I would have had security escort your ass out and tended to her. But I'm with you because I love you, and I only came here with good intentions."

"How did she get my number? And why was it an Atlanta number?"

"I don't know how she got your number, shawty, I was getting to all that when you came. And she most likely used a burner app to get a number for a different city."

"You've been in there 45 minutes! You should have been found all this out!" I finally looked down at him, still sobbing.

"I was late. I'd gotten there like 10 minutes before you showed up and showed out." He rubbed my back and then my stomach, but I moved his hand. "Can you meet me at home, please?"

"Yeah."

On his way up he kissed me, and then closed my door. Pulling out of my park, I gave him a warm smile. Fuck him. I wasn't going home. I was going to Marisol's and letting him worry about where I was.

CHAPTER FIVE

Santino

Tonight, the football coaching staff was throwing a party for all of the people who got drafted to the NFL. It was a good four of us, which meant a lot to my coach. He worked hard, and he made us do the same, so best believe tonight felt like a sweet victory.

"Why you so quiet?" I asked Bella who was by my side tonight, dressed in a sexy red number with her golden hair hanging down her back.

"No reason. I'm just taking it all in."

Ever since a couple weeks ago, she'd been hella quiet around me like she had something to say but didn't know how to. The paranoia in me had me thinking it was because of that shit with Crystal, but I knew there was no way she'd find out about that.

Speaking of the devil, my phone buzzed in my pocket so I pulled it out to look at it on the sly as Bella chatted with my teammate Gerald's girlfriend Victoria.

Crystal: *It needs to happen tonight or I will be talking to my father* *in the morning. No excuses.*

The first night I was supposed to go over there, I came up with an excuse as to why I couldn't. She was mad, and started shooting out threats, but I calmed her down with some sweet talk. The next night we scheduled, I drove over there, but couldn't go in so I made up another excuse. Next time, I did the same thing and kept doing so until I had to go away to Los Angeles for a week straight to visit the Rams. The fact that she had to go home to Arizona frequently, and could only come here to Vegas on weekends helped me out tremendously. I couldn't imagine if she was here seven days a damn week begging for dick.

Anyhow, soon I realized that all I had to do was hit her up and talk that good shit, and she'd be cool. Crystal honestly just wanted to be with me, but was just going about it all wrong. Unfortunately, though, I knew if I didn't come through with the dick tonight, she would fry my ass. I planned to just hit her from the back until she came, fake my nut, and then bounce.

"You look good tonight," I leaned over and kissed Bella lightly.

The way she looked into my eyes all weird made me feel some type of way. In my defense, I hadn't done anything but text shit I shouldn't have been texting. But I guess I felt guilty about what I *was* gonna do tonight.

"Thanks, so do you. I'm proud of you, baby. I remember you used to talk about this day when we were back in high school."

"I know. My two dreams were getting drafted to the NFL, and marrying you."

"You really want to get married? I mean we're young, and you're gonna be this big football player with women everywhere."

"I've been a star football player for the majority of my life, and have had women throwing themselves at me for just as long. I know what I want, Bella, and that's you." I frowned a little because I'd never heard her talk like this.

"Just making sure."

"Well you don't need to because I already told you what it was. I love you more than anything, including football." She blushed, and turned away wearing a wide grin, so I hooked her chin with my pointer finger to make her look at me. "Say it back."

"I love you too, Santino."

I pressed my lips against hers, but hard, not caring if her lipstick got on me. Our tongues entangled as I ran my hand up her smooth thigh.

"I'm gonna eat your pussy good tonight," I mumbled against her lips as I touched between her legs. It was so warm, which in turn made my dick spring up.

"D'Stefano, please," one of my teammates at our table named Corbin chuckled. Like Gerald and I, he too got drafted, but to the Raiders.

I noticed Trevor was very quiet, sucking his teeth every now and again. I hated this person he was becoming, and missed my homie that was loud and always coming up with bullshit to make us laugh.

"Trevor, man, enjoy the festivities," I looked to him.

"Ain't shit for me to enjoy," he sneered before gulping down some of his drink.

"Aight. Let's go dance, baby." I stood and helped Bella up so we could go to the dance floor.

For the next couple of hours of the party, Bella's mood had improved. She was laughing, joking, and making good conversation; basically, being herself. By 10pm, I was ready to go because I wanted to get this shit with Crystal over with. I was hoping my dick would even get hard. Shit, who am I kidding, it definitely would.

"Alright y'all, we're gonna call it a night." I gripped Bella's hand as I rose from the table my coach, his wife, and a few others were sitting at.

"We're leaving?" Bella spoke lowly and I nodded.

"Alright, D'Stefano. Congrats again," my coach smiled before turning his attention back to his wife and talking.

"Thanks," I replied, then dapped a few of my teammates up. I saw Trevor on the way out, but I just ignored his ass.

Bella and I left the dining hall, and I walked her back to the dorm. When we got inside and onto her floor, she tried to lead me into her room but I stopped her.

"What?" she frowned, staring up at me angrily.

"My parents came into town tonight and I promised them I would come talk."

I hated lying to her, which is why I tried not to. But in this case, I had to do what I had to do in order to stay out of jail. Telling Bella the truth would do nothing to help the situation. She'd just try to fuck Crystal up, and then Crystal would for sure snitch after that. I'd done all I could do at this point to stay faithful to Bella physically, and it was time I pay my dues.

"Okay, will you be back in time to see me tonight?"

"Yeah I will."

I kissed her and then jogged down the hallway. When I looked back, she was watching me still, and hadn't gone into her room. When I got down to my car, I texted Crystal to let her know that I was on my way.

Crystal: Can't wait.

I lit a blunt and hot-boxed real brief, and once my nerves were calm, I headed over to her father's house. I sat in the car for a few moments, thinking like I always did, but I eventually got out because I knew this shit had to be done. I texted Crystal to let her know I was outside, and she told me to come through the unlocked side gate and into the pool house. I did so, and when I got into the pool house, she was lying on a blow-up bed wearing lingerie.

"About time, Santino," she licked her lips and set some red drink down on the ground. "I've been seeing you on TV lately due to your signing, and when I do I have to go please myself in the shower because I get so hot."

"Thank you for the compliment," I shook my head. "Where do you wanna do this?" I removed my tuxedo jacket.

"Slow down," she giggled, getting up off of the blow-up bed and walking towards me. She tried to kiss my lips but I moved away.

"I told you, just fucking. That's what you wanted, right?"

"Did you not text me and say you wanted to kiss me so bad?"

My fake sweet talk was already biting me in the ass.

"Crystal, come on and let's just fuck. I've had a long day and I'm not in the mood for lovemaking. I want some freaky shit."

I had to come up with something to keep from kissing her. As a man, kissing was worse than fucking in my opinion. I know women see it the other way around, but not us niggas. I'd fuck a bitch all over this pool house, but couldn't kiss her if she paid me. Sex was just sex to us men, but kissing meant something else and I couldn't do that to Bella.

"Ooh," she bit her lip as she unbuckled my slacks.

Crystal dropped to her knees and pulled my dick from my boxers. She began sucking on the tip with her full ass lips, making my shit get harder and harder. Her mouth eased down, so I gripped the back of her head to start slowly fucking her face. Her mouth was drenched with saliva, and since she appeared to have no gag reflex, I began pounding her face like it was a pussy. Soon enough, I came all in her mouth and she swallowed like the hoe she was.

"This must be your distant cousin from out of town," I heard Bella's voice and froze the fuck up. "Because you told me you were here to meet your parents, but all I see is this bitch sucking your dick."

"How did you get in my house?" Crystal yelled as I stuffed my dick into my slacks and tried to buckle them.

"Bella," I finally turned to face her now that my bottoms were intact. She was crying and shaking her head at me. She looked so hurt, just like the day I broke up with her back then. "Baby, let me… explain to you!" I yelled the last part because she hauled off and started fucking Crystal up.

They fell onto the blow-up bed, and Bella was on top of her delivering vicious punches as Crystal pulled on her hair. I was finally able to pick Bella up off of Crystal who was crying and bleeding. I really didn't care at this moment, because she was lucky I stopped Bella when

I did. Running out with Bella in my arms, I didn't stop until I was at my car. I let her down to her feet, and she began sobbing.

"Baby—"

WHAM!

She socked the shit out of me to the point where I fell on my ass in the dirt after stumbling a little bit. No wonder Crystal was screaming like someone was killing her.

"Take your fucking ring and drive me back home! I'm done with this relationship, Santino! Why ask me to be your wife if it wasn't what you wanted, huh? To keep me from being with someone else?"

"No. Shit," I could barely get my thoughts together after that blow. Rising to my feet I said, "She was blackmailing me, Bella."

"Here you go with that same lame ass excuse! What did you do for her to blackmail you? And you better not tell me the same shit you told me about Perry!"

"I can't tell you what it is, Bella, I—"

"Take me home."

I unlocked my car and when I tried to open the door for her, she pushed me. Not wanting another punch, I went to my side and climbed in. The whole drive home it was quiet, except for the light sniffles from her. I wanted to console her but she wouldn't let me touch her. When I pulled into a park back at school, she tried to get out but I locked the door.

"Bella, please believe I love you and tonight wasn't something I wanted, baby. I've been pushing this off for the longest trying to figure a way out, but I couldn't, baby. I—"

"Save it, Santino. You lied about having dinner with your coach, and then lied tonight. I'm finished and I never want to speak with you again." The calmness of her voice scared the shit out of me.

I watched her get out, then decided it wasn't gonna be that easy for her to leave me. I rushed up behind her and hugged her body, until she started elbowing me, and crying loudly. Turning her to face me, I gripped her jaw and kissed her lips repeatedly as she pushed on my abs to get away from me.

"I love you, Bella, don't do this." I hugged her into my body and kissed her some more.

"Let me-me go!" she tried to scream.

"Ah!"

I released her and crouched down when she kicked me in the nuts. She ran off as I fell to the ground in pain, and just watched her go inside of the dorm building. As I laid there on the gravel, an idea finally came to me. Something I wish I'd thought of from day one. Limping back to my car, I pulled my phone out and dialed Oden.

"Come on, answer, man."

"You better have a good reason for calling me this late," he had the nerve to say. I could hear music and people in the background, so clearly he wasn't asleep.

"I need a favor, man."

"Fuck I look like, Santa Clause?"

"Well unless you like fancy orange jumpsuits, you'll do it."

Sighing, I could hear him inhale on his blunt before saying, "Come to Palace."

CHAPTER SIX

Anton

$\mathcal{I}$ was sitting with my lawyer in this conference room that Selinda, her lawyer, my lawyer Hugh, the judge, and I were gonna be meeting in. I couldn't believe I was dealing with this shit, and I really wanted to just say fuck it. On the bright side, I would be free from her ass so that was a damn plus.

"I don't even get how she can do this when I had a test done," I scoffed, shaking my head.

"Because you went about it all wrong, Anton. I told you to go get it processed the right way, yet you decided to have it done with some people who were not official."

"Hugh, they were official. They're nurses, they have all the certifications needed to do DNA tests, aight?"

"I'm sure they do. But when I say official, I mean someone who is not on your payroll. She's using that as a reason so in turn, we have to do this," he explained.

"She slept with my friends, man, like come on. What lawyer in their right mind would even represent her ass?"

"And that is part of our argument."

"Argument for what?" I turned in my chair to look at him. My watch brushed across the smooth wooden table.

"Well, the judge is gonna question the reason you had this done the way you did and so forth. We're just gonna be honest about it and let them know that her record isn't the cleanest and you didn't trust her. That's all we have. She is mainly doing this for money. If you're the father she gets child support, and if not, she plans to sue you for having your friends pull guns on her. But just relax."

"Aight."

Hugh and I sat there in silence for a few more minutes before Selinda walked in with her lawyer. None of us said a word to each other, but her lawyer was smirking at me like he had something up under his sleeve.

"Hugh," her lawyer finally said, reaching his hand across the table to shake my lawyer's.

"Bill."

"Good morning, everyone." The judge walked in and sat at the head of the table.

She was black with a short haircut and a face full of makeup. She reminded me of my mother when she wasn't hitting the pipe and didn't have HIV. At least her soul was at peace now.

"Morning, Judge Graham," we all replied, somewhat simultaneously.

"Now, I understand we are in this room because Ms. Green here feels like the previous paternity test was incorrect?" she looked through some paperwork, and then focused her attention on Selinda with squinted eyes so she'd explain.

"Yes, your honor." She pushed her glasses up.

Since when did this bitch start wearing glasses?

"Elaborate, Ms. Green, please."

"Well, I was tricked into getting a DNA test for my son when Anton invited me over to his home. His friends roughly dragged me to a bedroom where I was held at gunpoint—"

"Gunpoint?" the judge exclaimed. I just took a deep breath so I wouldn't show any signs of distress.

"Yes, gunpoint, your honor. And while I was being held in that room with the two very aggressive and scary friends of his, he had some women claiming to be nurses swab my son, Antonio."

"Okay, thanks, Ms. Green. Mr. Nickerson I'm gonna ask you to please explain yourself. What Ms. Green is claiming is beyond serious."

Hugh gave me a nod, telling me to go ahead and explain my reasoning for having the test done the way I had.

"Yes, uh, I only did what I had to do to get the test done because for months, Selinda refused to get a DNA test. She'd been harassing me and my girlfriend, and I knew the only way to get her to let me be was if I got a DNA test done and proved I didn't father her child. My friends did not hold guns on her," I lied and Selinda gasped. "But they did block her from trying to fight the nurses while they swabbed her son."

"I see. And you both agree that the results from Mr. Nickerson's nurses stated that Mr. Nickerson was not the father?"

"Yes," Selinda and I said in unison.

"Is the nurse who delivered the results available today?" the judge asked and I swallowed a lump in my throat.

"Uh umm, no she left the state and no longer works for me."

"Mr. Nickerson, what is it that you do, or what illness do you have to where you need a personal nurse on hand?"

"He sells drugs!" Selinda blurted out dumbly. Bitch only knew one thing about me and it was my dick. Thank the Lord.

"No, your honor, I do not sell drugs. This nurse was someone I hired to take care of my mother who'd been diagnosed with HIV. DNA testing was one of her specialties as well so I got her to do one on Antonio."

The judge nodded with a sympathetic smile for my mother.

I didn't lie much, so when I did, it was always a good one.

"Mr. Nickerson, lastly, why do you feel that her son is not your child? Selinda put in her statement that you guys were in a committed relationship."

Committed relation—... Anton do not reach across this table on that hoe.

"Well, for one, we weren't in a relationship—"

"Yes we were," Selinda blurted and folded her arms. The judge just glared at her, letting her know not to say another word.

"Anyway, we weren't in a relationship, and I know for a fact that she'd slept around during the time she got pregnant."

"Yeah right, nigga—"

"I think I've heard enough. Ronald, bring me the results, please."

Some guy dressed like a mall cop brought the brown folder to her, and she opened it up to read. I knew I wasn't the dad, but my hands were still sweating like a muthafucka.

"Oh, I forgot to—"

"Ms. Green, talk time is over," the judge cut Selinda off. "According to these results which have not been tampered with in anyway, Mr. Nickerson, you are not the father of Antonio."

"Thank you, your honor, thanks so much," I couldn't help but grin as Selinda shot daggers at me. Dumb bitch. Told her stupid ass this was a waste of time. I mean, she had to know deep down that her son wasn't mine, so the fact that she did all this shit blew my mind.

"This case is over, thank you." The judge started rising from her seat.

"But what about his friends holding me at gunpoint?" Selinda yelled.

"Yes, your honor, my client suffered emotional distress over that," her lawyer finally made a peep.

"Did she call the police?" the judge inquired.

"No, I didn't, but I was very scared of his friends because they're violent and—"

"You weren't scared of them when you let them fuck!" I barked.

"Alright, order in here!" the judge hollered, face twisted all up. "If you two want to have a lover's quarrel, do it in the parking lot, not in this room. And Ms. Green, the baby is not his so stop trying to ruin his life. Jealousy isn't a good look."

"But your honor…"

The judge was already on her way out before Selinda could finish.

The four of us left the room, and once in the parking lot, I talked with my lawyer for a little bit about how everything went down. He suggested that I file a restraining order against Selinda, and I agreed. Before, I felt like that shit wasn't for niggas like me, but unless I wanted to kill Selinda's ass, I needed to get her out of my life legally.

"Will do, man," I told him before we parted ways.

On the way to UNLV, my phone rang, and I smiled when I saw it was Tasmine.

"Hey, beautiful?" I answered using my Bluetooth.

"Hey, are you here yet?"

"No, baby, I just got out of that damn case. And don't even ask what the results were because you already know."

"I do. But I was asking because I really want some caramel corn and cheese corn all mixed together; Chicago style."

"The fuck? Where am I gonna find that?"

"At CVS! They have the Popcornopolis one, and that's what I really want. Bring me that and some ginger ale for my stomach."

"Aight, anything else? Because I'm not gonna see you until after my class."

"No, that's all I need so Khyle, Bella, Perry and I can study."

"They ain't bring snacks?"

"Yes, but we forgot that. Let me know when you get here. We're in the library. Bye, baby."

She hung up before I could even say anything else.

I headed to the CVS on Flamingo Road, and parked in the handicap spot once I got there. I wouldn't be too long and I wish them niggas would try to tow me. I went inside to buy what Tasmine wanted, and a candy bar for myself to snack on while I watched my class on my laptop, before I headed out to my car. As I was rounding the hood of my whip, an all-black truck rode by me slowly.

POP! POP! POP!

Before I could even process the next thought, bullets came flying out of the back window, ripping through my whole body it seemed. All I remembered were people screaming and in a tizzy as I fell to the floor. The last thing I saw was Tasmine's popcorn, before everything went black.

***

Some hours later...

I opened my eyes, and like clockwork, the pain shot through me. I felt it everywhere, even down in my feet. At first I thought I was dead, but I recognized the room I was in. This was where my crew and I went whenever we needed to recover. Wiping my eyes, I spotted Tasmine lying in the extra bed knocked out, looking like sleeping beauty or some shit. Everything she did, she looked beautiful doing it.

"You okay?" I heard a voice, and when I looked I saw Whitney, the nurse I had test Violet's son the second time.

Not feeling like I could talk, I just shook my head no. My throat felt scratchy, and that's when I realized I had tubes in my mouth. Whitney carefully removed them, and then poured me a few glasses of water, which I gulped down.

"Want me to let Oden and Truman in?"

"Yes, but tell them to be quiet. I don't wanna wake my baby up," I replied in a raspy tone before wincing in pain.

"Of course, Mr. Nickerson. I will bring your dinner as well."

Whitney left out, and then returned carrying a tray of food. Oden and Truman were behind her, and they both came and sat next to my bed as Whitney placed the tray of food in front of me. I inhaled the smell of the lemon herb baked chicken, mashed potatoes, and broccoli, before saying a prayer and digging in.

"I will give you guys some time," Whitney left.

"I see you still eat like a nigga in jail, so you must be feeling better already," Truman taunted me like always, prompting Oden to chuckle.

"Nigga, fuck you. Twig looking ass nigga," I spat jokingly, as I devoured the good ass meal.

"He's gotta be strong for the next batch of baby mamas that are gonna be coming his way. The Baby Mama Apocalypse," Oden added as he and Truman burst into laughter. "You need to be in the Guinness Book of World Records for most paternity tests done my nigga."

All three of us chortled in unison.

"This nigga everybody's daddy," Truman laughed.

We ragged on one another for some time like we always did, but then the room got serious. I knew they were gonna tell me something regarding my shooting. I was angry and confused, so I was ready.

"Marie was behind the shit. She's pissed about what we did to Billz, even though she was still trying to fuck Truman *after* his death," Oden explained.

"Yeah, and Roone was working with her."

"He was?" I bucked my eyes and Truman nodded. "I always wondered why that nigga decided to turn on you. She must have promised him that drug empire."

Roone had been trying to convince us to take over the drug game and combine it with our vehicle shit, but we didn't fuck with that. We knew how to flip cars and that's what we were sticking to. Wasn't our fault he couldn't catch on like Lloyd.

"She sure did," Oden confirmed.

"How y'all find this out?" I quizzed.

"Bernie's baby mama, Carly. Marie tried to get her to help. Carly is tired of all the bullshit though, so for a hefty sum, she spilled the beans on Marie's ass. She wants us to get rid of her too," Oden replied.

I low-key felt bad for Bernie and his family. We killed him when he was just trying to make peace on Billz behalf, but we had to do what we had to do. I was happy to hear they helped his baby mama out though.

"Yeah, we sent our goons out to get Marie, the police nigga she was working with to get Oden booked for murder, and his daughter,"

Truman explained, pressing on one of his fingers with each thing he named. "We already got the niggas who actually shot you. They didn't wanna snitch on Marie, but thank God for Bernie's baby mama."

"The policeman's daughter, why?"

"Shit if I know. Oden just wants the bitch dead for some reason. Once we get word that they have all three of them, we gone murk 'em."

"I want in."

"Nah, we need to do this shit ASAP, Tony. We can't wait for you to get better," Oden shook his head.

"Get me in there in a wheelchair or something. I have to put a bullet in somebody!"

"We will see what we can do," he looked to me.

CHAPTER SIX

Oden

One week later…

"Nigga, really?" Santino barked once my people pulled the sack off his head.

I had them snatch him from the gym, and bring him to my port so we could fly to Arizona where his bitch was that he wanted me to kill.

We were able to capture her father and Marie, but since the hoe he wanted us to get didn't technically reside in Las Vegas, it was harder to catch her. So while her pops and Marie sat in the warehouse being starved, beaten, but kept alive, we were gonna go get the little bitch. Plus, this gave Anton time to heal so he could off Marie like he wanted to. It was funny because he went from hating to kill women, to *wanting* to murk one.

"I thought it would be exciting for you," I grinned at Santino as Truman laughed.

"You could have just told me to meet you here. And where are we going?" he hissed, following behind me up the stairs to get onto my private jet.

"First off, calm down." Truman and I were still laughing, so I took a deep breath before I said, "We're going to Arizona to get Christina."

"You mean Crystal. But hey, since Bella knocked her ass out she hasn't been threatening me and shit so maybe—"

"Nah, the bitch gotta go. She was about to snitch." Truman ate some candy. All three of us were buckled into the plush ass cream seats, as the stewardess I hired prepared some snacks and shit.

"Exactly. She knows something happened to Leena, and she's gonna continue to use that shit against you to get some dick," I agreed.

"All she wanted was some dick? Why you ain't just give it to her?" Truman frowned, and Santino looked at him like he had two heads.

"Because I'm engaged and I love my girl, man. The last thing I wanna do is cheat, especially with a bitch who is blackmailing me."

"Not everybody fucks around on the woman they love, Tru."

"Man, I ain't been with no women since Chiina caught me at that hotel and she still won't take me back. I have yet to cheat on her since we made things official. Granted I *almost* cheated, but I didn't. In the words of Brandy, almost doesn't count. I'm gonna get her back, watch."

"Nigga, she put you out your own crib last night and you had to sleep on my couch," I reminded him as I took the glass of bourbon from the stewardess.

"Now why you got to say that shit with this nigga here, huh?"

Truman sucked his teeth as both Santino and I cracked up.

Khyle and I laughed at Truman for 30 minutes straight when he came to the door talking about Chiina had put him out his own crib.

The plane took off and we landed in Phoenix, Arizona about an hour and 15 minutes later. We then drove a car that my homie out in Phoenix let me use, all the way to Scottsdale. Santino directed us to the girl's house, and then I decided to have Santino go knock on the door. If he called her, what we did may track back to him and I didn't want that. I had connections in Las Vegas, but not too much in Arizona, so I didn't want him in any legal trouble.

Truman and I hid on the side as we waited for Santino to knock on the door. Some girl answered, and I guess it was her. She seemed to be off him for a little bit, but then she started crying and they hugged. As soon as she came all the way outside and closed the door, Santino led her back to the car. Truman came behind her and covered her mouth with a chloroform drenched rag, then once she passed out, we loaded her back into the car, and drove back to the airport.

My pilot flew us back to Vegas, and Lloyd picked us up in an all-black Suburban. He had Anton in the car who still wasn't at his strongest, but much better. On the way to the warehouse, Crystal started to come to after being out for the whole flight, so Truman just put the rag over her nose and mouth again to knock her ass out. She stayed out of it for the rest of the ride.

"Get his wheelchair," Truman told Lloyd once we started getting out of the truck at our destination. Santino was helping me carry Crystal inside.

"I don't need my wheelchair, I'm good," Anton retorted.

"So you gon' limp like some 60-year-old pimp?" Truman chuckled, holding the wheelchair in his hands.

"Yep. Gangsters limp all day, bruh."

The four of us laughed as Truman put the wheelchair back into the truck. We walked to the room that the Lieutenant and Marie were being held in, and the police nigga liked to had a heart attack when he saw Santino and I carrying his knocked-out daughter.

"Please let her go, she has nothing to do with this!" he hollered.

"You're right, she doesn't, but unfortunately for her, the apple doesn't fall far from the tree so she was on that snitch tip too," I replied.

"Fuck you! I've never liked you!" Marie hissed, shooting daggers at me, even though nobody was talking to or about her ass at the moment. She used to look so good before I had the homegirls ravage her.

"Oh, so that's why you only gave your pussy to all the homies and not me," I grinned, causing her to roll her eyes. I had to give it to her; she had heart through and through. She wasn't begging like Roone or Huelo, or any other nigga I'd had to ice.

"Yeah, because—"

POP! POP!

Anton sent two bullets into her face before she could finish her sentence, making Lieutenant Gaines cry his bitch ass heart out in fear. I glanced at Santino who had his eyes wide. He wasn't used to this, but he would get used to it.

"I never understood what you had against me, man," I cocked my head, looking at Lieutenant Gaines.

"It's just work, man. Big case equals big money and rewards. I promise to forget it all if you let my baby go," he begged for Crystal's life.

"But you gon' die anyway," Lloyd added, making the room chuckle.

"Yes, but — it's a big crime to kill a police lieutenant! You don't want to do this, trust me! They will come after you until the day you—"

POP! POP! POP! POP!

With my lips tucked in, I lit his ass up with that fire. I nodded to Truman so he could let the clean-up crew know that they needed to get here.

"Man, when she gon' wake the fuck up?" Santino asked, obviously anxious to get rid of this bitch now.

"I thought you ain't wanna kill her?" I half smiled.

"I mean I didn't, but now I understand that it's on some just in case shit, you know? I can see it now, her ass popping up at my house while Bella and I are married with four kids."

"Here this nigga go," Truman mumbled.

"Nigga hating because he ain't got no woman but Pilar's ass," Anton fired up a blunt as we laughed.

"Man, fuck y'all. Chiina is mine. I'm a good ass nigga. I mean, I wasn't before but I am now. Losing her and my son got me shook. Nigga can barely sleep."

"Cue the damn violins. Nigga, shut that sappy shit up!" I frowned, and the room roared with laughter.

"Nigga can barely sleep," Anton mocked him.

"I see y'all niggas can't never be serious," Truman sucked his teeth, smiling.

We waited for about 30 more minutes for Crystal to wake up since throwing ice cold water on her didn't work. When she came to, her eyes were closed for like 10 damn minutes before she opened them. When she saw a bunch of niggas dressed in black standing around, she shot up out of the rickety wooden chair and screamed.

"You want to?" I looked to Santino.

"Ummm, nah, these hands are for football."

"Nigga, you mean to tell me you got me out here to murk this bitch and now you're turning into a pussy?" I grimaced. His face was priceless, so everyone burst into laughter except him. "Nah, I'm fucking with you kid."

POP! POP!

Tired of that bitch screaming, I shot her twice in the head just as the cleaning crew arrived. I made sure they got everything squared away, and then we all left to pile into the truck so Lloyd could drop us off at home. He took Santino to the dorms first, and then headed out to Anton's, Truman's, and my townhouse complex.

"Your dick game must have been weak, Anton. Otherwise, why would she have you shot and not Oden? I mean he's at the head of this shit," Truman started up cracking on Anton again.

"Probably because I wouldn't allow her to hop on it anymore like you, community dick."

"Ooohhhhh!" Lloyd and I instigated.

"Nah, it was because you ain't break her off with a baby like you did for the rest of these Vegas hoes!" Truman snapped back, making us chortle.

This shit continued all the way to our townhouse complex. Them niggas were crazy.

I walked into my spot and all the lights were cut off in the living room so I knew Khyle was probably sleep. I entered the bedroom to see her sitting up against the headboard, holding our son in her arms. She gave me a weak smile so I knew she was tired.

"Why are you up, baby?"

"He couldn't sleep, and every time I put him down he cried. I just wanted to make sure he was out for good this time."

I made my way over to her, and kissed her lips before gently removing him from her arms. I rocked him lightly as I left our bedroom and went into his. His hair was getting thicker already, so I knew he'd gotten that from me. I pecked his round bouncy cheek once, before lowering him into his crib and turning on his crib light and mobile. I watched him sleep peacefully with a smile on my face. He was so small and it was crazy to know that one day he would be some big ass nigga. Laughing at my thoughts, I rubbed his back and left the room.

I showered quickly, brushed my teeth, and then grabbed some water from the fridge while still in my towel. When I got in the bedroom, Khyle was lying down with her long hair swallowing the pillow. I got some fresh boxers from my drawer, and slipped them on before climbing into bed with her.

"You can sleep in tomorrow, and when you wake up, I'm gonna have breakfast for you," I rubbed her hair back before kissing her lips. I so badly wanted to fuck her but we had four more days left.

"But you can't cook, baby."

Chuckling I said, "Don't worry about that. Just know you will have a breakfast set out for you. I have one meeting tomorrow, but after that, I will be right back to spend time with you and the baby all day."

"You promise?"

"Yeah, I do."

She turned her back to me, so I hugged her body from behind, moving her hair out of the way. I kissed the nape of her neck, then her shoulder before plopping my head against these plush ass pillows.

"I love you, Oden Bishop," she whispered.

"I love you more, Khyle *Bishop*."

***

The next afternoon...

"Good afternoon, boss. Your 1pm meeting is in the conference room already, and as asked, nothing else is on the schedule today," Winter smiled when I came into Palace.

"Thanks, Winter."

I hurried to the conference room to meet with *Maxim* magazine. They wanted to host a party here for this Victoria's Secret model that topped their Hot 100 Women's list. This would be big for the club and my pockets, so I really wanted to book it. I was flattered that they even found my club and wanted to use it. I knew we were on the up and up, but *Maxim* was big shit.

"Good afternoon— Naomi, what are you doing in here?" I frowned, angry as fuck as I entered the conference room. I didn't have time for her games.

"We have a meeting, honey, or did you forget?"

I forgot her ass was into party planning for magazines. When we were together, she worked for *Jet*, and handled all their deals when they held events.

"Right." I sat down. "So, I read what you guys wanted, and all the requirements can be met. I do need half of the fee upfront which is $50,000, if you guys want to book us. I think we could really pull this off for you, because not only do we—"

"Oden, baby, you have the job. I only came because I wanted to see you, but you know I wouldn't let them choose another venue."

"Naomi, I want this because we deserve it, not because you think some shit is gonna pop off between us. And if that is your reason, give up on us now, please before you embarrass yourself."

"Here are the contracts. I'm sure you've had your lawyer look over the emailed copy?"

"I did."

I didn't know what Naomi was attempting to do, but I was gonna make this money regardless. She could think whatever she wanted, as long as that *Maxim* party happened here at Palace.

CHAPTER SIX

Perry

Woke up this morning feelin' bool and balm, ain't have to drank no drank, a nigga's nerves was calm. Was it 'cause last night I had some bomb. She got ratchet in the red dress we had a bomb...

The strip club portion of Palace nightclub was "jumping" as Bella would say. YG was rapping through the speakers, and I only knew it was him because Khyle played him faithfully. This stripper named Brown was on stage dancing to the music, and like every time she graced the stage, the guys in here were going crazy for her. The huge platform would be covered in money when she was done, and you couldn't do anything but admire her.

"Booth six," Monica walked by me on the way to the bar.

I smiled when I saw it was my new favorite customer, Cash. He'd been coming here multiple times a week, and I always looked forward to it. Last night when he was here, he asked for my number, and since he said he'd text me later I went to my dorm with Bella to sleep. I didn't need Austin all in my face, and since Bella and Santino were no longer, I didn't have to worry about walking in on them having sex. Our room was covered in apology flowers and chocolates though.

Anyhow, Cash and I stayed up texting all night, not really talking about much, but the conversation was interesting. I had Bella help me with some of the replies until she fell asleep.

I felt a little bad about flirting with Cash because I had a boyfriend, but Khyle said it was because I rushed into a relationship with Austin instead of just dating. That could be right, but all I knew was that I wanted Cash to do all the things to me that he whispered in my ear whenever I delivered his booth food.

"Good evening, fellas, can I put in some food orders for you?" I smiled once I was inside of booth six, aka Cash's booth.

"Sit down for a second," Cash sipped his drink.

"Umm," I looked over my shoulder, "I can't. My boss is gonna go crazy."

"Who, Oden? Truman? Tony? Which one, they're all my homies, and they won't mind."

"Well, Tony is the boss for tonight, but I was talking about Winter. She's strict and we're really busy tonight."

"Aight then, how about you come home with me after your shift tonight?"

"I would need to stop by my dorm to get a few things, if that's alright? You can follow me there," I nibbled on my lip, liking the way his eyes scanned my rather skinny frame. I'd gained weight since freshman year, but I was still on the small side.

"That works. But my boys here wanna order some chicken strips and fries."

"Coming right up."

I put the order in on my tablet, gave Cash a smile, and then walked down the steps. When I did, I saw Oden leaving, and that woman who was helping him plan some event for next weekend following him out. She stayed on him like white on rice, and though he always appeared to be annoyed and standoffish with her, it was my duty to let Khyle know… as her friend. Pulling my personal iPhone out, I quickly took a picture of them leaving the establishment.

I continued working, taking orders from booths and tables, and spending a lot of extra time in Cash's booth. He was so fine, and I just couldn't help the tingle I felt down below every time he smiled at me, or simply spoke to me.

"How is everything?" I stopped by his area, holding my tablet low so I could show off the crop top I was wearing.

"Good. Sit down for a second," Cash asked again. And even though I already told him that I couldn't, I decided to oblige. The strip club was popping and so was the club upstairs, so I was sure Winter and Anton wouldn't be checking for me any time soon.

"K," I finally replied, pushing my hair behind my ears.

I sat down on the comfy plush couch next to him, and took a deep breath to inhale the scent of his seemingly expensive cologne. For a minute, we just shared smiles, as his eyes ran amuck all over me. It made me slightly uncomfortable because I didn't want him to find a flaw.

"Relax," he laughed.

"I am relaxed."

"Then why are your shoulders up here?" he mocked me, pulling his shoulders up to his ears damn near. We both laughed as I tried to relax my body. "That's better. I know I'm not that intimidating, am I?"

"Actually, you kind of are."

"Why?" he cocked his head, and his facial expression showed just how perplexed he was.

"The way you carry yourself, and I know that if someone is hanging out or affiliated with Oden in any way, they are no saint."

"Well you have that right, that I'm no saint. But I don't think I'm intimidating, maybe sometimes, but that's only when I have to be to get this money and make sure I keep it."

"I like intimidating guys, so that's a good thing."

"Oh word?" his eyebrow raised, as his teeth sunk into his bottom lip.

"Yeah—"

"Perry!"

I looked to see Winter standing there with her hand on her thick hip. She was scowling, and I knew that meant I was in deep trouble. But if she thought she was gonna get me fired, she had another thing coming.

"Oh, sorry Winter, I was—" I started down the stairs.

"You were fraternizing with the customers instead of working!"

"Aye, chill out, baby. I asked her to sit with me," Cash rose to his feet.

Even though he was in the elevated booth, it seemed like that was naturally his height. His demeanor was so commanding, that Winter stopped going off on me and just looked up at him in silence.

"Of course, Cash," she finally replied, pulling me with her. When we were out of earshot, she said through clenched teeth, "Do not do that again. If you do, I will let Anton know, and he will most likely let you go."

"And if I see you trying to sleep with Truman again, I will let Oden know so he can fire you," I smiled widely and pranced off, leaving her standing there like a fool.

I guess she wasn't hip to the fact that I was the queen of playing dirty.

About two hours passed of me being on my feet, and I saw it was time for me to go. Oden still had me on these doggone four-hour shifts, and I needed to talk to him about that, or whoever did the schedule.

"Let me clock out and get my stuff," I told Cash before darting to the back and getting my purse and keys.

When I walked back through the club floor, I didn't see Cash in his booth. Coming outside, I started to feel stupid like he played me, until I saw his all-white Range Rover parked next to my BMW. I only knew what type of car he had because Khyle, Bella, Tasmine, and I searched him on the Internet and found all his social media. I guess *all* didn't apply since the only thing he had was Instagram and Snapchat.

"Hey, you can follow me, and then I will follow you," I approached him. I just loved his scent.

"Or I can follow you, and then we just get in my whip and go to my house."

"K."

We drove to UNLV, and both got out so I could go up to my room. As we approached the door, I heard Bella arguing with someone that sounded like Santino. I gave Cash a nervous smile, and then entered slowly to see just what I'd suspected. Bella and Santino were basically screaming at the top of their lungs at one another. He tried to grab her into a hug, but she slapped him so hard, *my* ears rang.

"I told you that you had no more chances!" she hissed, tears running down her face.

"Baby, I know, but let me explain to you why I had to—"

"There is no excuse for you lying to me. How long have you been sleeping with her?" she sobbed. I felt kind of bad for Bella. He'd hurt her way too much.

"Baby, I never slept with her, I—"

"So she just had your dick in her mouth for no reason? Get out!"

"Sorry," I mouthed to Cash as I began packing some things. He just shrugged and sat down at my desk. I don't even know if Bella and Santino realized two other people were in the room.

Finally, I had everything I would need for the perfect night to spend with Cash, so we walked towards the door.

"You have to go, I have a breakfast date tomorrow," I heard Bella say just as I closed the door behind me. Oddly, I heard kissing after that.

"Are they always so angry with one another?" Cash inquired as we made our way to the elevator.

"No, actually they're usually all over one another, kissing, giving one another hickies, having sex. It's somewhat refreshing to see them not gnawing on each other."

"You cold," he laughed and so did I.

We left out and he put my bag in the trunk of his car, before opening the passenger door for me. Upon getting inside, I inspected the beautiful detailing of the interior of the car. I could immediately tell that he picked all of this out and had it customized; he was just that type of guy.

Things felt different with him than with Austin. Don't get me wrong, Austin was a great guy, but he wasn't on the same level as Cash. Cash was what these hood rats called a boss, and Austin was simply a corner boy doing well for himself. I needed a man like my friends had.

"Cold?" Cash asked once he cranked his car up and began adjusting the radio to what he wanted to hear.

"A little. It's rare that I get cold out here, but I think it's the fact that you have leather and it's been sitting in the night air."

"Most likely."

He leaned back so far that he was pretty much driving from the back seat. He bobbed his head sexily to the rap music as he toyed with his chin hairs, until we pulled up to a nice family home on Fiore Bella Boulevard. It was in a beautiful neighborhood in South Summerlin.

"This is your home?" I questioned as he swooped into the driveway and shut his engine off.

"Sure is."

He got out the car to get my bag, and then came around to my side to help me out. I was skeptical because I felt like maybe he had a wife and kids. I didn't even ask him about that. Hell, I didn't ask *anything* personal, like what he did, or how he knew Oden, nothing.

I wasn't really the fighting type; I hurt people in other ways, so I wasn't quite prepared to box with his wife if he had one.

"Wait, Cash," I pulled my hand from his as soon as we stepped inside of the beautiful home. "You live here alone?"

He frowned and closed the door, then hugged me from behind.

"Yes, I do, unfortunately. If you act right, maybe you can move in."

"Why do you have this house if it's just you?" I inquired further as we walked deeper into the beautiful home. I looked at every single picture lining the hallway, but only saw photos of him that had to be taken when he was younger. "Why not a simple condo like Oden?"

"Well for one, I don't know if you've noticed, but Oden and I are two different people," he grinned, leading me by hand to his huge den. "And secondly, all my life I lived in a small as house with only two bedrooms that I had to share with my four brothers. I like space, and since I have the money, I wanted to get a house."

"I see. I'm sorry, I didn't mean to question you—"

"No, it's cool. That's good that you ask questions because most women don't, and then get the shock of their lives when they find out their boyfriend is married with four kids."

"True."

"Want some wine? Weed?" he flashed me his sexy smile, before licking his lips.

"I'm trying to slow up on smoking, but I will take some wine."

"Alright. Have a seat and get comfortable, I will be right back."

I sat down after taking in the beautiful den for a little longer. I could see he had a pool out back that appeared to be clean like this den. I bet his whole home was spotless, but I was sure he had a maid. I felt my purse vibrate, so I took my phone out to see I had a text from Austin.

Austin: Yo where you at?

Me: Working. Oden decided to start giving me extended shifts.

Austin: But I thought this shift in particular was over at midnight.

Me: Got crowded so he just said I could stay until 4am. I have to go, I will get fired if he sees me texting.

I quickly powered off my phone just as Cash came back into the dining room with a huge bottle that didn't look like wine, and two glasses.

"Ran out of wine, but I have some Ace if that's cool."

"That's champagne, right?"

"It is," he laughed, setting everything down on the beautiful glass table outlined in gold. He poured some of the champagne into a flute for me, and then some into a short round glass for himself.

"Where is your flute?" I asked before taking a sip of the crisp and surprisingly tasty champagne.

"I'm not really a flute type of nigga."

"So you just have these for your female companions?"

"Pretty much, I ain't gon' lie to you."

"What do you do, Cash? How old are you? And did you just move to Las Vegas?"

"Damn, right to it I see. Well my grandfather died and left my siblings and I one hundred thousand dollars each. I invested the majority of my money into the MGM hotel so I could own a portion of it, so now I make money in my sleep. I'm building my chips now because I want to buy a bigger percentage. What else did you ask?" he cheesed, stroking his beard and biting his lip.

I re-crossed my legs to stop the flow.

"Umm, uh, oh, your age and if you're new in town."

"Right, well I'm 27, and no, I've lived in Las Vegas all my life."

"I've never seen you and I grew up here too."

"Well, we don't quite hang in the same circles, love. I mean, if you never started working at Palace, I might have never met you."

"True," I giggled, sipping my champagne. I reached the flute out so he could pour me some more. "How do you know Oden?"

"I met him some years ago through his grandfather who was in the hotel business. His grandpa was like my mentor with that."

"Interesting."

"Now your turn. I already know you were born and raised here in Nevada, and I can guess you're about 20 since you can't serve drinks at the club. But what are you in school for?"

"Yes, I will be 20, March 22. As far as college, I was hoping to become an oral surgeon but I don't really know if I have the energy to go through all that schooling. These past two years have been enough."

"I think you should do it. We could be dope together. I will eventually be rich from owning the Las Vegas MGM completely, and you will be a paid ass Dentist."

"That would be nice. We'd be like the Huxtables or something," I laughed, thinking about it. I loved that he still had that bad boy demeanor but wasn't into anything illegal like Austin.

Tossing my champagne back, I straddled Cash's lap and pressed my lips against his. They were so soft, and he knew how to kiss me gently without it seeming like I was kissing a girl or a kitten. His hands groped my skinny frame, and the way he squeezed my exposed thighs made me feel thick, which I loved. The kiss we shared was slow and sensual, yet passionate.

Reaching my hands down to his crotch, I began to unbuckle his jeans but he stopped me.

"We're not there, ma. You ain't even told me you had a boyfriend yet," he surprised the hell out of me. How did he know I had a boyfriend?

Moving out of his lap, I felt stupid. I didn't even know guys could turn sex down.

"Umm, we're on the outs right now; me and my boyfriend."

"It's cool. I just want to know everything about you before we go there. This dick will fuck up your head, baby." He looked to me before downing his drink. "And before I get you all attached to me, I have to know more about you."

I blushed at the thought of he and I sleeping together.

We talked all damn night until we passed out on the couch, cuddled up. I liked where this was going, but the fact that I had Austin still worried me. I knew he wouldn't let me go so easily. He was changing.

CHAPTER SIX

Bella

The next morning…

I just opened my eyes, and now I was staring up at the ceiling thinking. My heart had been broken into one million pieces, but I refused to sit around and mope about it like I'd done in high school. Santino had fucked me over for the very last time, and there was nothing he could do to convince me to take him back. I loved him still, which was odd to me, but I didn't want to be with him. I wanted someone who would be honest with me about how they felt, and not propose just because it sounded good. Santino had bruised my ego badly for the second time and I couldn't deal with him any longer.

It was Friday morning and I agreed to let Trevor take me to breakfast. I knew he was Santino's good friend and frankly, that was the sole reason I even agreed to go. Trevor was not my type, not because of his looks, but because he was no different from Santino. I'd seen him play many of girls, so he would never be someone that I pursued a relationship with. Not to mention, he was a good friend to Santino so he could never be a real candidate in the race to be my next man. I even found it odd that he asked me, but since I wanted to hurt Santino, I asked no questions.

Peeling the covers off of my body, I noticed Perry's bed was empty. I kind of remembered her coming in last night, but I was too into the argument I was having with stupid ass Santino to really pay attention to anything else. Thank God you needed a card key to get into our rooms, or a serial killer could have walked in and stabbed Santino and I since we weren't paying attention to shit else.

"Fuck," I massaged the bridge of my nose as I grabbed my toothbrush, paste, and Listerine.

I saw my phone sitting on the sink counter, and when I hit the home button, I had texts from Khyle, Tasmine, my brother Brandon, Allegra, and of course, Santino. Rolling my eyes at the latter, I started brushing my teeth.

As I was flossing, my phone lit up, signaling that I had a Facebook message from Austin. He and I weren't even friends on Facebook, at least not to my knowledge, so this was odd. I hoped he wasn't trying to fuck because I was about to hurt his feelings. Perry wasn't my best friend by any means, but I didn't do shit like that.

After I spit my mouthwash out, I unlocked my phone and went to read the message.

Austin: Is Perry still asleep?

I looked over my shoulder at her bed even though I knew her ass wasn't here. At this point I was confused because I thought she was with him. Suddenly it hit me, that she was probably with that new guy she had us stalk that evening. Perry was becoming a little player.

Me: Yes, she is. She isn't feeling too well which is why she isn't answering. I will let her know to call as soon as she wakes up.

Austin: Right. Thanks.

I contemplated cursing him out for low-key calling me a liar, but I didn't care and I had somewhere to be. As I gathered my things for the shower, I dialed Perry.

"Hey, Bella, is everything okay?" she answered as if I would ever call her ass in my time of need. I'd have to be desperate.

"Perry, Austin Facebook messaged me asking if you were asleep in the dorm with me."

"Oh shit." She sounded as if when I called I'd woken her up. "Umm, what'd you say?"

"I told him that you were knocked out and not feeling good, but he sounded like he didn't believe me. Where the hell are you?"

"I'm with Cash."

I figured that.

"Well you better hurry up and call that boy before he pops up at the school. I have a date and therefore I will not be here to continue the lie."

"Alright, I will be there maybe this evening. Cash is gonna take me shopping and out to eat."

"Perry, that may not be a good idea. You need to let Austin know the deal."

"Oh, like you let Dean know the deal as soon as you started

sleeping with Santino?"

Bitch!

"Okay, first of all—"

"Relax, Bella. I know what I'm doing even though it may not seem like it. Austin will be okay, I will call him."

"Okay, Perry."

We hung up and I went to get into the shower. After toweling off, I spread my lavender scented lotion all over my damp body, and then followed it with the spray. I decided to wear some cut off jean shorts and a halter-top. I wanted it to be somewhat sexy in case Santino saw me, but not too sexy because I didn't want Trevor to think he was about to fuck or that I even thought about his dick.

By the time I was putting my sandals on, I heard a knock and then my phone chimed. I saw it was an Instagram DM from Trevor saying he was outside. I told him he couldn't have my number but that we could talk through Instagram to see where things go. As you know, I just didn't want him having my number, but he thought I was some damaged girl, not wanting to move too quickly.

"Hey," I answered the door, and his eyes immediately darted from my face so that he could scan my body. I rolled my eyes on the sly, but quickly smiled when we regained eye contact.

"Damn, Bella. I always told Sanz you could rock a curtain and look beautiful."

"Thank you. Too bad that wasn't enough to keep him. Let's go." I closed the door behind me, and adjusted my purse on my shoulder.

Trevor and I walked down to his car, which was like a '98 Honda Civic, and he pulled the door open for me. It wasn't dirty, but it smelled like must, feet, and just a nasty nigga. It was obvious that he'd had a bunch of his sweaty ass teammates in his car, and didn't crack his windows. After getting myself to the point where I wouldn't throw up in this man's whip, I closed the door. This was exactly why I bought vent air fresheners for Santino's car. His never smelled, but I feared it would and wanted to prevent it.

"Can we crack the windows?" I asked Trevor, not wanting to offend him by just doing so.

"Oh yeah, sure."

I rolled down the manual window as he peeled through the parking lot with his music blasting. It was so loud that I couldn't even hear myself think, and his little car was just rattling away. The fresh air from outside seemed like a luxury at this moment because of how terrible it smelled in here. His cologne was even being masked by the stench.

After driving for about 10 minutes, we pulled into the shopping center where Baby Stacks Cafe was located. It was funny that he chose this place because Santino loved their pancakes. It'd be funny if we saw him here with his lying ass. I realized I was frowning at the thought of Santino when I looked into the side mirror.

"Ever been here?" Trevor asked as he parked his car.

"Yes, they're pretty good. I love the omelets."

"Yeah, them jawns are off the chain. Roll up your window, shorty."

You need to leave them cracked so you can vent this funky shit.

I just did as he asked, and then we got out of the car. I had never been so happy to be outside in the Las Vegas air, with that sitting heat and all. But being trapped in his smelly ass car had me appreciating the little things in life.

"Table for two, please," Trevor approached the hostess.

To my surprise, the place was semi crowded. We still didn't have to wait, but it was way more people than I expected. I guess because most were off on Fridays. Santino and I usually went on Thursday mornings since we didn't have class, and it'd be like a ghost town in here.

Once we were seated, we both ordered some juices and then started looking over the menu. I already had a taste for the Mexican skillet before we'd even pulled up, so reading the description again just confirmed it for me.

"So why did you ask me out, Trevor?"

He looked up from the menu and said, "Why you think? You're beautiful as hell."

"Thanks, but I guess I should rephrase that question. Why did you ask me out knowing I'm Santino's ex? I thought you guys were good friends."

"We used to be."

"Until?"

"Until he got drafted and started thinking he was better than niggas. Shit, he probably made the homie Huelo disappear because he was jealous."

Laughing I asked, "I'm sorry, why would Santino need to be jealous of Huelo? I mean, Huelo was cool, but come on."

"Hey, I don't know. All I know is I don't fuck with Sanz anymore because that nigga is Hollywood as fuck.

"Does he know you're out with me?" I quizzed.

"No, and I don't care if he finds out. It may be good for his ass for trying to play you."

"Yeah."

We ordered our food, and once it came we both tore into it. Trevor was pretty funny, so I did enjoy the conversation we had over breakfast. Afterwards, he drove straight back to the dorms because I was sleepy from eating.

As Trevor pulled into a park, I said, "Trevor, something in your car smells terrible."

I didn't want to say anything but I had to. When we'd gotten back into the car after breakfast, the funk had gotten worse but it wasn't the same must, feet, and sweaty balls scent like before. It was something else, like mildew or rotten food.

"Oh damn, for real," he laughed and looked in the back seat. Finally, his eyes stopped searching and he picked up an old Del Taco burger that had enough mold for 10 loaves of bread.

"Ugh, oh my gosh!" I shrieked, hopping out of the car as he laughed.

"Shit, I remember biting this and throwing it in the back seat because it was nasty as fuck."

"That is disgusting, Trevor!" If my lip turned up anymore, you'd be able to pull it over my head.

He tossed the burger into a nearby trashcan, and then we started towards Dayton Hall since we lived in the same building. As soon as we hit the corner, my heart stopped because I saw Santino talking to his teammate Gerald. Before I could distance myself from Trevor, he'd already seen us and was rushing over with Gerald on his heels. I thought I would get a kick out of Santino seeing Trevor and I, but I'd clearly forgotten how psycho Santino was.

"Fuck is going on here, Bella?" Santino grimaced.

"Uh umm, Santino—"

"We just came back from our date nigga. Is there a problem?" Trevor cut me off and got in Santino's face. That was a bad idea.

"Oh yeah?" Santino grinned, before sizing Trevor up.

WHAM!

It seemed like Trevor flew 10 miles due to the force of that punch. Before he could get himself together, Santino delivered another, and another, as Gerald and I both screamed for him to stop. Trevor claimed he was from West Philly, so I honestly expected more from him in the fighting department.

"Santino, baby, please stop!" I cried, as Gerald finally got a hold to him. "Trevor—"

"Nah, I'm good," Trevor hopped up. "I'll hit you up, Bella," he smiled, teeth covered in blood, before he walked briskly into the dorm building. Santino tried to break free from Gerald, but luckily, his other teammate Jimmy helped stop him.

"You're so ridiculous. You can fuck other bitches but when I move on it's a problem," I spat, before switching my hips into the building purposely. I knew Santino was right behind me because I could literally feel the heat radiating off of him.

"Come here!" he grabbed my arm but I snatched it.

Pinning me against the wall, he stared down at me angrily with his fine ass, allowing his cologne to dance up my nostrils. I wanted him to just fuck the shit out of me right here in the lobby. I didn't care if other students were here.

"Bella Bacigalupi, you will always be mine. And any time I see another nigga in yo' face I'm gonna fuck his ass up, on sight. I told you that hoe blackmailed me, baby, and I had to do what I had to do to make sure I didn't lose all that I'd worked for, including you."

"No, move, liar. And you lost me anyway, so what good did your plan do?"

I slipped from under him and made my way to the elevator. We rode it up together, and then I walked down the hallway with him trying to hug and kiss on me. I wanted to let him but I had to be strong.

His right arm wrapped tightly around my midsection, and then he grabbed my crotch with his left hand before whispering into my ear, "This is gonna always be my pussy."

It was like someone cut a water hose on in my panties because they were immediately drenched. I had to snatch away from him, fearing he'd be able to feel it through my jean shorts.

Santino followed me into my room, just as Austin slapped the shit out of Perry. His back was to us, so he didn't even know we were in there. He then wrapped his hands around her throat to choke her as she cried and tried to fight him off.

"Aye, nigga, what's yo' problem!" Santino yanked on Austin's shoulder, spinning him around. "Why don't you fight a man, nigga," Santino gritted, mouth twisted up. My baby stayed fight— I mean, my *ex* baby stayed fighting.

"You better back yo' pretty ass up out of my face before you get smoked, boy," Austin sneered, looking Santino up and down while exposing his handgun.

"Oh my gosh!" both Perry and I squealed at the sight of his gun.

"Nigga, I dare you," Santino stepped closer to Austin. Their noses were almost touching.

"Oh, you fucking him too?" Austin moved back from Santino finally.

"No, Austin, I—"

"Fuck out of here." Austin darted out of the room.

"Santino, mind your own business next time!" Perry hollered at him through tears, and then rushed from the room, chasing after Austin.

"Get out, I'm about to take a nap," I said.

"Me too, then."

He closed the door, and then picked me up to carry me to the bed. I hated and loved how strong he was. He removed my shoes, and then slid out of his, before we both got in my bed. Gripping my body from behind, he pulled me into his strong chest and kissed my neck.

"Santino, we're still done."

"Mm hmm," was the last thing I heard him say before I dozed off.

CHAPTER SEVEN

Truman

"Are you ready to see everything, Mr. Morrison? It's all so beautiful, she's gonna love it," my jeweler Michelle grinned.

"I hope so, because I spent a pretty penny on all of this shit. I hope it works in my favor too."

"I think so. I mean the only way I wouldn't forgive my man after seeing these jewels would be if he killed my mother. Now it was anything like that, right?"

"No, she doesn't even know her mother, only her aunt. And I definitely didn't do anything like that. I broke her heart though."

"This should mend it then, but if it doesn't, it will definitely patch it up. Let me go get everything. Have a seat, and some champagne."

Rubbing my hands together, I closed my eyes and said a quick prayer. I needed Chiina to forgive me, and I felt like this would help. I'd already apologized, pleaded my love, gave her flowers, and I proposed prior to all this, so there wasn't much left to do. I felt like I was out of options, so hopefully this would work.

I hated coming to her aunt's to see my kid, and her not talking to me or looking at me. One time she sat in her room and cried the whole time I chilled with my son, as her aunt shot daggers at me in the living room. I told Chiina she could continue to stay at my crib since she'd kicked my ass out, but she refused so this was where we were at currently.

"Champagne for you, Mr. Morrison," Michelle's assistant walked up to me with a glass.

"Thanks, man."

I admired some of the other pieces while I waited for Michelle to bring out the jewelry I'd purchased for Chiina. She finally emerged after a couple minutes, and when she displayed the necklace, bracelet, and watch, even I was in awe. She was right, Chiina would have to forgive me after gifting her with this shit. I hadn't seen this many diamonds since I bought Pilar a necklace, and even then, I don't think it was this much. This shit cost enough to buy a seven-bedroom house in Las Vegas, and I'd spent it all on jewelry for my lady.

"Nice, right? I think she will love it," Michelle smiled down at all the diamonds.

"Me too, shit," I said, and we laughed in unison.

"Let me just bag it up for you."

I stood there and watched Michelle place the items into the correct red velvet boxes, and once she put them into a bag, I thanked her and left.

I knew Chiina would be home because she was off today; I made sure of it. She didn't want any of my money, so she was now back at work, assisting with booking VIP tables. I allowed her to manage the club's tables while Winter did the strip club's tables. I didn't want them working together for obvious reasons.

I made it to Chiina's aunt's house, and just parked right in front. I was happy to see her aunt wasn't home, because that bitch worked my damn nerves. She had valid reason to hate me but still.

I ran over what I was gonna say in my head, then grabbed the gifts and got out the car. I rang the doorbell once I approached the door, and after a few moments, Chiina answered.

"I wasn't expecting you, Truman. TJ and I are having our day together."

"I can't come see him whenever I want?"

I looked down at her beautiful face that had not a spot of makeup. She was wearing a big t-shirt so I could see her sexy, golden legs. It was hanging off of her shoulder, allowing her curly hair to brush against the exposed part of her shoulder that I wanted to kiss.

"I guess," she moved back so that I could come inside.

I couldn't help myself, so as soon as the door closed, I hemmed her up against the wall and kissed her lips. She didn't kiss me back but I didn't care. As I leaned in for another, she turned away so I gripped her jaw and made her look at me. I pecked her gently again as her small palm rested against my abs like she wanted to stop me.

"Truman, did you come here to see him or me?"

"Both."

"Just come see the baby for a little bit so you can leave," she scoffed, switching off down the long hallway until we made it to the living room.

My dick immediately started hardening as I followed her into the living room. I was craving some pussy, not just any pussy, but Chiina's. It was something about it, like I knew it was mine. Nothing was better than fire ass pussy that you knew had your name all over it.

We took a seat on the sectional where my son was lying on his circle pillow that he always slept on. Since he was knocked out, I just rubbed his small back before planting a kiss on his cheek.

I never knew I would be a father this soon. I didn't even think I would have kids, so it was crazy that I was really trying to do this whole family shit. It surprised me that I wanted to be a family man so bad, because the mere thought of it used to make me cringe. But I loved Chiina and my son more than I loved anything else in my life, so this was where my happiness lied.

I realized that was the case because whenever we broke apart like this, I felt empty as fuck like something was missing. Everything else in my life was gravy as far as my money, business, and my health, but my mood stays on low when I don't have my kid and my girl, so I know it's real.

"When do you think we should take him for pictures?" I inquired.

Chiina stared at me for a second before a pretty smile burst through her face. She pushed her hair behind her ears nervously, and rubbed TJ's hair back.

"Probably when he gets to be almost 10 months. I didn't know you thought about things like that, so I'm a little surprised."

"You shouldn't be. What you think, I just be talking out of my ass when I say I love you and want this?"

"Umm, yeah. Your mouth says one thing but your actions prove otherwise. How can you say you love me, but creep out of our bed at night to go sleep with an employee at a hotel?" Her facial expression showed how disgusted she was. "Like, just thinking about it pisses me off, Tru."

"I get it. When I think about it I feel stupid and disappointed in myself."

"Yeah right."

"Chiina, I'm serious. For as long as I've been having relationships with women, I've never been faithful or even attempted to be. I always played the part but was doing dirt on the low. This is the *first* time I've tried to be faithful and actually somewhat succeeded, so hell yeah, I was disappointed in myself. Not to mention I hate to see you hurt like that. It's still hard for me to discipline myself when it comes to the opposite sex, but I'm trying and you cannot say that I haven't improved."

"Yeah," she mumbled, looking off and grabbing her bottle of juice. "I just don't know yet, Truman. I need time to think. I don't trust you and I don't want to be married to you while you're out doing God knows what. I couldn't imagine being stuck with you in that situation."

Damn, that shit low-key hurt hearing her say she wouldn't wanna be stuck with me. I understood her though. I mean who would want to be legally tied to a spouse that was out doing dirt? I know I wouldn't so I couldn't blame her I guess.

"I understand, shorty, and I'm not gonna rush you. I just want to know if I even have a little bit of a chance."

She cocked her head to the side as her eyes searched my face.

"I guess you have a teeny chance because of the baby and because for some reason, I'm still in love with you."

"Good, I wasn't gonna give up anyway," I grinned, making her chuckle. "Oh, I got you something." I picked the bag up from her aunt's laminate flooring and handed it over to her.

"What is it?" she peeked into the bag.

"Open it and see."

She set the bag on the couch next to her, after pulling out the first velvet box. Slowly lifting the top to expose the bracelet, her jaw dropped in admiration, which made me smile.

"Truman," she whispered, eyes scanning the bling nonstop. "There's more than this?"

"Yeah, get all the stuff out of the bag."

After placing the bracelet's box down, she reached in and opened the necklace, then the watch. I got up to sit next to her so I could help fasten the necklace around her, and she placed her small fingers on it as she looked down.

"You like it?" I questioned.

"Of course."

"I bought this for you as a gift, baby, because I love you and I feel like you deserve something nice like this. You're my girl, well I want you to be, and mine will always have the best shit."

"Thank you," she half smiled.

"Can I have another kiss?"

She nodded, so I pulled her into my lap. She gripped the sides of my face as we kissed slowly but passionately. Once she felt my dick getting hard under her, she pulled away.

"You won't be getting that for a long time if ever again." She got up. "Are you hungry? I was in the middle of making roast, mashed potatoes, and steamed spinach."

"Hell yeah, you make a chocolate cake too?" I was excited. I almost forgot how good my baby could throw down. She was young, but because she had basically been on her own for a while, she had to learn to cook at an early age.

"Yes, I did. I added chocolate chips like you like too," she giggled, as I followed her to the kitchen, carrying my son lying on his pillow. This nigga was so small and fat, that he was portable as fuck. I laughed at my thoughts.

"So, you knew I was coming then?"

"No, I just made the cake like that for you so much that it became natural. I like it that way too now."

We entered her aunt's big ass kitchen, and Chiina laughed when I set TJ in the middle of the table like he was the roast. As I waited for her to take everything out and make the plates, my phone chimed. I looked down to see it was Pilar's ass trying to come back from the damn dead in my life again.

Pilar: I miss you.

Me: Stop it.

Pilar: *So you for real don't care if I fuck another nigga?*

Me: *Nope, and haven't you already been doing that?*

She didn't respond, instead she tried to call me, so I quickly hit ignore and cut my phone off. If my boys needed anything they'd text my work phone, and since I was here with Chiina and my kid, my personal could afford to be off for the moment.

"Hell yeah," I rubbed my hands together as Chiina set my plate in front of me, along with a glass of red Kool-Aid.

She sat adjacent to me with her plate and a glass of water like always since she said the Kool-Aid was way too sweet.

"I see you were hungry," she chuckled.

"I was." I stuffed some of the tender ass, seasoned ass roast into my mouth. "I missed shit like this, baby. I love you like for real." I leaned over and kissed her sweet-smelling neck.

"Well you don't have this back yet, but we will see."

After dinner we ate chocolate cake, and by that time my son was up. Chiina and I played with him until he got fussy, and that's when she put him to sleep. It was around 8pm by that time, and she said her aunt was on a business trip so I could spend the night. At the moment, she was getting the den ready so we could watch some movies, while I rushed home to get a few things.

I swooped into my park, on cloud nine damn near. I'm telling you a nigga was walking on sunshine. It was crazy how two people could literally change my mood like that. That's how I knew I needed to get my shit together and make my family whole.

I hit the alarm on my car and then tread up to my door. When I unlocked it, I saw two open bottles of my wine on my coffee table, along with two glasses. Pulling my gun from my waist, I made sure the safety was off and walked to the back. I saw my bedroom door was closed, so I counted down from three before bursting in.

"What the fuck!" I hollered at the sight of Pilar getting her back blown out by some nigga in *my* fucking bed.

"Oh shit!" the dude rolled off my bed, dick swinging and shit.

"Get the fuck up out of my house before I put a cap in you, bro," I said through gritted teeth, trying not to catch a murder case. I had never been disrespected like this in my life.

The guy didn't even bother getting dressed, he just quickly snatched his clothes up and rushed past me. Pilar, however, took her time slipping her lace panties up with a smirk, laughing wryly.

"You think this shit is funny?" I hissed, itching to shoot her disrespectful ass.

"Yeah, I do. You were so busy chasing behind little Lolita that you forgot to get your house key back. My place is being remodeled and I needed a spot to fuck the nigga you didn't care about me doing it to." She slipped into her heels. "We were gonna spend the whole weekend here."

"Pilar, get out before I kill you. On everything I love, if when I count down from five and you're still here, I'm shooting you."

"Trust me, I'm gone. I just wanted you to see how it felt to watch the person you love be with someone else."

"I don't love you."

"Some time ago that would have made me cry, but I couldn't care less. I'm happy to be free from your dog ass. Deuces, nigga, and don't forget to wash your sheets, we've been going at it for hours," she whispered the last part before giggling and sauntering out of the bedroom.

POP!

I shot out the chandelier in the hallway, prompting her to scurry out like a roach.

"Psycho ass nigga!" she yelled before I heard the front door slam.

I couldn't believe that stupid ass bitch. And to think I felt bad for dissing her. Shit, that hoe could kiss my ass now. I was done with her, and if she ever got in my face again, I was shooting her between the eyes.

However, tonight I was gonna worry about my family, so I just packed my shit up and went back to Chiina's aunt's house. Tomorrow I'd get them damn locks changed though.

CHAPTER SEVEN

Tonight, Bella, Tasmine, Perry, Shayne, and I were all out to dinner at Top of the World, a rooftop restaurant with an amazing view. We wanted to do something, and since a party wasn't really gonna work for Tasmine, Shayne, and I at the moment, we decided to just have a nice dinner. Not to mention, I wanted my friends to become more acquainted with my sister. She was gonna invite Marisol, but I told her to hold off because I was still slightly annoyed by her.

"I saw Trevor the other day and he's still looking fucked up," Tasmine said, making the table laugh.

"Who is Trevor?" Shayne questioned.

"This guy that I went out with," Bella sighed and Shayne nodded. I could tell Bella felt bad for getting Trevor fucked up, but I mean what did she expect? Santino was crazy and even crazier about her.

"You mean a guy you used and ended up getting him knocked the fuck out? You know Santino is psycho, yet you still went out with another guy; his friend at that," I said.

"I know, and I didn't think it all the way through. I was just upset at the fact that he'd cheated on me. It didn't quite register until Trevor and I hit the corner, and I saw all that anger in Santino's eyes."

"Well, what are you gonna do? Are you going back?" Tasmine inquired.

"Nope. He had no room for mistakes, yet he made one."

"Didn't he explain the situation to you?" I frowned. We didn't want to get into too much detail with grimy Perry here, because it was no telling what she'd do with that information.

"No, I haven't really let him because when I see him I just want to fight. I knew he'd been lying which is why I had Tasmine take me to that same location we followed him to. I wanted to be wrong, but I watched that bitch give him head and him enjoy it."

"Well, I'm sure she's still feeling the effects of that ass whooping you gave her," I joked, making everyone chuckle.

"Oh, I know she is. And if she wants another dose I can give it to her."

"I knew I liked you," Shayne winked at Bella.

The waiter set down our plates, and after we held hands to pray, we began digging into our food. I looked into my son's carrier to make sure he was fine, and then went back to eating. I could tell everyone was starved because no one was saying a damn thing. All you heard was the clinking of silverware, and people humming a little at how good the food was.

"So what happened between you and Austin?" Bella glanced at

Perry before looking back down at her plate. Bella had already told us that she and Santino walked in on Perry getting slapped, and how she got angry with Santino when he defended her.

"We're good, everything is great. I decided to let Cash go, and work on what I have with Austin," she lied through her teeth. I could tell by her constant nodding and refusal to make eye contact.

"You just decided to let Cash go? You talked about him nonstop and had us up all night scouring the Internet for him," I said, brows dipped.

"Okay, so I didn't let him go. But things are better with Austin. I thought about breaking up with him, but I know he's gonna get angry and I'm scared. Then Cash, he refuses to take me seriously while I have a boyfriend."

"Can you blame him?" I chuckled.

"You seemed to be mad when Oden told you the same thing," she came for me.

"Ye-yeah, I was. And I'm happy he treated me that way because it forced me to break off a toxic ass relationship like the one you have, P," I fake smiled.

"Oh, Khyle, I forgot to tell you and show you something," she cleared her throat and then reached for her purse. "Oden has been spending a lot of time with this girl. One night I saw them leave the club together."

My stomach dropped as I watched her scroll on her phone. I wanted to be angry at her for watching my man, but then I guess I was thankful that she saw. Placing my fork down, I put my hand out for her phone that she had outreached to me. I saw a picture of a girl walking behind Oden as they left, and I could tell they were talking. Realizing the photo was live, I held down on it to see that not only were they conversing but that it was Naomi.

"Thanks," was all I said as I handed it back to Perry.

"Who is the bitch? You know her?" Shayne looked at me, anger all throughout her face.

"No, I don't," I lied. I couldn't wait to get home.

After dinner, the girls and I got dessert, and then went our separate ways. When I got to Oden's townhouse, I put my baby to bed and then went to the back to get my handgun that my father had recently given me. I guess he had an inkling that Oden was dangerous, so he wanted me to be able to protect myself if something popped. I thought it was ridiculous, but at this moment I was happy. I'm sure this situation in particular wasn't what my father had in mind, but I didn't give a fuck.

Walking back to the living room with my gun, I sat down on the couch and sent that nigga a text to find out when he was gonna get here.

Oden: *About two more hours baby.*

He was lying because he'd told me a week prior that he was getting off early tonight since he'd planned it. I didn't respond, I just made myself some herbal tea, and turned on the television. I started getting tired after about an hour and a half, so I eventually dozed off, but the sound of his car woke my ass right back up. I straightened up my appearance a little bit, and then sat back down on the couch, gun in hand.

I got nervous as I listened to his keys jingle in the door. When he walked in, I simply said, "Hurry up and close the door."

"You okay, baby?" he asked, seemingly a little bit worried.

"I told you I wouldn't tolerate you cheating on me, Oden."

Frowning in confusion, he replied, "And I haven't been. I never have and you know that. What is wrong with you?" He set his keys down.

"Why is that bitch living over here and all up in your fucking job, nigga! Niggas know I'm your bitch now, and you're parading her around like I don't fucking exist, embarrassing me! I just had your fucking baby!"

"Khyle, shorty, who are you— whoa, whoa!" When he started towards me, I pulled my small silver gun from behind my back and aimed it at him. "Are you serious right now?"

"As a heart attac,k nigga. Why have you been fucking around with Naomi? You think I'm just gonna let you leave me and be with that bitch? I will shoot the both of your asses tonight!"

"Okay," he started laughing, clapping his hands and shit like it was a joke. "Khyle!" he shouted when I shot a hole in his vase to let him know I wasn't fucking around.

I loved this nigga and it'd be a cold day in hell before I let him run off into the sunset with that ugly ass bitch Naomi. I'd kill him, and then my baby and I would be the only ones riding off into the sunset with *his* damn money.

"Answer me before I blow your head off, nigga!" I barked, still aiming the gun at him.

"Babe, Naomi plans parties for Maxim magazine, so I have to work with her to get the party for this weekend together. Remember I said that? I told you about the party," he spoke softly to me like I was crazy… and I guess I was.

"So you don't love her?"

"No, baby, I don't. I love you even though you just threatened to kill me and shot up my damn vase."

"You don't miss her? She was your first love," I said, waiting to shoot him if he said the wrong thing.

"I didn't love her like I love you, Khyle. I liked her, a lot I will say, but what we have is deeper than that, baby."

"Okay, last question," I sniffled. "Why were you two hours late today? You were supposed to get out of the club and meetings tonight, two hours ago."

"Can I come closer?"

"Only a little bit." He started towards me and when he was close enough I told him to stop.

"Because I had to get this." He reached into his pocket and pulled out a gray velvet box as he knelt down. He lifted the top and displayed the most beautiful diamond ring I'd ever seen up close.

"Wh-why did you get this?" I felt myself on the verge of crying.

"I got it because I planned to ask you to marry me tonight. I love you and my son more than anything in this world, Khyle, and I feel like this is the only thing missing between— can you get the gun out of my face so I can talk?"

"Sorry," I chuckled and set it on the coffee table.

"Like I was saying, I feel like marriage is the only thing missing and I'm ready. If you're not, we can be engaged until you are, but I want you to be my wife, Khyle Luke. So what do you say, huh?" He gave me that beautiful grin after licking his lips and running his hand over his wild curly hair.

"You still want to marry me even though I planned to kill you?" I whined, making him laugh heartily.

"Unfortunately, yes. You're crazy as hell, but that just lets me know you love me. And like I told you, shorty, I would never step out on you, so don't even put that shit in your head, aight?"

"K. Well yes, I will marry you, and I want to this summer."

"Works for me." He slid the big ring onto my finger, and my mouth just couldn't close as I stared at it. "Can we celebrate tonight?" he started kissing on my thighs.

"Just two more days to go, baby, but I will make it good I promise." I cupped his chin and pecked him. "But sit up here and I will take care of you," I patted the couch.

He quickly sat on it and unzipped his pants, so I got down on my knees and took him into my mouth. With my eyes on my ring, I sucked his dick so good I should have asked for payment after.

I couldn't believe I was gonna marry the love of my life. A horrible night had definitely turned into a great one.

CHAPTER SEVEN

Oden

That weekend…

Thug ass nigga when I'm eatin', don't interfere. Maybach, rear view mirror, saw the one time comin'…

I stood inside of my glassed VIP, watching everybody dance wildly to YG and spend hella money on drinks. I glanced at Anton and Truman who were smiling just as widely as I was. This night alone was gonna have the club's profits through the roof.

"Nigga, this was the move right here," Anton nodded his head to the music.

"Tell me about it," Truman replied.

"Hey guys, can we take some pictures, please, with Valerie," Naomi walked up with their *Maxim Hot 100* girl and some photographers. She was sexy but I didn't see why she was number one. I was sure she'd break in half during any kind of sexual activity, because she was way skinnier in person. I know my shorty wasn't thick, but she had more meat on her bones than old girl right here.

"Sure," I responded.

We stood up there taking picture after picture, until finally the damn photographers had, had enough. Anton walked down to the strip club so he could check on shit, and then Truman went downstairs to do the same with the rest of the club.

"Mr. Bishop, I wanna thank you for allowing them to throw my party here. I love your club," Valerie smiled. She was a brown-haired white girl, very beautiful and looked exactly like what she was: a Victoria's Secret model.

"No problem, I'm just happy you're enjoying yourself. Naomi really made sure we went all out for this," I said, glancing at Naomi before landing my eyes back on Valerie.

"So since this is my party, do I get to make a wish of some sort?" Valerie licked her lips, staring up at me.

"Valerie—" Naomi tried to cut in but she gave her a look. "Refresh my drink please, Naomi."

"Sure." Naomi took the glass and walked off.

"So what do you say? Can I ask for something and you promise me that no matter what it is you'll grant it?"

"I can't promise that," I smiled, trying to be professional when really I wanted to tell this hoe to scram.

"Oh, I think you're gonna enjoy my wish, so I will take my chances and just ask." She moved closer to me. I kept my stance, staring down into her pretty face. "You smell so good, what is that?"

"Cologne."

She giggled at me being so short before whispering, "How about I give you a blowjob that will rock your world, and then you bend me over and fuck me while I stare down at the club goers."

Leaning closer to her face I whispered back, "I'll pass."

The face she made showed how shocked she was at my response, letting me know she'd never been turned down before. I had no interest in smashing her because for one, I was engaged, and two, it was bad for business. If I was gonna cheat, it wouldn't be with her.

"Did you seriously turn down one of my famous blowjobs?"

"Yeah, I did. And it can't be that good if you're calling it a blowjob. I like bitches who tell me they'll straight up suck my dick. Enjoy the night. All your drinks are on me," I winked, before leaving the area to go in search of Naomi.

I wanted to get at her because last night Khyle told me how she came to our doorstep talking hot shit about how she was gonna get me back and all this other nonsense. It was one thing to say it to me, but to knock on my door and say it to Khyle like she thought she had it like that, was another. I don't know why Khyle hadn't mentioned it before, but I planned to get in Naomi's ass for real.

"Can you come talk to me in my office," I said when I found Naomi by the bar.

"Umm, of course," she nibbled on her lip and followed after me.

We went to the back and took the newly installed elevator up, then stepped off. When I got closer to where the offices were located, I saw Winter and Truman arguing.

"Aye aye! What the fuck are y'all doing? Both of you should be working," I hissed, looking back and forth between them. Honestly, I was a little annoyed by Truman and the fact that he was back here arguing with this bitch like he hadn't been damn near in tears over Chiina. His bullshit was starting to irritate me, which had never happened before.

"Oden, tell her to stay off my bumper before I fire her ass," Truman looked to me. I exhaled heavily, happy that this wasn't some lover's quarrel. "If Chiina catches her following me it's gon' be a murder scene."

"I'm not trying to be on his *bumper*, I just want to know why he's been dodging me and not speaking to me!" Winter cried. She was for real weeping, tears and all.

"Naomi, go in my office please," I said. She hesitated, but went inside and closed the door behind herself. "Truman, tell me you haven't been sleeping with Winter. I thought you were trying to grow up for your damn family!"

"I didn't fuck her! I was going to but I didn't! Tell him!" Truman barked at Winter.

"We didn't, but I know you're feeling me! You can't just do this! I love you!"

"Oh my gosh," Truman grumbled, placing his hands over his face. "You see this? I've never even touched her!" he outstretched his arms. "How the fuck does she love me, bro?"

"Truman, just go back out on the floor, aight?" He started off and Winter tried to follow him, so I grabbed her arm lightly. "Winter, whatever feelings you have for Truman, remember not to bring them here and that he is your boss. Most importantly, he is involved and has a family. Whatever he made you think prior, get it out of your mind. I need you to be on your job. There are girls on the floor that you are supposed to be supervising. If I catch you following Truman, looking at him, or even discussing your feelings for him I will fire you. Got it?" I stared deeply into her eyes.

"He doesn't love her he—"

"Winter."

"Got it," she mumbled, dropping her head.

"Thank you. Now please go to the strip *club area,* and stay away from Truman, especially while Chiina is working tonight."

Truman was right, Chiina would go ape shit and ruin this whole party if she spotted Winter trailing Truman around the club. We were playing with fire by having them both work here and in the same job, but we couldn't just fire them because of personal shit. However, if Winter kept up this fatal attraction mess, I wouldn't step in when Truman gave her a pink slip.

"Okay. Oh, and boss? That girl Perry is sitting with booth six a lot instead of working. I tried to intervene, but the guy she was all up on acted like he was gonna kick my ass."

Would I ever catch a fucking break?

"Tell Anton, not Truman. *Anton,* okay?"

She nodded and switched down the hallway.

"Sorry about that Naomi." I came into my office and closed the door behind me.

"Personal work drama? You guys need a TV show or something. I can probably make that happen," she laughed.

"No thank you, even though I'm sure it'd be a hit." I went to sit next to her on my leather couch before exhaling heavily.

"You okay, babe?" She rubbed my back, reminding me of what I came to talk to her ass about.

"Yeah, Naomi, I'm good. Look umm, why did you show up at my crib talking shit to my girl?"

"What? When?"

"Don't play stupid. The day we came home with our son, you showed up telling her all this shit about how I loved you first and that I was gonna leave her."

"Don't remember," she shrugged, smiling a little. "Alright, I did it. But I know everything I said wasn't a complete lie, was it?"

"Yeah it was," I chuckled angrily.

"You're full of shit, Oden Bishop. I refuse to believe that you don't love me even a little bit. I mean we were together for years and during the majority of them, we were head over heels in love."

"Yeah, and then you started acting up, so even though we were together my feelings started to change. But the past does not matter anymore, Naomi. At this moment and for forever, I will be in love with Khyle, the mother of my son and my soon to be wife."

"You don't wanna get married you—"

"I already asked her earlier this week, and we're getting married this summer. If it were up to me, we'd be getting it done tomorrow at some chapel."

"Oden," a tear slipped from her eye. "I'm sorry for how I acted during that last year we spent together and I'm sorry for getting married! My divorce will be final in a week, and we could—"

"We can't! Naomi, we can't do anything! I'm trying to let you down easily but you're not fucking getting it! I do not love you anymore! Things with Khyle are different! I'm a different man for her and with her!" I shot up off of the couch, irritated beyond belief.

"Different how?!" she hollered back.

"Because I've never cheated on her!" I shouted. "There! You wanted to know how, I told yo' ass, and now you're standing there looking dumb as fuck!"

"You-you actually were cheating on me?" she sniffled.

"Not at first, no, but after you accused me so many times, hell yeah! I was already on trial for the shit every time I walked through the door, so I thought why not. And you know what, I didn't feel bad after fucking a different bitch every night either. That's some shit I could never do to her. Now does that explain to you how different my feelings are?" My chest heaved up and down as I panted angrily. I was tired of this shit. If I had to hurt her damn feelings for her to get off my dick, then so be it.

She said nothing for a little bit, as she just looked at me like she didn't know me.

"I'm gonna go check on the party." She wiped the tears from her eyes and darted out.

Pulling out my phone, I messaged Anton because I wanted to see if I could go home for the night.

Me: Everything good? I wanted to call it a night.

Tony: Yeah we got it. We've already taken pictures and shaken all the hands. Right now everyone is just partying and getting drunk.

Me: Aight I'm out.

I texted Khyle to let her know I was coming home now instead of at around 5am like I'd initially told her. I did that because I wanted her to be up. I felt like a kid to his mother with shit like that. I hated coming home to see her already asleep.

I went back through the club one more time to shake some more hands, take any last minute pictures, and let people know I was leaving. I felt Naomi's eyes on me as I spoke to one of her co-workers, but I just ignored her. When I was done, I left out the back and hopped into my Porsche, headed home.

I walked into my townhouse, and saw the lights were dim. There were red candles lit here and there, making the room smell sweet. Scanning the area, I saw Khyle sitting on the dining room table wearing a pair of heels, the kind with her whole foot out basically; my favorite. As for the rest of her body, she was completely naked. Her legs were open, and she was leaning back with her hands holding her up and her long ass hair swinging. My dick was rock hard immediately, which had never happened to me.

"Close the door and come here," she demanded coolly.

I did as she asked, and made my way over to see three kinds of sundae syrup sitting on the table next to her. I tried to touch her but she brushed my hand away. I was about to nut in my damn slacks in a minute, just from looking between her legs, at her sexy flat stomach, and her perfectly round breasts.

"What's your favorite flavor?" she asked. "Caramel, strawberry, or chocolate?" She touched each of the syrups.

"Caramel for sure, but I do like strawberry and chocolate too," I bit my lip.

She nodded before taking the chocolate and covering her brown, dime sized, nipples with it. When she was done, she set it down and just looked at me.

I made my way over to her and started sucking her nipples like that shit was going out of style. I flicked my tongue and sucked until there wasn't a speck of chocolate left. Hearing her moan out each time I put pressure had my dick making a tent in my pants.

Licking my lips, I watched her put the strawberry syrup down her stomach, before she lied back on the table flat. I licked that off, sticking my tongue in her navel to make sure I got it out. I trailed my tongue up her stomach, planting sloppy kisses every now and again as I cleaned the syrup off of her. Once she was clean yet again, she brought the caramel syrup over her pussy and started to drizzle it. With the way my mouth was watering, you would have thought her pussy was an actual sundae.

I sat down in the chair so her pussy was right in my face, and dug in. I placed my palms on the back of her smooth thighs to push them towards her stomach a little, as I sucked on her pussy like a lollipop. She was crying out, massaging my hair as I went to town. I'd missed eating her out, so I was like a starving dog at the moment; not to mention I loved caramel.

"I'm gonna cum, mmm," Khyle whimpered as I made my mouth and her pussy become one.

"Cum for daddy, baby," I mumbled against her clit, before latching back on to it. She came, and I licked it up before diving back in like an Olympic swimmer.

Gripping her small waist, I pushed her pussy further into my mouth, forcing her legs to spread wider and drape over my shoulders. Pressing her legs into her stomach again, I dipped my tongue into her opening, and then brought it back up to flick over her button. Her whines and whimpers were driving me crazy at the moment, making me go harder.

"Oh! Oh fuck, baby, I'm gonna cum so hard," she called out, so I sucked her clit harder, holding her thighs against her stomach. "Oden!" she cried, her moans high pitched than a muthafucka. In a minute, the neighbors were gonna be thinking I had Mariah Carey up in this bitch. "Mmm," she trembled violently as her nectar spilled down my chin. I just kissed her lower lips gently, swiping my tongue in between very slowly every now and then.

Pulling away finally, I stood and she sat up to help me undress. Once I was butt naked like her, she took the caramel syrup and put some on the head of my dick. She began sucking the damn skin off, making me lose my balance for a second. I gripped the table and just watched my rod pound against her throat, and her take it like a G. Seeing her ass naked with them heels on, sucking my dick like a little porn star was the shit right now.

"Khy, fuck." I rubbed her hair back as she went to town on my dick.

Shit was sloppy as fuck, and she was deep throating me like never before. If I hadn't have proposed earlier this week, I would have right now.

I gripped the back of her hair tightly, and started humping her face. She took it like a professional, and when she looked up at me with that innocent pretty face while sucking me up, I was done. Biting down on my lip, I tried to hold back but I couldn't. I spilled my seeds down her throat and she swallowed it up.

"Where do you want me?" she asked, nibbling on her full bottom lip sexily.

"Bounce on it," I said, sitting down in the chair.

She straddled my lap, and I positioned my dick at her opening. She grasped my shoulders as I pushed her down on my pole gently. Her pussy was so tight that it was strangling my dick, but it was slippery wet at the same time.

"You know you got the best pussy, baby," I sucked on her collarbone, as I moved her tight wet hole up and down my shaft.

"Ahh, ahhh," her voice trembled as I pounded her middle.

I trailed my lips from her collarbone down to her titties, and cupped them so I could suck her nipples some more. She started getting used to my size again, so she was bouncing on her own slowly, as I licked her nipples. When I'd gotten my fix, I tilted my head back so we could tongue kiss.

"Uuuh, uuuh," she moaned into my mouth as I beat her pussy up by humping upward.

Soon after, she came so hard her body shook. I felt a flood on my dick as I groped her mid section and sucked on her lips. I picked her up off of my dick, and then bent her over the table. I bit down on her shoulder as I slid inside, and once I was all the way in, I started fucking the shit out of her.

"Whose pussy is this, Khyle?"

"Yo-yours, baby," she damn near cried just before I smacked her on the ass.

I spread her cheeks so I could see my dick pound her middle, and just the sight almost made me nut immediately. I grabbed her hair and started slamming into her, making her cum almost right after. I bent down to kiss all over her smooth back while winding my hips, giving her time to recoup a little bit. I smacked her ass before grasping it, and then beat it up until I busted all inside of her.

"I love you, you know that?" I grabbed her breasts from behind and brought her back into my chest. "Huh?" I panted, sucking on her ear.

"Yeah, I love you too," she was finally able to get out.

I pulled out of her, turned her to face me and picked her up. She wrapped her legs around my waist, and kissed me passionately, before I blew the candles out.

"You know I'm not done with that pussy right?"

She just giggled and slipped her tongue into my mouth as I

carried her to the bedroom. I was horny as fuck, and making sure she kept them heels on all night.

246

Shorty Is In Love Wtih A Real One 4

CHAPTER SEVEN

Tasmine

Louisville, Kentucky...

Anton and I had flown into Kentucky yesterday evening, but we didn't stop by my parents' house because we needed time to get our heads together... well at least I did. I was scared shitless to face them, but Anton was calm like always, swearing that it would be okay.

I was three months pregnant now, and hadn't talked to my parents since they told me to come home. I didn't enjoy being like this with them, but I wasn't gonna just do whatever the fuck they wanted me to do. I loved Anton, my friends, and everything I had going on in Las Vegas, so coming back to Kentucky for college wasn't an option. Why couldn't my people just be cool about the shit? I didn't need this type of stress while I was pregnant.

"Relax while you got my baby in there," Anton touched my stomach as we pulled into my parents' driveway.

"I'm trying to, but I just don't know what will happen."

"Nothing bad. What's the worse they can do?" He threw the car in park, and looked at me with his handsome face.

"Kill us both."

"I wouldn't let that happen." He got out of the car and then came around to help me out. I used my key to enter, and saw my parents sitting in the living room already. Thankfully, Tasia and Mia were in there as well.

"Heeeeeey!" Mia screeched, hopping up and running over to me. She hugged me tightly and then pulled back to touch my stomach. "Where is it?" she frowned.

"It's a little lump here, don't you see," I joked, glancing at my father who wouldn't look my way.

"I don't see shit. Hi, Anton."

"Move, crazy," Tasia said to Mia before hugging me. "Hey, Tony," she waved.

"What's up?" he nodded his head up and hugged both Tasia and Mia.

"Mama, Daddy, Tasmine and Anton are here. Did you guys want to go into the dining room or—"

"Tasia, they don't need you to speak for them. You guys leave us be in the living room," my dad sternly replied.

Tasia and Mia left without another word, so Anton and I went to sit down on the sectional, opposite of my parents. I could see the hate in my dad's eyes and the disappointment in my mother's.

"Mr. Randall, Tasmine and I—"

"This is my house and I will be the one to start this conversation. I don't need to hear a damn speech about how much you claim you love my daughter and how well you're gonna take care of her. What I wanna know is when you plan to make an honest woman out of her?"

"Daddy—" my father put his hand up to stop me.

"I haven't really thought that through, Mr. Randall. I think we need to take things one step at a time. After the baby, we can look into getting married."

"You haven't really thought about it?" my mother reiterated with a deep frown.

"No, I didn't say I hadn't thought about it, I said I hadn't thought it through meaning what would be a good time, etc. I have absolutely thought about marrying Tasmine, and that was before she got pregnant."

"And what about these other kids you have with about four or five other women? Have you *thought through* about marrying them too, or is my daughter special somehow?" my dad scoffed.

Really Tasia? I thought, shaking my head. I knew Mia hadn't said anything so it had to be her that told my parents about Selinda, Kai, and Violet.

"Those were false accusations of fatherhood that I was able to disprove, sir."

"You don't plan to pull something like that on Tasmine, do you? I mean, I wouldn't want to have to come down to Las Vegas and put a hole in your head."

"Daddy!" I shrieked, but he didn't even look my way; he kept his eyes on Anton. My dad wasn't the tallest or strongest man in the world, but his personality was one of a seven foot, 300-pound wrestler. My mother said that was what she loved about him; he feared nothing but God despite his somewhat small stature.

"Mr. and Mrs. Randall, I know you said you didn't want to hear me profess my love for Tasmine, but it's the only way I can possibly get you to understand that this isn't all that bad. I mean she's about to be 20 years old, she's in college doing great, and she's at least pregnant by a guy that loves her. I understand that you want her to have a degree, a job, and a husband before she has a baby, but you should have enough love for her to accept what's happening in her life."

"Don't tell me how much I should love my daughter!" my dad hollered.

Aww shit…

"I'm not trying to tell you anything, sir, but I want you to think about her instead of yourself! She's pregnant and at this time, she should be calm and relaxed, yet every night she's stressing and crying over what the fuck y'all are putting her through and I'm tired of the shit! I'm tired of seeing her upset over something stupid as fuck like y'all not accepting the fact that she's having a child! It's a part of life, and if it's that easy for you to just dismiss her out of your life because of it, then maybe she don't need y'all!"

When Anton finished, it was quiet as hell in the living room. You could hear a mouse piss on cotton if you listened good enough. My parents were angry, but Anton was angrier, and I didn't even know he had been all this time. I had no idea that he heard me occasionally cry at night.

"Tasmine, sweetie, it's not that we don't love you or care about you anymore, it's just that we are upset with your behavior. The only girls that get pregnant before marriage are irresponsible ones who open their legs to anyone, like your friend Khyle," my mom explained.

"Mother, Khyle is not irresponsible, nor does she open her legs to anyone; neither of us did. We both made babies out of love whether you and Dad believe it or not. Like Anton said, this may not be the best time, but it happened and the baby is coming. I didn't come here to get you guys' approval, I came here because I love you and I want us to act like family again. But if you can't accept my relationship and my baby then I just won't deal with you." I stood up and started to walk off with Anton behind me, until my dad called my name.

"Just promise us that you will finish college, Tasmine. And Anton, promise us that you will marry her or at least do right by her if you don't last," my father spoke. I could see his heart was broken, and that made me feel bad again.

"I promise, Daddy," I smiled, hoping this was a breakthrough.

"Mr. Randall, I'm serious about your daughter. Contrary to popular belief, I don't just get anyone pregnant. Not that I got her pregnant on purpose," Anton replied to my dad, making all of us chuckle lightly.

"I hope not," my mother chimed in. "Well, why don't you guys stay here in the guest room instead of wasting money on a hotel."

"We can sleep in the same room?" I grinned.

"Only if you leave the door open. That's my final offer," my dad said, crossing his arms.

"That works," Anton nodded.

"Are you guys hungry? I made lunch already," my mother offered.

"Yeah, of course."

Anton and I followed behind she and my dad, but once they got far enough to where they couldn't see us, he leaned down and kissed my lips a couple times.

"Didn't I tell you it was gonna be alright?" he raised one brow, smirking.

"For now. Let's see how long it lasts," I giggled. I admit, I was pretty happy to see my parents had somewhat accepted my child. I would have hated to sever my relationship with them. I knew there would still be some bumps in the road though, because my dad didn't get over things as quickly as others.

"Don't be so negative. I love you with yo' pretty ass."

"I love you too, handsome."

CHAPTER EIGHT

Shayne

$\mathcal{I}$ only got through one damn night at Marisol's before Lloyd marched my ass back home. I still wasn't talking to him though, so I'd been sleeping in the extra bedroom in his townhouse.

I honestly didn't know why I was so upset. He didn't cheat on me, and he hadn't planned to which I guess wasn't too surprising because I ran circles around that Elodie bitch in the looks department. But I guess the fact that he went behind my back to fly her out here and all that bullshit, and how he hid the fact that he knew who was playing on my phone from day one bothered me. Not to mention, he didn't even resolve the shit. What was talking to that thirsty hoe gonna do? Only good thing that came from that lunch was that I must have scared the shit out of her because she hadn't bothered either of us.

"I'm hungry," Lloyd came and stood in the doorway of the guest room. I took the petty route and made *myself* some dinner. Instead of responding, I simply shoved some of the mashed potatoes into my mouth, and kept my eyes glued to this movie on Netflix. "Shayne."

"Yes?" I raised a brow, eyes still on the television.

"I said I'm hungry. You ain't cooked shit since I got you from Marisol's." He sat on the edge of the bed and took my feet into his lap to massage them. As badly as I wanted to toss my drink on him, I didn't, because this damn massage felt like heaven.

"Okay, baby, what do you wanna eat?" I asked, grinning. Wasn't cooking his ass shit.

"I can't stand yo' evil ass," he chuckled, already peeping game.

"No, I'm serious. What do you wanna eat tonight?"

"I want what you got," he looked at my plate, licking his sexy chocolate lips as his strong hands massaged my feet. "What is that, fried pork chops?"

"Mm hmm, with mashed potatoes and grilled carrots."

"Damn, baby, make me that too."

"Too complicated. What about pasta?"

"Aight, I guess. My damn stomach is feasting on itself so I will take anything at this point."

"Okay, so go get that Top Ramen from the cabinet, put it in the microwave, and pour some Alfredo sauce over it. Voila, nigga."

"Shayne!"

"What? You think I'm gonna make your stupid ass some food? Think again, nigga!"

"You are so damn extra, shawty! I ain't even do shit and you've been mad for the damn longest! Do you even know why you're mad?"

"Yes… umm, because you didn't put that bitch in her place."

"I didn't get a chance to because you came up in there, breaking glass and causing a fucking ruckus by trying to have a prison fight! I was gonna talk to her and get her ass straight!"

"What is talking gonna do, Lloyd? That bitch is obviously missing a few marbles! For one, she somehow got my phone number, and two, she'd been calling me for weeks and just breathing on the phone. Only psycho hoes do that!"

"Nah, that's how Elodie is. She did it to this other chick I dated for a hot minute, and after I talked to her, she left us alone. But baby, I think you scared her off. Turning a wine glass into a weapon was crazy."

"Well, until I have some stone-cold proof that the bitch is gonna leave us alone and let us be a family, then I don't wanna have shit to do with you."

I rolled my eyes and scarfed down the last of my pork chop and mashed potatoes, before placing the empty plate on my nightstand. I did feel a little bad because my baby looked like he wanted to chew my arm off because he was so hungry. I couldn't break though, because he would never take care of Elodie if I did.

After staring at me for a little bit as I pretended to be enthralled by the TV, Lloyd got down on the floor. He gripped my thighs roughly, and placed them over his shoulders. Before I could protest, he pushed my thin panties to the side and began sucking my clit gently. Being pregnant had me horny as a teenage boy, so once his tongue and my pussy made contact, I was through.

Spreading my legs wider, I palmed his head of beautiful curly hair and began grinding my pussy into his mouth. The way he lapped up my juices and moaned as he ate me out was such a turn on.

"Mmm, shit, Lloyd," I whimpered, feeling my orgasm rip through my body.

Pulling my panties to the side some more, he pressed his mouth into my middle, and fucked me with the tip of his tongue for a little bit. He then let his tongue travel the length of my vagina, before pushing my right leg outward and devouring me. I could feel my juices drenching the comforter as I called out to the high heavens.

"Oh fuck, oh fuck, I'm gonna cum, mmmm," my body trembled as I came hard as hell.

DING! DONG! BOOM! BOOM! BOOM!

Someone ringing the doorbell then banging on the door like the police, jarred Lloyd and I from our positions… yet a-fucking-gain. After giving one another a look, we quickly fixed ourselves, and I rushed to the door on Lloyd's heels. He looked through the peephole and sucked his teeth.

"Who is it?" I quizzed, watching him pull his gun from the kitchen drawer.

"They're covering the peephole," he responded before snatching it open. Before the door was even cracked, Pierce came barging in on one hundred, slamming the door behind himself.

"Where is she?" he started walking through the townhouse like he owned it, and like Lloyd wasn't out of his mind crazy.

"Aye, nigga! Fuck wrong with you coming up in my crib like that!" Lloyd hissed, doing something to his gun.

"Where is she!" Pierce hollered to me, completely ignoring Lloyd as if he didn't even see him standing there with a gun.

"Who!" I yelled back, scared of the evil look in Pierce's eyes.

"Alanna! You told her to leave me and I know it!"

"Get out of her face, nigga!" Lloyd shoved Pierce back.

"I looked in her old phone and saw she texted you a couple times saying she couldn't break up with me and you telling her to grow a pair! You conniving ass bitch!" Pierce barked and started towards me.

PHEW!

Lloyd shot him in the leg, and he collapsed to the floor, crying out in agony.

"Oh my gosh!" I shrieked.

"I told you stay out her face, muthafucka," Lloyd spoke calmly.

"Fuck you, nigga! I can't stand this stupid ass hoe! From day one she ain't been shit but a damn pain in my ass! And now— ah!" Pierce cried out from the pain. "And now, she don' got my girl to leave me." Looking dead up into my eyes he said, "I'm gonna kill you. You think I won't? I will kill you, bitch." He meant it, I could tell.

WHAM!

Lloyd smacked Pierce with the butt of his gun.

"Apologize to her."

"Pierce, Alanna already wanted to break up with you! I simply told her to do it if she was gonna do it! I don't care about either of you, and couldn't care less if you stayed together honestly!"

"Apologize!" Lloyd roared, prompting both Pierce and I to jump.

"Fuck that slut," Pierce looked up into my eyes, still cradling his bleeding leg.

PHEW! PHEW! PHEW!

Bullet after bullet pierced his face, no pun intended. His head exploded like a piece of fruit, before he fell back, staining the hell out of the carpet with his blood.

"Oh my gosh! What are we gonna do, Lloyd! We're gonna go to jail! There's blood every fucking where!" I cried, scared out of my mind.

"Chill, shawty," Lloyd said, dialing on some phone that looked like it belonged in the mid 2000's.

He walked into the kitchen and talked to someone for a little bit as I just stared down at Pierce's dead body. For some reason, I felt like he was gonna jump back up on some Michael Jackson *Thriller* shit.

"Come on, go shower. I know them panties are soaked," Lloyd said, turning me towards the bathroom. He was right. I didn't get to quite handle myself after cumming hard as hell from that head.

I hopped into the hot shower, and washed everything, including my hair. I felt dirty, scared, and anxious about what would happen to Lloyd and I. Technically, I didn't pull the trigger so I could run for the hills, but I loved Lloyd with all my heart. I wouldn't be able to deal with him being in jail, especially while I had his baby.

Any other nigga, I would have thrown the deuces up and called the police on my way out, but Lloyd… never. If he wanted to drive the body somewhere to bury it, I would go. If he needed my help digging a shallow grave, I would oblige. He was my other half, not completing me, but complementing me. I couldn't lose him and I would do whatever was needed to make sure I didn't. However, I still had a bone to pick with him over that Elodie shit.

As I was racking my brain, I saw Lloyd come in and brush his teeth before slipping back out. Once my hair was clean, I washed my face and then my body, before stepping out. When I walked out the bathroom, Pierce's body was gone, and so was his blood. I felt like I was losing my mind, so I walked closer into the living room.

"Aye, don't step where he was, the floor is still wet," Lloyd surprised me. He was sitting in the kitchen drinking something brown.

"Where is everything?" I asked.

"Something called a clean-up crew, shawty. Oden sent them."

"So what now?" I made my way over to him, and he pulled me between his legs to kiss me.

"We act like nothing happened. And if by some chance you get questioned about Pierce's whereabouts, act like you ain't seen the nigga in months, aight?"

"I just… never mind," I shook my head.

"Talk to me." He patted my butt as I tightened the towel around my body.

"I feel like this is all my fault."

"How, baby?" His brows dipped, and his handsome face was knotted up in confusion.

"Because I ruined him. When I met Pierce, he was a good guy

with a promising career in football. And then after he got with me, he became nothing more than some weasel that was emotionally damaged and weak. The look in his eyes tonight was so crazy. I felt like I didn't know him. I feel like if he'd never met me he would be alive and well still."

"Shayne, Pierce was a grown ass man, shawty, but he was weak and that had nothing to do with you. A real man would have seen that you weren't fucking with him and kept it pushing. A real nigga would never let a female knock him off his square no matter how much he loved her."

"So if I left you, you're saying you'd be okay?"

"No, what I'm saying is I would work through that shit. I would miss you like crazy and definitely try to get you back, depending on the situation, but I wouldn't let that shit define me. A relationship is supposed to enhance your life, not diminish it. I would never let the fact that you left me have me out here fucking up my money and whatever else I got going on in my life. That's what weak niggas do. Just like if I left you, I would expect you to still be a great mother to our son and still excel in dance. Don't blame yourself for anything except loving a man who wasn't strong enough to deal with you."

"When did you get so smart?" I grinned, draping my arms over his shoulders.

"I'm from the south, baby, we're all intelligent; well, most of us."

"Hmm, I should have been moved down there then."

"I'm trying to tell you," he said, making us both laugh.

"I love you, Lloyd, but I'm still upset with you for that Elodie shit.

I want you to prove to me that it's fixed."

"I will. Now make me a pork chop and then go lie down in the bed with your legs open." He bit his lip and kissed me, before lightly shoving me towards the stove.

"Let me change out of this towel first."

"Nah." He pointed to the stove.

I rolled my eyes playfully, but got to making his food.

CHAPTER EIGHT

Santino

"*B*ella! Come here!" I hollered after her once she stepped out of class.

She looked over her shoulder to see me, and then took off running. For the first few seconds, I couldn't believe it so I was frozen; but, once I got my mind right, I darted off behind her. She was pretty fast, but of course I was faster. Once I got close enough, I slowed down so I wouldn't run her over, and picked her sexy frame up from behind.

"Fuck you running for?" I growled in her ear. "And you thought you could out run *me*?" I placed her to her feet after kissing the corner of her mouth.

"And who the fuck are you, nigga?" she rolled her eyes, panting heavily as we started walking.

"Santino D'Stefano, wide receiver for the Los Angeles Rams. You ain't heard?" I responded cockily, flexing my muscles. She smiled even though she didn't want to, and looked away. "Let me talk to you though." I hemmed her up against the side of the gym, and she rolled her eyes… again.

"Talk about what? We have nothing to talk about Mr. Wide Receiver."

"So you don't love me anymore?"

"I do, but that means nothing to you; it never has. I loved you when you dumped me in high school, and I loved you when you fucked that bitch."

"I didn't fuck her. What you saw was the first time I'd ever done anything sexual with her, Bella. Let's go somewhere we can talk in private."

I knew I would get nowhere with her if I didn't go ahead and tell her the deal. Just saying that I was getting blackmailed wasn't enough for her, and truthfully, it wouldn't be enough for me if I walked in on her getting her pussy ate.

I loved Bella, and I planned to marry her and be with her for the rest of my life, which meant her knowing all of my secrets and demons. She and I were best friends at the end of the day, and I trusted her more than I trusted the homies. If anybody should know what's going on with me, it should be her.

"Fine. But you're not fucking me."

"We'll see." I grabbed her ass and she smacked my hand away.

"I'm fucking with you, come on."

I led her to my car, and then opened the passenger side so she could get in. I then jogged around to the driver's side, and slid in before locking the doors.

"Talk, Sanz. I have to study for my test I'm taking later this week."

"Aight. So remember when I told you I went to talk to Oden about murking Huelo, but changed my mind?"

"Yeah."

"Well, I changed my mind for two reasons. One being that you were right about the fact that I shouldn't have been worrying about Huelo, especially because he got himself killed. But the second reason was because Oden saved my life."

"How?" She turned in her seat to face me.

"Because of Leena; she ran up on me with a gun. I don't know what the fuck she was thinking, or where she'd gotten an idea like that from, but that's what happened, and Oden… took care of her. To make a long story short, Leena told Crystal, the girl you caught sucking me up, about her plans for me, so Crystal caught on to the fact that I had something to do with Leena disappearing. She threatened to tell her dad, who is a lieutenant of LVMPD, if I didn't sleep with her. I knew it would look bad because that would be two people associated with me that went missing, and I couldn't take that heat."

"So that's why you…"

"Yes, baby. Trust me, I tried for weeks to keep her at bay, and the only thing helping me was that she only came out here for the weekends which bought me time. If she had have told and they started investigating me, I would have lost my NFL contract and probably went to jail for accessory to murder for Leena, which would in the end cause me to lose you."

"You wouldn't have lost me, baby."

"Bella, I couldn't have expected you to stick around for me while

I served a life sentence in jail." I took her hand into mine and kissed it. "I did what I did not because I wanted to cheat on you, or because I wanted her, but because I felt like I had no other choice."

"So what happens now? I can't deal with you sleeping with her just to keep her mouth shut, Santino. I love you, but I can't do that."

"It's taken care of already, so you won't have to."

"It is?"

"Yeah, it is. Crystal, Leena, nor any other woman can try to come in between us again, Bella. So can you put your ring back on?"

"This ring will be on for good this time, right?" she smiled as I pulled it from my glove compartment and slid it on her finger.

"You tell me, shit. I never wanted you to take it off. You better always keep this shit on though. I've been fucking losing my mind these past few weeks that we've been apart."

"Me too, but I was trying to get over it."

"I know… you had me punching on bitch ass niggas," I scoffed thinking about how Trevor's ass was on that bullshit. He, Huelo, and I were thick as thieves here in Vegas, so the way he flipped still had my mind blown.

"I'm sorry about that. I just wanted to hurt you the way you hurt me is all."

"Trust me I know. You would never stoop that low for no reason. That's why I ain't even mad at you."

"You whooped his ass though, baby," she giggled.

"Course I did."

I leaned over the seat and brought her lips to mine. I hadn't felt them in the longest, so right now I was in heaven. They were so soft, and it was almost like they were made for me. She toyed with my ears as our kiss got heavier and heavier, and before I knew it, my hand was going down into her jean shorts.

"Later, Sanz. I have to study right now."

"How about I get us some food, and when I come back I can help you study?" I bit my lip and squeezed her thigh.

"Fine," she rolled her eyes for the tenth time today but with a smile. "Go to Felipito's, pleeeeaaassse! I want some tacos."

"Anything for you."

She kissed me once again, and then got out of the car. I watched her walk away in them little ass shorts, and shook my head. My dick was craving some of that right now, so I needed to hurry up and go get this damn food.

Cranking my car, I turned up the radio and sped out of the school parking lot. I made it to Felipito's, which was around the corner from the school on Tropicana Avenue. It was a drive-thru spot, but I always liked to walk up to the window and order because I was paranoid as fuck. You could watch them niggas and make sure they were being clean with your shit when you walked up instead of driving through.

I swooped into an empty park, and made my way up to the window to order tacos for Bella and a carne asada platter for myself. After paying, I got my receipt and went to sit down at the small cement tables outlined in red.

"Look who it is," I heard someone say as I texted my mother back.

My mom had been hitting me up nonstop trying to talk, but I had nothing to say to her or my father. Right now I needed to focus, and my parents' drama was always a distraction. I hadn't been fucking with them since my dad put me out, and funny enough, they didn't seem to care until my name was all over everywhere from signing that Rams contract.

"Fuck you want," I sneered, looking over at Trevor. He was strolling up with two other niggas that I had never seen before. Something about them told me they weren't from here.

"Oh, I'm just wondering if you're trying to go for round two in this bitch," he said, and his homeboys laughed.

"Why? Because you found some bums to help you out?" I chuckled, pocketing my iPhone. If they wanted these hands then I'd give it to them; all of them.

"Bums? Nigga, fuck you!" one of his minions hissed, cracking me up. Trevor placed his hand on his homeboy's chest to tell him to chill. That was best because I'd have his skinny ass taking a nap with just one hit.

"These ain't no bums, Sanz. These are my real friends from Philly, who would never go Hollywood on me like you."

"Yeah, because they have no reason to go Hollywood. The bum life ain't shit to brag about."

"Man, Trev, let us fuck this nigga up," the angry one shot daggers at me.

"Well, you won't have a reason either when we're done with you."

"What?" I frowned, rising from my seat. As soon as the word left my lips, they each pulled a metal bat from behind their backs and charged me.

WHAM!

Trevor swung and hit my knee. I decked him between the eyes, and he went stumbling back, knocking down one of his homies.

WHAM!

His other friend hit me in the back, so I turned to him and started fucking him up. Before I knew it, I felt bats coming from everywhere. I started going crazy on Trevor as his friends whacked me, because I knew my career would be over. I saw nothing but red and I was ready to kill these niggas.

POP! POP! POP!

Suddenly gunshots rang out, and I heard people screaming. Trevor and his friends darted off, but not before bullets flew through all of them. They dropped like flies as I ran for cover, while trying to figure out where the bullets were even coming from. My legs and back were killing me, but not enough to keep me from saving myself.

"Call 911!!!!" the bitch working at Felipito's hollered.

The cars in the streets were driving slowly as fuck, being nosey and trying to figure out who shot Trevor and his friends. His homies were lying on the concrete lifeless, as Trevor rocked back and forth, howling over his leg wound. I limped to my car, trying to stay under the radar, and just got inside, not moving. I didn't want to pull out just yet, because the people around may get suspicious and think I was fleeing because I was guilty.

Few moments later, the ambulance and some policemen showed up. I saw the young girl who worked at Felipito's talking to the officer, and she pointed to my car a couple times. When the officer was done with her, he made his way over to me, so I just got out of the car. Fuck!

"Santino D'Stefano?" the officer grinned, catching me off guard with his chipper mood.

"Uh, yeah," I replied nervously.

"Can't wait to see you play for the Rams later this year. But hey, are you alright? The young lady told me you got jumped just before bullets started flying."

Thank God she didn't say some bullshit.

"Yeah, they got some licks in. I'm a bit bruised, but I'm okay," I said as I watched them wheel Trevor's crying ass onto the ambulance, while two other people zipped his friends up in black bags.

"And did you see where the bullets came from?"

"Nah, I didn't. I was getting whacked, and then all of sudden I heard gunshots. Them three stopped hitting me, and then rushed off but not before getting blasted."

"Probably just some reckless gangsters," he sighed and wrote down what I said. "Do you think I could get your autograph?" he pulled a Rams hat from his coat pocket like a weirdo.

"Uh, sure, yeah man." I signed the hat. "You carry this hat all day?"

"No, funny enough I just bought it and here I am meeting one of the Rams."

"Yeah."

"Have a good day, D'Stefano. And ice those injuries, we're gonna need it this year."

I simply nodded and then went up to the window of Felipito's.

"Aye, where is my food?"

The young girl looked at me like I was crazy for still thinking about my food, but then handed me the bag. Shit, I paid for it and I was hungry.

I got back in my car and drove back to campus. Word traveled fast because as I walked to Bella's and my dorm, people were trying to stop me and ask what happened to Trevor. As I made my way between the gym and the dorm hall, I saw Oden leaning up against the cement pillar with Truman, smirking.

"What's up?" I nodded my head and dapped them both with my free hand.

"Nothing much," Truman responded.

"Be glad he and I were in the mood for burritos," Oden looked to me, before he and Truman burst into laughter.

"Shit," I chuckled. "Thanks man, them niggas were gonna take my knees out! And aye, y'all are good, I didn't even see where that shit was coming from," I whispered.

"Been doing this shit a long time," Truman said.

"Yep, so even when I'm not prepared for shit, like just then, I'm still good at what I do."

"Well I appreciate y'all, man." I was lucky that Trevor and his friends didn't get to really do too much thanks to Oden and Truman. I was sore, but I could tell it wasn't anything major.

"Just get us some season tickets," Truman joked… at least I think he was joking. I was gonna get them the tickets though just in case.

I guess having friends on the dark side did have its benefits. Twice Oden had saved my life, and I couldn't be more grateful.

CHAPTER EIGHT

Anton

Violet called me and said that she needed me to drop some food by for her son, and since I didn't have to be in court until 10am, I decided to just swing by there before. I had Tasmine with me, but I told her ass she had to stay in the car. My baby was usually a pretty calm person, but now that she was pregnant, she was a bit feistier. For example, she was initially okay with me helping Violet, but right now she was hot as fish grease over me bringing food for Athen.

"So whenever she calls you're just gonna hop up?" Tasmine shook her head with her arms folded.

"No, but she said she really needed it and couldn't leave him, so I thought why not. I told you I was gonna be helping her. Her child's father is a fuck nigga anyway."

"Just hurry up! You have other shit to do today!"

"I love you too." I caressed her small bulge and kissed her cheek.

I grabbed the Target bag from the back seat, and then jogged to Violet's door. I knocked lightly, and when I got no answer I rang the doorbell.

"Come in!" she yelled.

I entered the house and closed the door behind me. Before I could call her name, her sister Vanessa walked into the living room wearing some lingerie. You had to be fucking kidding me. And the bitch had the nerve to be smiling like we were for real about to get shit popping.

"Where is Violet?" I quizzed.

"She went to work. I guess she forgot to tell you she decided to go back," she giggled, throwing her hair behind her back. I never realized how much they sounded alike until now, but no wonder I got a call from the house phone instead of just a text like usual. "So are you just gonna stand there or do you wanna touch?"

"Did you seriously pretend to be your sister to get me over here for this bullshit?" I scoffed.

"Yeah, I did. I know we have a connection and that's why we've been so rude to one another, Tony. I think it's time we take our frustrations out on one another in a different way." She moved closer to me.

Laughing, I said, "I'm sorry, it's just I can't believe this shit right now. All that you've done to fuck me over, and now you want some dick? You've always wanted the dick, huh?" I looked down into her eyes, smiling. She thought I was flirting but I was laughing at her ass.

"I did, but you never saw me, only my sister. I knew her baby wasn't yours, but I wanted you to stick around, so I got my coins together and bribed your little nurse."

"Wow, conniving."

"I know," she chuckled. "Why don't you come to the bedroom with me?"

"Get down on all fours," I told her.

"Oooh shit, kinky!" she instantly dropped down, arching her back to look sexy in her lingerie. I took my phone out and she asked, "What are you doing?"

"I just have to get a picture because I can't believe this shit right now," I winked.

She flipped her hair around and posed for me a couple of times, before rolling onto her back and cocking her legs open.

As I went into my text app, she looked up at me, awaiting my next move.

Me: Your sister is foul af. Got me over here by pretending to be you.

I shot the text to Violet with a few pictures of Vanessa looking stupid as fuck attached.

"Come on, Tony. I'm so wet," Vanessa purred as I put my phone up.

"Just sent your sister them pictures of you failing miserably at trying to be sexy and seduce me. Do better, shorty." I turned on my heels and headed for the door.

"Fuck you, nigga!" she hopped to her feet and closed her robe over her body. "I got niggas begging to fuck me everyday!"

"I knew you wanted this dick from day one. Thanks for proving me right," I chuckled, pissing her off even more. I set the Target bag on the table near the door, because I'm sure Violet wouldn't mind the extra.

BAM!

Vanessa slammed the door hard as hell, almost pushing me out. I couldn't do anything but laugh because she was a such a dumb ass bitch and stayed taking L's. I mean first she tried to tamper with the paternity test and got caught, and just now she tried to hop on a dick that didn't even get the least bit hard from seeing her. My dick has never been softer.

My phone chimed once I got in the car to see Tasmine knocked out, holding a Ziploc bag of graham crackers.

Vi: Wtf!!! I'm so sorry, Tony!

Me: No worries, but watch your back, she's jealous of you.

Vi: Nothing new. Thanks for sending the pictures. It won't happen again.

"Oh, umm, what happened?" Tasmine jumped up, wiping the corners of her mouth and looking around like she thought someone had their dick in her mouth while she was asleep.

"Nothing, baby. You can rest, and I will wake you up when we have to go inside of the courthouse." I rubbed her exposed thigh. I barely finished my sentence before her head hit the headrest. I just chuckled and cranked the car.

Around 10:15am...

I was currently standing in this courtroom next to my lawyer, as Selinda sat a little ways down from me with hers. She'd been pouting like a child since we got in here, because she was upset about me filing a restraining order. I didn't like being this close to policemen and courts and shit, but I had to do what I had to do to make sure Selinda was out of my damn life for good. It was like the DNA test wasn't enough for her to back the fuck off.

After we had the second test done, she tried to file charges against me for emotional distress because Oden and Truman held her and Kai at gunpoint. That fell through I guess, so she keyed my damn car and drew graffiti on the side of the dealership. At that point, I decided to take my lawyer's advice seriously and get this restraining order, because Selinda was doing the most.

I didn't want to kill her because she had a son to raise, and losing a mother was the worst shit ever. But, I had to get her out of my life somehow so this was second best. If I didn't, next she would be sneaking into my house and kidnapping my kid for ransom money.

"You should have filed that day you got the second paternity test back," my lawyer Hugh whispered to me.

"I know, I was going to, but then I felt like she wasn't gonna bother me anymore now that we had two tests proving I wasn't the father."

"I know, but she's obviously off kilter, Anton. You should have known that wouldn't get her to stay away."

The judge had been writing something down, but now that she was done, she had her attention focused on my lawyer and I. I glanced back at Tasmine, and she gave me a warm smile as she smoothed down her hair.

"Mr. Nickerson, you say you have proof that Ms. Green has been stalking you and deliberately sabotaging your personal items?"

"Yes, your honor. These are pictures here of my car that she keyed, and of my dealership that she spray painted obscenities on." I handed the photos to the bailiff so he could take them to the judge.

"I did not do that!" Selinda hollered like an idiot. I was gonna get this restraining order based off how she'd been acting since we stepped in here alone.

"Ms. Green, if I have to ask you to be quiet again, we're gonna have a problem," the judge threatened.

"Sorry," she mumbled.

"How can you be sure that Ms. Green caused this damage, Mr. Nickerson?"

"I have security camera snapshots taken by my dealership and club cameras of her doing both, your honor." I handed those photos over. The judge took one look at them and then granted my restraining order.

"I didn't even get to talk!" Selinda yelled as her lawyer tried to calm her down.

"There is nothing for you to say, Ms. Green. It's obvious that you're bothering the plaintiff, so I hereby order you to stay away from him. When I say stay away, that includes phone calls, text messages, social media, his place of business, and anywhere else that you know he will be. If you violate this order, you will be jailed, Ms. Green, and the sentence will not be light. Court is adjourned." She banged her gavel, and I damn near hopped over the brown banister to leave.

"You should have gotten one of these a long time ago," Tasmine said as I draped my arm over her shoulder and kissed her.

"Tell me about it, man. I don't know what life is like without fake baby mamas and crazy hoes," I joked as we walked out with my lawyer.

"I promise you, Anton, it's much more enjoyable," my lawyer laughed. "Congratulations." We shook hands and hugged, then he walked off.

"How would you like to celebrate?" Tasmine quizzed once we were inside of the car.

"By being knee deep in that pussy." I kissed her and she blushed. I was about to celebrate in that shit all night long.

CHAPTER EIGHT

Oden

"Now these are nice, beautiful."

I walked down the line of Maserati's in five different colors. I had 20 cars sitting here, fresh from Italy that were about to be shipped back overseas to customers. Business was so much better and more profitable now that we got more cars at once, due to not having to steal them. I was able to cut so many muthafuckas out of the equation, which meant more money for Truman, Anton, Lloyd, myself, and my team. I couldn't stand Cecil's weak ass, but damn was I happy I went to meet Giovanni in Modena.

"Are they all sold yet or are there still deals to be made?" Anton asked as he took a pull on his blunt.

"Well, 18 of them are sold, so we have two more sitting but they'll be gone soon, right Truman?" I looked over my shoulder.

"Handling that as we speak. And the yacht party in California is on too." He typed on his phone.

For spring break, all of us, including our ladies, were going to

California and having a yacht party. It was to celebrate the success of the club, the liquor line, the car business, and the dealership. All of us, even my underdogs were making a lot of bread, so we wanted to celebrate how blessed we were.

"We also have to celebrate that young restraining order," I squeezed Anton's shoulder as he grinned widely as hell.

"Damn man, about time you got that pit bull under control. Oden, we gotta celebrate the fact that even though we both smashed Selinda, she never brought that paternity shit this way," Truman said.

"Shit, one of y'all niggas probably *are* the damn dad now that I think about it."

"Nah, I didn't even cum while I was smashing. I had to have her suck me off to cum, and I kept the condom on," I laughed, shaking my head. Selinda's pussy was weak as fuck.

"And that condom was in tact when *I* finished," Truman added. "But, I will let y'all know if these last two car deals go through. For now, I'm about to see if Chiina will come spend the night with me."

"She still ain't took yo' weak ass back, huh?" Anton chuckled.

"Man, she pretty much has. She's been spending the night at the crib a lot, but I ain't fucked yet. I'm hoping I get lucky tonight."

"So you're for real done with Pilar?" I questioned.

"I been done with that, but I guess since she wasn't feeling that decision, she decided to do some foul shit. We ain't talked since."

"Foul shit like what?" Anton raised a brow.

"Maaaaan." Truman wiped his face. "Caught her fucking some

Terry Crews looking ass nigga in my got damn bed."

Before he finished, Anton and I were bent over laughing hard as fuck. I think it was so funny because this nigga had dogged Pilar out for years behind her back, and she got him in the worst way. Only thing that probably would have made it better was if she did the shit at a time where he was in love with her. I could tell he felt more disrespected than hurt, because his feelings had shifted to Chiina. I'm surprised he didn't kill Pilar's ass for that shit she pulled, because Truman was crazy.

"Man, you're lucky she ain't have yo' heart anymore. You would have been sick. If Chiina did that, you'd probably kill yourself," Anton chortled and so did I.

"Please don't even speak that shit into existence. I don't even wanna think about another nigga touching Chiina."

"Damn, I'm gon' have to find Pilar and dap her ass up for that one. You change your sheets?" I laughed along with Anton.

"That was a Mortal Kombat 'finish 'em' move," Anton added and we doubled over in laughter.

"Fuck y'all. I got a whole new bed, *and* changed my damn locks." He tried not to laugh but because Anton and I were still cracking up, he couldn't help it. "I'm gone." He walked out, and we just followed behind, fucking with him until we got into our own cars.

∗

Saturday Night...

Tonight I was throwing a party at Palace for my shorty just because. Her birthday wasn't until August, but I just wanted to do something to show her how much I appreciated her. I felt like she had enough roses and jewelry, and I wanted her to feel like she should be celebrated… and she should.

Everyone in our circle was here; shit, even Perry and my homeboy Cash. She was currently straddling him, attempting to grind in his lap, and even though I wanted to tell her ass to chill out, I had to remember tonight was supposed to be fun for everybody. I'm still trying to figure out how they even meshed.

Frat girls still tryna get even. Haters mad for whatever reason. Smoke in the air, binge drinkin'. They lose it when the DJ drops the needle…

Everybody danced to "Black Beatles" by Rae Sremmurd, holding their drinks in the air and just having a good time. It was so many damn people here, so I knew we were almost at capacity. I had banners all over this bitch with Khyle's name, so people would know exactly why we were here.

I smiled watching Khyle and her friends dance, as they looked over the balcony at the rest of the club. Tonight, I allowed 18 year olds and up to come in, and made people 21 and over wear wristbands so the bartenders would know who they could serve and who they couldn't.

"Having a good time?" I walked up behind Khyle and kissed her neck as she continued to sway to the music up against me. I felt my dick getting hard, so I wanted to take her back to my office and fuck, but I was gonna wait a little bit since we'd only been partying for like 45 minutes.

"Of course I am." She smiled over her shoulder at me before

bending over and grinding on my dick a little bit. I could already tell she and Bella had gotten twisted before coming in here, but I wasn't gonna complain at all.

I chuckled at Tasmine because she was playfully gagging at Santino and Bella kissing. I admit they were sucking face pretty hard, and the shit kind of looked painful. They were drunk as fuck though, already.

Looking down at Khyle's ass popping against my dick, I pulled her up and hugged her around the neck from behind.

"You know I wanna fuck you now, right?" I whispered in her ear before sucking her neck. "I wanna bend you over my desk."

She smelled so good.

"Gotta lick to stick," she giggled, grasping my forearm, which was draped around her from behind. She moved her body against my crotch some more, and chuckled when she felt my wood.

"You already know I wanna eat your pussy 'til you cum," I said in between sucking her neck. I saw her close her eyes and nibble on her lip. "We will be back," I told our people as I pulled Khyle towards the back.

"Get it, O!" Truman's crazy ass hollered after us before whispering something in Chiina's ear.

As soon as Khyle and I got into my office, I lifted her onto my desk and started pushing her dress up. Our lips crushed together, and our tongues connected soon after. She must have had something sweet because I could taste it in her mouth, which made me kiss her harder.

"Why are you so sexy?" I mumbled against her lips as I yanked on her panties.

I pulled away from her to watch her lace thong come down her smooth thighs as I sank my teeth into my bottom lip. The littlest shit was sexy to me when it came to her.

"I don't know," she giggled drunkenly.

I threw her panties to the side, and yanked her towards the edge of the desk. She stared up at me innocently with drunk eyes, and that shit had me wanting to fuck the shit out of her for some reason. I touched between her legs, and as I was going down to feast I heard the music stop. Not like it was loud all the way back in my office, but you could usually faintly hear something and I didn't.

"Hold on, baby," I said, picking her panties up and handing them to her before quickly washing my hands in my office bathroom.

I left out and heard her follow after me once she had her panties back on. As I got closer to the main area of the club, I realized no music was playing like I thought. Khyle and I entered the VIP section where all of our friends were, and that's when I spotted Naomi at the deejay booth with a microphone. Was she fucking serious?

"Oh! There he is!" Naomi grinned once I came to the balcony of my VIP. She was adjacent to me, where the deejay was.

"Aye, she's tripping," Anton tapped me.

"Why didn't you stop her ass—"

"Oden, baby, you know that I love you and I always have. You told me…"

"This bitch has got me fucked up!" Khyle hissed, and tried to rush over there, but I stopped her. "Let me go! You won't handle this bitch so let me do it!" Khyle went ape shit as Naomi continued to talk.

"I got it, baby, relax. Anton, please," I said and he grabbed Khyle up.

"And even though we've been apart so long, I know that you love me too, and what you have with that girl is just temporary," Naomi continued as I started towards her.

"Move!!" I heard Khyle growl at Anton, trying to get to Naomi so she could fight.

"Naomi, what the fuck—" I tried to grab the microphone once I reached her, but she backed away, still rambling.

"By saying that Oden, I wanted to know if you'd marry me?" She dropped down to one knee and pulled a ring from her breasts.

"What the hell?" someone from the dance floor down below yelled.

"Gimme this shit and get yo' ass up," I gritted in Naomi's ear before yanking her back to her feet. "Cut the fucking music on, nigga, and if you ever in life let some shit like this happen again, I will personally stop you from breathing," I glared at the deejay as he hurriedly cut the music back on with wide eyes. "Bring yo' stupid ass." I yanked Naomi towards the back.

When we made it into the hallway, I let Naomi go and continued to my office with her behind me.

"Talk that shit now, bitch!" I heard Khyle's voice, and when I turned around she was on Naomi's back, pulling her hair and punching the side of her face.

"Oden!" Naomi screeched, spinning around, trying to find a way to get Khyle's ass off of her.

Just as I rushed over to pry my shorty off, Anton came back here out of breath.

"Nigga, I told you to hold her!"

"She broke free! She's stronger than she looks my nigga!" Anton hollered back as I handed Khyle to him. She was still swinging and kicking, trying to get back to Naomi who had a busted nose.

"I ain't done!" Khyle shouted as Anton carried her back to the VIP.

Covering my eyes in frustration, I said, "Get in my office, Naomi."

As I followed behind her, I shot Winter a text to let her know we needed the first aid kit. Closing my office door behind me, I leaned up against it and took a deep breath. What the hell was I gonna do with this woman?

"What the hell was that, Naomi?" I frowned as she sat on my couch with her busted ass nose. *Got damn,* I thought. Her shit was definitely broken.

"I just wa-wanted you to know how I felt," she cried, lightly touching her nose and wincing in pain.

"Naomi, I told you the damn deal, yet you decided to do this shit in a club full of people, and while my fiancée is here? What the fuck were you thinking?"

"That you would see I was serious about us."

KNOCK! KNOCK!

I hopped up and opened the door to see Winter. She walked in with her lips slightly parted before her eyes landed on Naomi. She immediately got to working on her nose. I waited until she finished putting gauze on it and left to call Scott so he could take Naomi to the hospital, before I finished speaking.

"Why can't you understand that I'm serious about Khyle? I mean I've tried to be nice about it, then I tried being rude, but you can't seem to understand me. I cannot have you pulling shit like this on me, Naomi. You of all people know that I don't tolerate this type of shit from anybody. The only reason you're still walking this Earth right now is because I do genuinely have love for you, shorty. But in a minute that shit is gonna be out of the window."

"I'm sorry, Oden," she began sobbing violently. "I made a mistake with you and it's just hard to accept that you don't wanna be with me anymore. I can't stop thinking about you and when I try to date other guys all I do is compare them to you. I'm miserable, and I hate seeing you with her or hearing you talk about her. It's hard for me," she wept. "And then she has your baby." She broke down.

"And you know what, I get it, but you need to get yourself together before you end up dead on the side of the road somewhere, Naomi. I love Khyle, and I don't take too kindly to things that jeopardize what we have. Look at me," I hooked her chin. "If you do anything else, which includes flirting with me, pulling stunts like the one tonight, or speaking to my girl, I will body you and that's on my grandfather's grave," I spoke sternly, looking into her eyes to make sure she understood. "I won't talk or give you a chance to explain yourself. I will walk up on you like a thief in the night, snap your neck, and put your body in a meat grinder." My voice was calm.

Her jaw dropped open slowly as her eyes searched mine. Naomi was my girlfriend for a cool minute so she knew what I was capable of. But hey, if she wanted to continue to play with fire, I would gladly flame her ass up.

"I understand," she nodded. "Can we be frien—"

"No."

"K," she whispered.

KNOCK! KNOCK!

"Hey boss, Scott has the car ready," Winter came in.

"Go," I told Naomi. "Winter, please make sure my girl does not get close to her. We ain't trying to have any murders in the establishment."

"Got it," Winter chuckled.

After getting my thoughts together, I went back out to the club. I saw Khyle talking to Bella, Tasmine, and Chiina, so I came up behind her. She moved from my embrace, and I just tossed my head back because I wasn't in the mood for her to have an attitude.

"Come here," I pulled her to the back of the VIP.

"What?" She snatched her hand from me once we got there.

"Why you mad?" I tucked my bottom lip in, looking down into her pretty face. I had my hands behind my back, but I was backing her little cute ass into the wall.

"Because you didn't let me hit her!"

"Baby, you broke her fucking nose! What more do you want? To kill the bitch?"

"Maybe. And she embarrassed me."

"She embarrassed herself, Khyle. She proposed to a nigga that everyone in here knows is taken. For God's sake, I'm throwing a party for you, so niggas already know the deal! She's the one who ended up looking dumb. She proposed to me, and then got her nose broken."

"I guess."

"Can we please try to enjoy the rest of the night? This is the one night neither of us have to watch the baby, thanks to Shayne, so let's enjoy it. And I'm sorry about what she did. I swear it won't happen again; and if it does, she won't be with us anymore."

"Okay. I love you." She looked up at me and intertwined our fingers. Yeah, her ass was twisted, because her mood never switched that quickly.

"I love you more." I pulled her into me, and then leaned her head back so I could get a kiss.

I had a feeling Naomi caught my drift, but if she didn't, I had my meat grinder waiting at the warehouse.

CHAPTER NINE

Perry

Cash and I were in his bed kissing, and I could feel his erection pressing against my vagina. I wanted to have sex with him so badly, but he refused. Until I was a single girl, he wasn't gonna do it with me, and by now I was dying.

I wanted to be with Cash, but I was afraid of Austin. He'd become controlling, and I guess it was because he took my virginity. At least that's what Google said.

I missed the old Austin, the one who let me be my own person and always had something fun for us to do. That man only lasted a few months. Now, I had to lie to even get out of his sight, and he always wanted proof. I felt like a prisoner, and I hated it.

I'm sure Cash could help me break free, but Tasmine said that would end terribly. And since she was good at predicting storms in our lives, I decided to listen. I wasn't hip to the thug life as people called it, so I didn't want to start anything up between two people like Cash and Austin.

"Just come on," I whispered to Cash as I rubbed my hands up his shirt. His large hand groped my thighs as he laid between them, which felt so good. He was lifting my dress, when suddenly he stopped. "What's wrong?" I opened my eyes and looked down to see what had his attention.

"How you get this fucking bruise on your thigh?" he questioned, face all twisted up.

"Uh well, I bumped into my desk in my dorm room."

"You lying? You know I don't like when I'm lied to, Perry." He got off of me and sat up on the edge of the bed.

"I was supposed to go to his house but I didn't because I was with you and he—"

"Who the fuck is *he*?"

He knew the answer, but I think he just wanted me to come out of my mouth and say who it was. I really didn't want to, because Austin's party was tonight and things needed to go smoothly. However, Cash was good for being able to tell when people were lying to him, and I didn't wanna go down that road.

"Austin," I mumbled lowly, but loud enough for him to hear.

"So that's why you're still holding onto that nigga? You're scared of his ass? What you think, if you come this way I'm gonna let something happen to you?"

"No, I just didn't want you guys fighting or anything. Cash, I will talk to him tonight, and I'm sure everything will be fine."

Staring at me for a little bit, he just nodded his head and said,

"Yeah, aight."

***

The party...

Spoiled, she ain't got no patience. She gon' have these bitches hatin'. Got them diamonds on me skatin'...

Austin's party was being held at his residence, and it was packed wall to wall. People were currently dancing and singing this song by 21 Savage word for word. All of Austin's friends flew out from New York, and some of his new ones from Las Vegas were here too. I was relieved that Khyle, Tasmine, and Bella agreed to come with me tonight, because I didn't quite get along with Austin's friends' girlfriends. They were so different over there on the east coast, and we just didn't mesh.

I'd done a lot to get this party going, including paying for all the food, alcohol, and party games. When I started planning months ago, I was so excited to make him happy, but at the moment I wished I could get my money back for half of this stuff. I was over him, our relationship, and having to lie just so I could go to the mall with my friends. They knew everything about Austin, so you can imagine that they too weren't in the mood to celebrate his birthday.

"So what did Cash say?" Bella asked as she, Tasmine, and Khyle helped me uncover all the food I had catered in the kitchen. I had no help with anything, so I was happy that they decided to assist me.

"About?" I played dumb, moving around the kitchen.

"About you being here at this party tonight, Perry. When are you gonna just be honest and break up with Austin?" Khyle sucked her teeth. I believe out of everyone she wanted to fight Austin the most.

"I will but not tonight, because it's his birthday."

"Fair enough. I mean let him enjoy this, and then tomorrow, sit him down and tell him that you're not happy and that you found someone else. Make sure he understands that you stopped being happy before you met Cash," Tasmine stressed. I didn't want to tell Austin about Cash at all, but Tasmine said that was a bad idea.

"Aye, what you doing in here?" Austin barged in, holding a bottle of Peach Cîroc. "I been looking for yo' ass!" He was drunk and clearly high as well.

"Oh sorry, what did you need, baby?" I smiled awkwardly. I could feel Bella, Tasmine, and Khyle's eyes on Austin and I.

"Just keep yo' ass close. I don't need you being a fucking hoe at my party," he gripped my arm tightly as hell, so I knew he was gonna leave a bruise.

"Stop!" I yanked myself from him. Usually I wouldn't have said anything but 'yes sir'; however, my friends and other people were here, and I was embarrassed.

"Come here," he tugged me out the kitchen, and I heard my friends coming after me. However, before they could grab me, Austin pulled me into a bathroom and closed the door. "Who you disrespecting, Perry?"

His eyes were dark, and it was like no soul lived inside of him. I didn't know who he was anymore, and it made me sad as hell, not to mention scared.

"I wasn't disrespecting you, Austin, I just don't want you grabbing on me like that in front of everyone. It's embarrassing."

"Let her out!" I heard Bella yell before banging on the door and twisting the knob, trying to get in.

"Oh, you telling your friends our business? It's cool though, because that's why I've been getting my dick wet elsewhere. You wanna be on that bullshit I'm gonna let you. Take yo' ass upstairs and stay there until I say you can come out." He threw me towards the door, and after I stepped out, he brushed past me and my friends.

"Perry, you okay?" Tasmine questioned as Khyle called him a bitch. He just kept walking, and I kept my eyes on him, furious. I couldn't believe he'd been cheating on me. Austin was gonna learn the hard way to never fuck with Perry Monique Washington… yes, my middle name is Monique.

"Yeah, I'm fine. Can you guys finish in the kitchen? I will be right back."

I rushed up the stairs to Austin's bedroom before they could respond, and locked the door behind me. Pulling my phone from my boot, I quickly dialed Cash.

"What's good? Where you at?" he answered.

"I'm at Austin's party that I told you I was throwing for him rememb—"

"Wow."

"I know, but he hit me again and told me I had to stay in this room until he said I could come out. I'm scared, Cash. I think he's gonna mess me up good tonight," I laid it on thick. I truly did think Austin was gonna fuck me up, but he hadn't quite hit me tonight so I was lying a little bit.

"Text me the address from the burner app I told you about."

"K."

We hung up and I quickly sent Austin's address from the burner app to Cash's burner number. He quickly replied telling me to get out of the house, so I rushed out of the bedroom and downstairs to the kitchen.

"Come on guys, let's go," I told my friends.

"Can we jump that nigga first?" Khyle inquired, eating one of the rib tips.

"No, no time. Let's go."

The four of us went out through the back way where the building's pool was, and left through the gate. We quickly jogged around to my car since I drove us here, and then I sped away from Austin's before parking by the townhouses a little ways from his.

"Umm, okay, what are we doing?" Bella asked.

"Just wait on it." *I* didn't even know what we were doing, but I wanted to see what Cash had planned.

About 10 minutes later, the four of us watched a black truck pull up. Since the door of Austin's house was open, the two masked men were able to barge into the party. I heard people screaming, just before the front door closed. I heard gunshots next, and then a few moments later, I watched the two men drag Austin out of the house, throw him into the truck, and speed off. I saw the license plate wasn't really a plate at all… it was just black.

"Oh shit, that was gangster!" Khyle joked, and even though we were still in shock, we all burst into laughter.

"Well shit, let's get the fuck up out of here," Bella said, just as people started coming out of the house, looking around and in mild panic.

As I drove the ladies to Oden's complex, a text came through the screen of my BMW.

"Oooh Cash," Tasmine giggled.

I rolled my eyes playfully before tapping it. I saw he said to come to his house, so I didn't feel the need to reply. I dropped the ladies off since Bella was spending the night with Khyle, and then hightailed it to Cash's place. When I pulled into his driveway, he was already standing in the doorway wearing sweats, socks, and no shirt.

"Hey," I got out and jogged up to him wearing a smile.

"What you so happy about?" he grinned down at me as he stepped back so I could come inside.

"I don't know." I hugged his sexy body, as he pressed me up against the door, closing it. "What did you do to him?"

"Taught his ass a lesson," he spoke lowly, while rubbing up my skirt. His hand went down into my panties, and I gasped when he pushed his fingers inside of me. "He won't be back."

"Mmm," I moaned, gripping his biceps as he plunged his fingers in and out of me. We were leaning up against his door, in the dark, already started. I'd been waiting to feel him like this for the longest, so I wasn't gonna stop him.

"You mine now," he said just as I let my juices flow over his fingers.

He pulled them out of me and licked them clean, before lifting me up and carrying me to his bedroom. We kissed hungrily as we undressed one another, and once we were both naked, he pushed me down onto the bed. Spreading my legs, he put them onto his shoulders and started licking. I'd never gotten head before, and I didn't see the hype until now.

"Oh God," I bucked my eyes as I stared at the ceiling in shock. The way he licked, sucked, and slurped me had my body feeling high.

His hands were running amuck all over my bottom half as he feasted on my center, and soon enough, I'd cum three times. He trailed his lips from between my legs up to my breasts to lick my nipples. He sucked my chin, and then covered my mouth with his, just as he started poking around at my hole.

Lifting my legs and placing them over his arms, he sucked on my lips to distract me as he pushed himself inside. I dug my nails into his back as he started to move in and out of me, delivering pain and pleasure. He was much bigger than Austin, and I was paying for it.

"Ahhh, ahhh," I whimpered when he started to go faster, pounding into me with force.

He pinned my hands behind my head, and stared down at me as he pummeled my center. My body jerked when I came, but that didn't slow his strokes up one bit. He leaned down to kiss me gently, then growled against my lips as he let loose… inside of me.

"I think I love you, Cash," I panted as he breathed against my neck, heart beating rapidly.

He just smiled cockily, before slipping his tongue into my mouth.

This felt different… but in a good way.

CHAPTER NINE

One week later…

Them stupid hoes Siena and Raquel got us good yesterday afternoon. Bella and I were sitting in front of the dorm just chilling, and them hoes dumped buckets of cranberry juice over our heads. They got away because for a moment Bella and I just sat there in disbelief at what the fuck had happened. I wasn't pregnant so I could easily whoop their asses now, which I would do, but it would be with a twist.

"I can't believe I'm gonna be watching this," Tasmine laughed, shoving popcorn into her mouth. "I'm gonna record this shit for memories."

Bella and I walked into the bathroom, and started pouring baby oil on the floor, starting from their side and bringing it all the way to the side Bella's room was on. We made sure to walk backwards as we doused the floor, so we wouldn't slip.

Once we were done, we simply closed the bathroom door, and

put the bottles into this trash bag that we were gonna throw out later. The three of us left the room, and then ran downstairs just to hang outside of the dorm. We were all getting on a party bus to Los Angeles tonight since the guys were throwing a yacht party tomorrow.

"Oh shit," I chuckled as Siena and Raquel walked by us and went inside of the dorm.

Like the hoes they were, they always had some niggas to see, so they showered after class every evening. But this time, as soon as they stepped foot in that bathroom, one of them would be slipping and sliding every damn where, James Brown style.

"You wearing a bathing suit on the yacht, Tasmine?" Bella asked.

"Yeah, I am. My belly is still in the cute stage. I don't look like a whale yet."

The three of us sat outside talking for a little bit longer, about 15 minutes, enjoying the cool evening air and the sunset. Funny enough, I just so happened to look over my shoulder to see Raquel storming out of the dorm building, looking like she was ready to be thrown in the fryer with her greasy ass. Her hair was stuck to her face, and the dress she was wearing was stuck to her body as the three of us died laughing.

No words were spoken as I hopped down off the cement pillar, before she and I started going at it. Like a stupid weak bitch, she immediately went for my hair, and grasped it as I punched her face. I heard someone else running up, so I assumed it was Siena. Before she could get in, Bella and her started throwing hands.

"Fuck her up, Khyle!" I heard Tasmine yell excitedly. "Damn, Bella!"

Raquel dipped down, tired of me beating her face in, and started punching me in the stomach. I kneed her ass in the face, and when she fell back cradling her mouth, I straddled her. Because my hair was so long, she grabbed it again as I wailed on her.

"What the fuck is yo' little ass doing!" I heard Oden's voice before I was being snatched into the air.

"Stupid bitch always starting shit!" Raquel hollered as she slowly got up off the ground, blood covering her teeth. Her eye was already swelling up. I didn't care though because she had gotten away with too much and deserved this.

I tried to wiggle out of Oden's arms, but he was way too strong. He then whispered in my ear for me to calm the fuck down, so I did. Truman was struggling trying to pull Bella off of Siena, but he eventually succeeded. Siena was crying and screaming because Bella ripped some of her real hair out, but that's what her ass gets for that cranberry juice shit.

"Bring her to the bus!" Oden yelled to Truman as he walked me over to it. He was still holding me from behind, and I was just pouting the whole way.

He let Tasmine get on first, before walking me on. Truman brought Bella on next, and then Oden made sure the driver closed the doors. Thank God we gave them our bags earlier, because I had a feeling Oden wouldn't let me off this bus for shit at the moment.

"Y'all are fucking crazy, man," Truman shook his head before sitting down, panting, pulling his phone out. "Let's go pick up Chiina and my son first, then we can get Santino, Anton, Shayne, and Lloyd in no particular order," he said and Oden nodded.

"What about Perry?" Tasmine questioned.

"She and Cash are gonna fly over in the morning, but ride back with us," Oden replied.

"Where is my baby?!" I snapped, mad at Oden still.

"He's in the back, and calm yo' ass down." He followed me to the small bedroom where my son was knocked out. I leaned down to kiss his fat cheek, and just watched him sleep for a little bit.

"Aye, who you getting an attitude with?" Oden grabbed me and pinned me up against the wall. "What I tell you about that?" He unbuttoned my shorts and started pushing them down with my panties.

"You should have let me finish fighting her," I whined as he lifted me up, removing his dick. "I—" I couldn't finish my sentence once he brought me onto his dick.

I gripped his hair as he moved me up and down, while pressing me against the wall.

"You stay so tight," he groaned before sucking the shit out of my neck. "Mmm, fuck."

"Ahhh, uuuh," I cried out as he pounded me with precision. I didn't want to wake my baby, but I couldn't help myself.

Oden slowed his strokes down, winding his hips, and I came immediately. He vacuumed my lips into his mouth, and started beating it up. I couldn't even kiss him back because I was crying out so.

"You gon' stop fighting?" he asked me, pounding my G spot on the fucking money. I swear my eyes had rolled to the back of my head.

"Answer me."

"Ye-yesssss. Ah, oh my gosh, I'm gonna cum," I sniveled, as he bit down on my lip.

"Cum on your dick."

As soon as he said that, I gushed again. He let me down, and then made me face the wall, before sliding inside of me from behind. He gripped my waist tightly and started slamming into me while biting down on my exposed shoulder. He reached around the front of me to toy with my clit, and a few moments later, we were both releasing and calling out.

"Nasty asses!" I heard Shayne yell from the front, so I guess they'd picked her up already.

"Aye," Oden pulled me back and hemmed me up against the wall when I tried to walk off and get my bottoms. "I love you."

"I love you to—" I couldn't even finish before his tongue was down my throat.

***

The next afternoon…

"Okay, go, Khyle, he will be fine," my mom shooed me. My parents were gonna watch my son while I went to the yacht party.

"Alright, all of his stuff is in this bag. If something happens, call me. He's perfectly fine so if he coughs or anything—"

"Sweetie, I've had two kids, I don't know if you know," she smiled, holding Oden Jr. His jaws were so fat that I had to kiss them once more.

"I'm sorry, I guess I get paranoid."

"That's normal. But once that second child comes, you'll be trying to pass them both off to the highest bidder."

"So you're saying you were protective over Shayne and not me?" I grinned, as we both laughed.

"No, I was just anal with Shayne because it was a new job for me. With you I knew more, so I didn't worry too much. It was easier for me to let your aunt babysit you."

"Speaking of Auntie, is cousin Delaney going to UNLV this upcoming year?"

"Yeah, she is. She's excited. I told her she's not gonna wanna hang with you and your friends and vice versa."

"Not true, Mama. I mean I can't party like I used to, but I can still do a lot."

"I know. Well go! Have fun on the yacht! My grandson and I are gonna go have some fun before grandpa wakes up. Isn't that right, cutie," she tickled Oden Jr.'s fat belly.

"Alright. Well bye, Mama."

I grabbed my purse and phone, then walked out of my house. When I saw Emery pushing her stroller up my parents' driveway, I was surprised even though I shouldn't have been. She always knew when I was in town, and she always dropped by. Only this time, not only did she have her baby, but her baby's daddy, Brian was with her.

"Fuck me," I mumbled as they got closer.

"Where's your kid?" Brian asked in that snotty tone of his. Nigga didn't even say hi.

"He's with his grandparents for the day."

"Damn, already dropping him off to go turn up?" he laughed, running his hand down his newly grown facial hair.

"Hi, Emery," I turned to her with a fake smile. My eyes immediately went down to her baby in the stroller. He was beautiful, looking just like raggedy ass Brian.

"Hey, Khyle. How have you been? I saw you were engaged," she nodded as Brian mumbled something smart under his breath.

"Yeah, I am engaged. I'm planning to get married mid-July if I can pull everything off in time." As soon as I finished, Brian said something else. "Nigga, you got a problem?"

"Nah, I just said you look good." His eyes roamed my body. I was wearing a two-piece that was covered up by a short, netted dress.

"Really, Brian?" Emery sneered.

"Aye, we not even together, man. Kill all that shit," he waved her off, still looking at my body. "I was your first, so that's always gonna be mine. I still remember fucking the shit out of you."

Both Emery and I burst into laughter because that was a lie. I'd told her plenty of times how weak his dick was, so the fact that he tried to act like he was a beast in the bedroom was hilarious to us both.

"Brian, you wasn't doing anything in the bed. Poor Khyle thought her body just couldn't cum, but it was you all along," Emery said, making us laugh.

"But I made you cum though, so hush yo' fucking mouth. If my dick was so weak, you wouldn't be begging to hop on this shit, and crying when I tell you I ain't gon' ever be with you," Brian snapped, shutting Emery up real quick.

His statement might have bothered me a year and some change ago, but now I didn't care that they fucked around.

"Well, it was nice seeing you both… I guess. I have to go meet my friends and my man at the dock for a party." I walked past them and to my father's Mercedes.

"Call me when that nigga leaves you for a bitch that don't have kids!" Brian called after me, trying to hurt my feelings. He was so ignorant that you would never guess he was in school to be a doctor.

"No, I will call you when I find some new kegel exercises for Jacqueline so she'll have walls again. I know it's a struggle putting that weak dick in that loose ass puss," I shot back as I got in the car, and I saw Emery cracking up.

After backing out of my parents' large driveway, I turned my music up and put my shades on before peeling down the street. I had no time for Brian or Emery.

CHAPTER NINE

Bella

Spring break was here, and currently I was in Southern California with my best friends and my man. After getting here on the party bus, we checked into the suites at the Beverly Hills hotel, and then went to dinner. The whole crew stayed up half the night, basically having a little intimate kickback in the suite with drinks, snacks, music, movies, and board games that someone was smart enough to bring. And today, we were getting on a yacht for a party. So as you can see, I was enjoying myself very much so far, and I still had a week to go. It was nice knowing niggas with coins.

The yacht was in the Marina, and it was two stories with a kitchen, bedrooms, dance floor, just everything. We were about to start sailing in the beautiful water, but we just had to wait until Khyle got here. She had to drop her baby off with her parents.

"Alright, she's here y'all so we can go," Oden walked in holding Khyle's hand. He let go so she could hug and say hi to everybody, even though we'd eaten breakfast together. When she walked back by to sit next to Oden, he gripped her waist and made her straddle his lap.

"Y'all have enough kids, don't you think?" I joked.

"Nope," Oden laughed, planting a kiss on her collarbone.

"I knew he was gonna say that," Tasmine chuckled, before turning her attention back to Anton.

Once the yacht started moving, a hostess came around and took orders for drinks. I was able to order something alcoholic, and I was hella happy about that. After having some drinks, and a few snacks that were being brought around, they turned the music on. We were in here basically having a full-on party, while admiring the scenery. I could definitely get used to having a house out here, because I would stay at the damn beach.

After hours of dancing, having drinks, alcoholic and non-alcoholic, talking, and just enjoying one another's company, it started to get dark. Everyone kind of sectioned off with their significant other, either slow dancing, watching the water, eating, simply talking, or even napping. I couldn't get over Perry and Cash kissing like two hot in the pants teenagers. I was just waiting for them to start fucking each other.

"Come on," Santino helped me up, and then led me upstairs where one of the rooms were. He closed the door behind himself, and smiled evilly.

"You're nasty," I giggled as I sat on the bed. He climbed on as well, and kissed my lips gently.

"Calm down, I just wanted to come in here and talk to you. It's cold down there."

"It is. But what did you want to talk to me about?"

"I wanted to know how you were feeling about me having to leave in June. You'll be in Arizona while I'm here in Los Angeles training."

"I will be sad of course," I sighed. I hadn't even thought about all that, but now that he was bringing it up, I felt like crying damn near.

"You know they helped me get an apartment out here in Los Angeles, so why don't you stay with me for the summer? Well you can go home for the beginning and then come to California for the second half, or vice versa." He squeezed my thigh.

"Yeah, we could do that, but what about when I start school?"

"We'll make trips, mainly me though. And once the season is over, I will be in Las Vegas more. But when we are apart, I want you to remember that I love you."

"I will. You better not find someone else."

"I couldn't, even if I tried, baby. You better not either. But don't talk like that. We won't be going days and weeks without speaking to each other."

I smiled at him as I caressed his handsome face. He was so sweet, and he always knew what to say. I was a little worried about us being apart come my junior year, but I think he and I both proved that our love could weather any storm. We were meant to be, and it was obvious.

"So, beautiful," he pushed my hair behind my ears and kissed me. Once our tongues started dancing, he made his way in between my legs.

"How is Trevor?" I questioned.

"Why?" his face was twisted up. He was obviously irritated, as well as surprised.

"Not like that. I just know he got shot, and I haven't seen him around campus. I usually see him when I leave my math class, or around the dorm."

"He lived, unlike the homies he was with. He can't play any more though." Santino sighed and rolled off of me.

"You feel bad?"

"I did for like a hot ass second, but then I remembered his sole purpose for rolling up on me was to injure me so that *I* wouldn't be able to play. So now I'm like, fuck him. His plan to sabotage me ended up backfiring. The only thing that really bothers me is how our friendship went from sugar to shit over something so stupid."

"Jealousy is a strong emotion, Santino."

"I know, but damn. As a friend, you'd think he'd be happy for me. It's normal to want what someone else has, but that's when you work harder to get there. You don't start hating."

"I agree." I caressed his hair as he stared up at the ceiling in deep thought. "Just know I'm proud of you, and I appreciate all that you've done to keep our relationship together. I wish your parents were—"

"Don't even go there. Sadly enough, I'm kind of happy I don't fuck with them like that anymore. I used to dream about the day that I'd get signed to a football team and be able to stop fucking with them. Shit, the only reason they care about me now is because of that Rams contract. They hadn't reached out to me once since my dad put me out, but now that my face is all over college sports shows and newspaper sports sections, they care."

I turned onto my stomach, and then leaned over to kiss his soft lips a couple times.

"I think that was all they cared about from day one," I replied and he nodded. "Where did you meet Crystal?"

I asked that out of nowhere… well sort of. I'd been wondering where the bitch came from. It seemed like she sprouted from the ground, blackmailing him. That's part of the reason I didn't believe him, because he never mentioned her before. She kind of just came out of the bushes, at least to me.

"I've known her for about as long as I've known Leena. They were best friends, and from day one Crystal wanted to fuck me. I'd thought about it while I was 'with' Leena, but I decided against it because I just felt like sexing Leena's best friend was fucked up."

"So she's been wanting to fuck you for years and never got the chance?" I laughed.

"Pretty much," he flashed his smile. "I mean she got what she got, but I never put it in her."

"Damn, so she never got to sample this?" I grabbed his dick in my hands and then straddled him.

"Nah, but you can right now." He gripped my hips, and started untying my bikini bottoms.

***

Back in Las Vegas, Nevada… A week and a half later…

"Santino, I do not like surprises," I whined, toying with my large engagement ring as I wondered where he was taking me. He had me blindfolded as he drove through the city.

He said nothing, and finally his car came to a stop. I heard him get out, and then come around to open my door as well. Taking my hand into his, he helped me out, and then closed the passenger side door behind me. We started walking, and after only about 10 steps, he stopped and snatched the blindfold off. I squinted my eyes at the bright sun, while enjoying the way it beat against my skin.

"Why are we at the Alicante townhouses?" I quizzed. This was the same boss ass complex that Oden, Anton, and their friend Truman lived in.

"Because this one is ours," he said, pointing to the door in front of us.

"Oh my gosh, are you serious?" I shrieked, staring at the door as if that would make it open up for me.

"Yeah, I am. You've been begging me for months to look at a place here, and everything finally went through. I got a nice little signing bonus from the Rams that finally hit my account so…" he shrugged and pulled the keys from his pocket.

"Gimme!" I snatched them and rushed to open the door.

When I walked in, my mouth dropped even though there wasn't a lick of furniture. It was so beautiful and clean. But most importantly, I would be living in close proximity to my best friends again.

"I saw some other places, but I liked this one best. And I wanted you to be close to your girls while I'm away. Oden and his crew too. I asked him to look after you."

"You know I can defend myself."

"I do. I saw Siena's face yesterday. She mugged me like I was the one who fucked her up," he sucked his teeth before we both laughed.

"Well, now that she and I won't be neighbors anymore, we most likely can end our feud."

"That needs to happen. I can't have you getting kicked out of school for fighting. I need you to get that medical degree so you can take care of me when I get hurt."

"I will, baby." I walked aimlessly around the condo for a little bit, and then came back to the kitchen. I hopped up onto the counter, and pulled my dress over my head. "Come take care of me."

He started towards me, taking off an article of clothing with each step until he was down to his boxers. Once he made it to me, he pecked me softly and repeatedly as he pulled my panties past my thighs. Throwing them to the side, he dropped down and started to kiss between my legs gently.

"Mmm," I moaned subtly as he started to suck hard yet slowly on my clit. He knew just what to do to get me to cum fast. I loved it passionate but rough.

He flicked his tongue over my button a couple of times before latching back on to it, while spreading my legs wider. In no time, I was grabbing onto the kitchen sink faucet, crying out as I came. Gripping my ass, he pushed my vagina further into his mouth and devoured my pussy feverishly as I grasped his hair.

"Oh, oh my gosh! Fuck," I whimpered, looking down at him as he gave me a tongue-lashing. My body froze, and then trembled as if

I were standing in a freezer once I came. "Shit, baby," I panted as he kissed my lower lips.

I dropped down to my knees, and he immediately started fucking my face once he got his dick from his boxers. I just closed my eyes and took every stroke like I was a professional. I licked, hummed, slurped, and deep throated him until he came so hard he lost his balance.

"Damn," he smirked, yanking me up from the kitchen floor and bending me over the bar. He pushed my left leg forward, and plunged inside of me.

"Ahh," I gasped as he humped me, trying to fit himself all the way in.

He gripped my neck from behind, and started slamming into me. Our skin was smacking together, and our moans were loud as fuck. I knew someone had to hear us. Grabbing my hair, he pulled my head back so he could suck on the side of my neck as he plowed into me from behind.

"Ahh, uhh! Oh shit!" I called out just as we both exploded.

"Your pussy never ceases to amaze me." He pulled out of me, and then turned me to face him so he could kiss me. "I love you, Bella D'Stefano."

Giggling shyly at the fact that he put his last name with my first name I replied, "I love you too, baby."

I couldn't wait to spend forever with him. Santino was the love of my life, and he would always be. He stole my heart years ago, and I never got it back.

CHAPTER NINE

Truman

The next evening…

I felt good about my relationship with Chiina. However, she still wasn't living with me and I still hadn't fucked. She acted like everything was all good, but the fact that we didn't live together or have sex worried me. Not to mention she hadn't quite said that we were back together yet. I blew out hot air as I parked my car in the back of Palace.

I got out, hit my alarm, and then tread up to the side door so I could get inside to my office. I hated going through the front because niggas would always start acting dumb, and bitches would get thirsty as fuck.

After dropping by my office to start up my computer and set my shit up, I decided to walk both clubs just to peep the scene. I knew Anton was still here for another hour, but I just wanted to see what exactly I was working with for the night.

"Hey, boss," Cara smiled as I walked by her.

"Shit, what's up? I forgot you came back to work today. I ain't never been this happy to see you," I laughed, giving her a hug.

"Why? What happened?" she chuckled.

"Your temporary replacement was a bit of a basket case."

"You slept with her?" she turned her lip up and rolled her eyes. "Truman, when will you learn?"

"No, I didn't sleep with her ass." She gave me a look that said she knew I was bullshitting. "Aight, I almost did, but I got caught so I didn't. But, in my defense, she tried to hook up after that and I declined."

"Well, I'm happy to see that you're progressing. Chiina is a sweet girl and she loves you a lot, so I hope you have it together this time."

"I do, damn, why does everybody doubt me?"

"Umm, because you have a pretty trashy track record, Truman. However, I will say that I do see a difference in you now that you're with Chiina. I see you trying when before you didn't really care. You know when you were with what's her face."

"Pilar, and don't bring her shady ass up."

Laughing, Cara asked, "Wait, what did she do?"

"Just know I can't stand that bitch."

"Oooh," she chuckled. "So tonight, we are fully booked. I wanted to ask you about potential celebrities. If any come in wanting VIP, should I move some people around or just let them know we're full?"

"Let them know we're full, unless they start trying to pay top dollar. And I mean big bucks, because I don't really like the moving around thing too much."

"Got it." She pranced off.

I checked out the strip club area, and everything looked intact, so I went upstairs to the club. As I made my rounds, I ran across Anton so I chopped it up with him for a bit. As I continued, I spotted a figure that looked like Chiina, laughing with some nigga all in her face. Darting over there, I grabbed her up and pinned her against the wall.

"Aye nigga, what the fuck!" the dude she was talking to yelled.

"Man, get the fuck on somewhere before I put yo' ass to sleep for good!" I roared. My heart was damn near beating out of my chest, and I could feel my blood boiling under my skin. Turning my attention back to Chiina, I glared down at her for a few moments before questioning, "What the fuck you doing in another nigga's face, Chi?"

"Calm down! I can do what I want, I'm not yours!"

"You not mine?" I palmed my chest, baffled. "You walking around here spending my money, got a ring on your finger that I paid for, and you got my baby. You honestly think you're single?"

Truman, don't put your hands on her. This is your son's mother, I had to say to myself.

"Yep. I don't know if I want you so get out of my face. I have work to do." She nudged me to the side and I swear I felt like I'd just hit a dip on a roller coaster.

My chest was aching as I watched her switch off. Her saying she didn't know if she wanted me cut deeply as fuck. I thought we were damn near back together, but clearly that wasn't the case. For the past few months, we've been carrying on like a fucking couple, minus the sex, yet she wasn't even feeling it. The fact that I was trying, made this shit worse. I hadn't even thought about another bitch. And to make matters worse, I was still on her at this moment. I didn't want anybody else.

This was exactly why a nigga didn't want to be in love. What good came from being attached to someone who could up and leave at any moment? I loved my mom, and her ass dipped. I loved my dad, and although he didn't abandon me, he belittled me so much that I had to cut his ass off in high school.

It was cool though. Maybe I would go back to my old ways. Life was gravy then. I shook my head at my thoughts. Oddly, my old lifestyle as a Lothario didn't sound appeasing anymore. I wanted to be a family man, and wake up to Chiina and my kid every morning. But oh well.

I trucked it back to my office, ignoring people that spoke to me, especially the thirsty ass females throwing pussy at me, that back in the day I would have caught. Once I got back to my office, I made myself a drink, and then sat at my desk, sipping. After polishing off and refilling the glass, I heard someone knock at my door before just walking in; it was Chiina.

"Fuck you want?" I hissed, throwing back the Bourbon.

"You." She closed the door behind herself and leaned on it.

"Really? Because I could have sworn you just said you didn't."

"No, I said I didn't know."

"Oh right, so much better. At least there's hope, right?" I smiled sarcastically.

She walked over to me after locking the door, and turned my

chair so that she could sit in my lap. For a moment, she just stared at me with that pretty innocent face I fell in love with.

"I said those things because I'm still a little hurt by how you've treated me in the past, Tru. But after thinking it over, I realized that you're doing a lot better now. And because I love you, I'm willing to put the past behind us and be together."

"Be together as in living with one another, right?"

"Yes."

I swished my drink around in my glass a few times before saying, "Being together as in getting married, right?"

"Married?"

"That's what that ring on your finger is for."

"I know, but I thought you just asked me to marry you because we were having sex at the time," she chuckled.

"No, I really want to marry you, baby."

"Okay."

"Let's go tonight."

"Truman."

"I'm serious. Why not? What would we be waiting for?"

"Nothing I guess."

"Aight then, let's go." I tapped her leg so she could get up from my lap. "And speaking of sex, can we please end the drought tonight?"

"It's possible."

That was good enough for me, so I shot Anton a text telling him the deal. He was cool with staying longer, so Chiina and I dipped.

***

Some odd hours later…

"We're really married," Chiina chuckled as she plopped back on the bed in our suite. I'd never seen her smile so much, and that shit had me feeling myself a little bit.

"I know. How does it feel to be Mrs. Morrison?" I laid down on top of her, in between her legs.

Rubbing the sides of my face, she said, "Feels like I got something I've always wanted."

"Me too, shorty. I may not have known I wanted it until recently, but I couldn't ask for more at this moment."

"I love you," she hugged my neck tightly.

"I love you too. Think of some places we can honeymoon. TJ is old enough to come along with us you know."

"Okay. And speaking of TJ, since my aunt is watching him tonight, let's have some fun." She started pulling off her little white dress that we'd bought in haste.

"Say no more," I said before kissing down her exposed body.

Who knew a nigga like me would be in love and married? I sure had no idea my life would turn out like this, but I'm thanking God that it did.

CHAPTER TEN

Tasmine

"You're lucky as fuck you're pregnant, shorty, "Anton huffed as he put a box of my stuff down. Since my sophomore year was coming to a close, we were slowly moving my stuff into Anton's townhouse. I was happy that Khyle and Bella were my neighbors because that was what I was gonna miss about the dorm life; being able to take a few steps and be at their door. Well, Bella's door since all I had to do was roll over and see Khyle.

"I appreciate you," I giggled before shoving some cookies into my mouth. "Just think of it as exercise, baby." I couldn't help but laugh because of the way he looked at me.

"Ain't no fucking exercise. This is fucking slave labor. I can't believe these boxes are so heavy and they only have clothes in them."

I just shrugged and turned the TV up because I didn't want to hear his mouth anymore. Today I didn't have class, and I always took full advantage of days I didn't have to go to school. I heard him mumble, talking shit under his breath when I hit the volume on his ass, but I didn't care. He just needed to hurry up so we could go to our

325

doctor's appointment and then get something to eat.

I sat there on the couch, chilling and eating as Anton hustled back and forth through the living room, carrying all of my shit. When he was finished, he came and sat next to me with a paper and a frame.

"What is that?" I quizzed, frowning.

"My restraining order against Selinda."

"You're framing it?" I chuckled.

"Hell yeah. Shit, you know how good I feel every time I think about this shit? So just imagine if when every day I leave, I see this by the door? It'll automatically improve my day."

"Makes sense. How do you feel about *actually* having a baby this time?"

"It feels good. That's where people mistook the situation. I wasn't upset about having a kid, I was upset that a baby I knew wasn't mine was being pinned on me. Not to mention, they were doing the most like popping up on my dates, causing scenes every damn where, like the whole shit was just stressful. If I honestly felt like them kids were mine, I wouldn't have been tripping."

"Even though you didn't like the girls?"

"I mean yeah. I smashed them so I would need to take responsibility. Every time you have sex, you risk making a baby. My thing was, if you feel like I'm the father, handle your business and agree to a DNA test. All that extra shit was uncalled for."

"Tell me about it. The night that hoe popped up on our date, I was floored. I'd never experienced anything like that before. I was so over you."

"No you weren't," he smacked his lips as he kept his eyes on fixing the frame.

"Excuse me?" I chuckled. "Yes the fuck I was."

"Then why did you come to my house for Thanksgiving? You still wanted a nigga, don't even lie."

"No I did not!" I half lied.

I was off him, but I would be lying if I said my mind didn't drift to him often. I guess I was more so bummed than over him, because I had a whole fairytale drummed up in my head about how we would end up.

"Well, all I know is you went from being 'off me' to carrying my baby, so either you're lying or I'm just really that nigga," he kissed my cheek.

"I guess I'm lying," I blurted before we both burst into laughter.

"You just couldn't let me be 'that nigga', huh?" he stood up to hang the frame onto the wall. I got off the couch, and made my way over to him, wrapping my arms around his torso.

"No, but in all seriousness, you really are 'that nigga'. Not just because you were able to snag such a beautiful, intelligent, sexy woman like myself," we laughed together, "but because when you put your mind to something, you get it done. I know so many guys who would have still been getting harassed by Selinda and Kai because they were too lazy to get shit done, but not you. And then the way you help Violet and her baby, just makes you so much more attractive."

"Yeah?" he raised a brow and I nodded.

Leaning down to kiss me, he cupped the back of my head as his other hand traveled down into my tights.

"No, Tony, we have to go to the doctor!" I whined.

"Just a quickie."

"No, this is an important one. After the doctor and food, we can come home and do whatever you want," I smiled, biting my lip.

Sucking his teeth, he kissed me and said, "Aight."

***

An hour and a half later...

I was lying back on the examination table in the dimly lit room, as my doctor spread that cold ass jelly on my stomach. Anton was holding my hand as we stared at the screen. Nothing was on it yet, but I guess neither of us wanted to miss a thing.

"Okay, let's see what we have here. Are you sure wanna know this time?" my doctor smiled.

We'd made appointments to find out before, only to cancel them. I wanted to wait and see what it was on the day I delivered, but I was getting anxious to design the baby's room, and get its name embroidered in things.

"Yes, we're sure," Anton responded.

"Alright." She started moving the device across my belly, as Anton and I waited on the edge of our seats. "Looks like you guys will have a beautiful baby girl," she beamed.

I could feel my face light up as I glanced at Anton. I wanted a girl badly for some reason, but Anton said he didn't care what we had, long as it was healthy.

"Love you, babe." Anton stood up to kiss me as tears spilled down my cheeks. I cried over every damn thing.

"Love you too," I sniffled, turning my attention back to the small screen and on my smiling doctor.

Seemed like lately my life was turning into everything I wanted it to be.

CHAPTER TEN

Shayne

$\mathcal{I}$ was sitting in the middle of the living room, doing some pregnancy yoga. I was due to give birth any minute now, and my doctor told me any type of activity would help. The treadmill was too hard, so I decided to try this.

I was currently in a sports bra and some leggings, but I was still burning the fuck up. As I fell back against the couch, palming my big belly, I heard the doorbell.

"Who is that?" Lloyd yelled from the back room before I could even get off the floor.

"Give me a second, damn!" I hissed, rolling my eyes hard as fuck. "How the hell would I know who it is already, dummy?" I mumbled under my breath. I ain't want him to hear because he would get in my ass.

I looked out the peephole, and saw it was Alanna standing there looking stupid. I mean she looked pretty with her hair straightened and her makeup done, but her facial expression looked dumb. She always looked like that when she had fucked up. Snatching the door open, I stood there, head cocked, waiting for her to speak.

"Hey, can I come in? I need to talk to you," she fidgeted. Suddenly, I remembered that Lloyd had killed Pierce, and I hoped she wasn't coming here to ask about him.

"Who is it?!" Lloyd barked again from the back.

"Alanna!" I spat, shaking my head at him before turning my attention back to her. "What do you need to talk to me about?"

"Well," she barged in and sat down so I shut the door. "I'm pregnant and I don't know what to do about it."

"And you expect me to what? Give you an ultrasound? I'm not understanding why the fuck you're here right now." I was annoyed that she had caused so much bullshit in my life.

"No, because I told Earl Jr. and he wants me to get an abortion! How could he ask me to do something like that?"

"I'm sorry, the fact that you're surprised is baffling to say the least, Lana." I sat down next to her since my feet were starting to hurt. "I'm so tired of hearing about this nigga. Like, I have nothing to give you anymore. He has never given a fuck about you, and everyone sees that but your ass."

"I'm just gonna get rid of it like he wants."

"So you're gonna kill your baby for a man that doesn't give two shits about you? At the least you should keep your baby because it still is a part of you, and then get that nigga for child support."

"All you care about is money, Shayne. I don't care about getting his funds, I want to be with him."

She was such an idiot that it made my stomach hurt. I even felt my son move, so he clearly felt like this bitch was dumb as fuck as well. *That's right, baby*, I thought.

"I'm not all about money, stupid! What I'm telling you is to not penalize your baby because you want to make some fuck nigga happy! And in addition to that, get him for child support since he doesn't want to take responsibility."

"I don't know why I came here," she stood up.

"Shit, me either. I couldn't care less about you, Earl Jr., or his wife who is also pregnant," I smiled, throwing salt on her wounds.

"I hope your baby is stillborn," she retorted, and I will be the first to admit that it shocked the hell out of me. I couldn't even react or respond right away as I processed her words over and over again.

"Okay, you need to go," I sniffled, feeling myself get emotional at the thought of my baby being born dead. "Go!" I shouted, making her jump. I swear if I see her ass after I give birth, I'm fucking her up just for that statement.

"Baby, you good?" Lloyd came rushing into the living room, just as I slammed the door behind that slut.

I said nothing, and just shook my head as I started to cry. Lloyd pulled me into his strong arms, which immediately helped soothe me a bit. I inhaled his cologne as I sobbed into his polo shirt.

"You think the baby will be okay, even though I'm such a horrible person?"

"What? You're not a horrible person, Shayne. And the baby is perfectly fine. We've had tons of scans to prove that shit." He pulled back some so he could kiss me, and then hugged me again.

"Alanna just said—"

"Alanna is a sad ass, weak ass bitch with nothing going for herself. I better not ever see you crying over something her doormat ass said ever again, you hear me?"

"Yeah," I whimpered. "Can you go get me some ice cream?" I asked after a few moments of silence. We just both burst into laughter, before he released me from our hug and grabbed his keys from the counter.

***

Couple days later...

"He's so adorable," Khyle cooed over my son, Landon. I'd just delivered him four hours ago, and although I was dead tired, I was scared to fall asleep. I wanted to make sure he was good.

"Thanks," Lloyd popped his collar before he and Oden dapped one another up. Khyle and I both rolled our eyes playfully.

"Were you able to get medicine?" Khyle quizzed.

"Yes, girl! After hearing about what happened to you, I was on that damn nurse like white on rice until she hit me with that epidural," I replied and all four of us laughed.

"There he iiiisss," my mother came floating into the room with my dad behind her, carrying flowers for me.

"Hi Mom, Dad," I smiled as I watched my mother kiss Khyle's

334

cheek, and then take Landon from her.

My father hugged and kissed Khyle, then greeted Lloyd and Oden before making his way over to me.

"These are for you," he handed me the flowers and pecked my forehead.

"You got Khyle red roses," I frowned.

"I know, but you said you liked sunflowers, sweetie."

"Oh yeah," I giggled, and then sniffed them. My dad just shook his head and walked over to where my mom was to look over her shoulder at my baby boy.

"Oh shit, ain't this your homegirl?" Oden said, pointing up at the little TV that was plastered to the ceiling basically.

"It is," Khyle said as I turned the volume up.

"Earl Marsden Jr. of the San Deigo Chargers was slain early this morning around 3am at his residence. According to sources, Marsden was visited by his mistress in the wee hours of the morning, where she shot him and then proceeded to kill his pregnant wife, before fleeing the scene. Neighbors claimed to have heard Marsden arguing with a female who they assumed was his wife, before gunshots rang out. The mistress, Alanna Benson, is currently in custody, and has *admitted* to killing the NFL star and his spouse. She will be charged with three counts of first-degree murder, since officials were able to prove that Mrs. Marsden was in fact four months pregnant. I'm Kathy McMahon, and this is KVVU news."

My whole hospital room was silent, as we stared at the television.

I couldn't believe Alanna. On the bright side, though, she had finally bossed up on that nigga… and in a major way.

"I never liked her," Khyle broke the silence, making everyone in the room chuckle.

"Less attention on her, and more on me and my baby, thank you," I giggled. Like clockwork, everyone began talking while my parents looked over my son.

I knew this Alanna stuff was shocking, but that hoe was dead to me ever since that stillborn comment, so she was not about to take the shine from my baby boy.

"You better not do no shit like that to me," Lloyd mumbled against my lips before kissing me, as he towered over my bed.

"Don't fuck up."

"Never. I love you too much."

"I think I love you too much… too."

"You better."

"Wait, what about Elodie?"

"Baby that situation is dead, I'm telling you. You scared her off."

"Someone had to," I batted my eyelashes making him grin.

As our lips met, I couldn't help but to close my eyes and smile. I wasn't the nicest or the greatest person in the world, but it felt good to see how far I'd come. I was no longer that selfish girl who only cared about people if it benefited her. I must say, life is so much better when you're not so self-serving. I just thank God for blessing me when a lot of times I didn't deserve it.

CHAPTER TEN

August 2…

$\mathcal{I}$ opened my eyes, feeling pleasure down below. And since I'd just woken up, I was paralyzed for a few moments. When I finally got the strength, I looked down to see Oden with his mouth between my hips. I pressed my head back into the pillow while massaging his beautiful head of hair as he feasted on me. Spreading my legs wider, I pushed more of myself into his mouth before letting out a loud moan.

"Oh my gosh, Oden!" I cried as he sped up, taking me over the edge, making me explode.

I tried to crawl away, but he gripped my ass and forced me to stay in place. Pressing my thighs into my stomach, he trailed his tongue up the length of my pussy, before flicking his tongue over my button, making me tremble at the feeling. All I could do was grip the sheets, damn near tearing a hole in them with my long nails, as my chest heaved up and down. He looked up into my eyes, as he sucked on my clit, and I just bit down on my lip as I came hard as hell for the second time.

"Damn," he whispered, touching between my legs as I laid there, panting like I'd ran a 5k. "You taste so good in the morning," he said before sucking my nipples. I just didn't respond, because I hadn't come back from that powerful orgasm.

"Is this how you're gonna wake me up every morning?" I finally spoke up with a smile.

"Maybe. You are my wife now," he reminded me.

We got married just a couple weeks ago, at the end of July. It was a beautiful wedding held outside in Los Angeles, since we had more grass and pretty trees in California. All of my family and friends were there, and so were Oden's homies. It was a big affair, and I'd never had so much fun or taken so many pictures as I had that day. It was truly one of the happiest days of my life.

I got out of the bed, and grabbed my robe so that I could go check on my baby. When I walked in he was just lying in his crib, trying to get his toes into his mouth.

"What are you doing?" I cooed, scooping him up and kissing him. "Mommy's gonna be right back, okay?" I pecked his fat cheek again, making him smile before placing him in his playpen.

Rushing down the hall, I joined Oden in the bathroom to brush my teeth. He'd already done his, so it was perfect timing. He stepped out of the bathroom, and then came in behind me holding a red velvet box. My brows dipped, and since I couldn't quite ask him what it was yet, I quickly finished brushing, flossing, and rinsing.

"Happy birthday, baby," he finally said, reaching the gift out to me.

"Oh my gosh!" I beamed, opening the box to see a beautiful diamond necklace. "Thank you, baby." I tilted my head back so that he could kiss me.

"Anything for you. I want you to wear it tonight when I take you out. Scott is gonna drive you around today to get pampered, go shopping, and have lunch with your friends on my dime. But make sure you get back here in time to get ready for dinner at 9pm."

"Yes, sir. What about Oden—"

"My son is rolling with me for the day. I'm gonna take him to see some hoes," he chuckled and flinched when I punched him playfully. "Nah, but I got him for the day. He'll be ready for dinner tonight too."

"Okay, but he's hungry and stuff so go—"

"I got it, Khyle. Just get ready for your birthday."

I giggled excitedly, and then rushed him out of the bathroom. I texted my friends, who already knew the deal, so I guess Oden told them, and then I hopped into the shower. Once I got out, I put on some lotion and then got dressed in some jean shorts, a tube top, and some Nike Air Max, before tying my hair up into a huge bun on my head. After securing my watch, I sprayed on my body mist and walked into the living room. I saw Oden feeding our son, and they were already making a damn mess but my son was having the time of his life doing so. I had a mind to say something, but just decided to enjoy my birthday and let them be.

"Bye, baby!" Oden hollered after me as he pretended Oden Jr.'s spoon was an airplane.

"Bye, husband."

I smiled down at my wedding ring as I made my way to the big black Escalade sitting in front of our townhouse. Just as Scott opened the back door, Bella, and Tasmine came running up to me. It was dope living in the same complex as them.

Perry was currently out of the country in Paris with Cash, so she couldn't come, obviously. She did text me and say she was gonna bring me a gift back from over there though.

The three of us got into the car, and after Scott got back in the driver's seat, we were on our way to the nail shop.

"Your man set it out for us today, and I am taking full advantage," Bella tossed her long golden hair from one side to the other.

"Me too, but I know you're excited about Oden playing babysitter for the day," Tasmine chimed in, rubbing her belly.

"Girl, who are you telling," I hi-fived her. "We have to get Anton to do the same once you deliver."

She was due in just two more months, but you could tell she was over it.

"Happy birthday, Khyle." Bella handed me a box.

I opened it to see three necklaces; one saying *Best*, the other *Friends,* and the last *Forever.*

"Oh my gosh, Bella. Here you go," I gave her the *Forever* necklace, and then handed Tasmine the one reading *Best.* "Thank you, babe!" I shrieked, after fastening mine around my neck. Tasmine and Bella did the same, before I hugged Bella.

"From me," Tasmine handed me a gift, but the box was bigger than Bella's.

I ripped the packaging open, and grinned widely when I saw she got me the Rihanna Creeper sneakers in the white/oatmeal color. I had every other one but couldn't find these. I don't know how she located them, but I didn't care.

"Thank you!" I squeezed her. "Aww, I love you guys."

"We love you too," they both said almost simultaneously.

342

CHAPTER TEN

Oden

That night…

$\mathcal{I}$ pulled up in front of my townhouse with my son strapped in his car seat. Like me, he was wearing a burgundy tuxedo that I had to get custom made. I glanced in the back seat at him and just chuckled at my mini me, as he drank from that bottle like his life depended on it.

"All you're missing is the big hair, little man," I touched his small foot.

Taking my phone out, I texted Khyle to let her know I was outside and ready to take her to dinner. I had a lot of surprises for tonight, because I wanted to make sure she enjoyed her birthday. My shorty meant a lot to me, and I always liked to make sure she knew how much I loved her and appreciated her. That was a surefire way to lose your woman; taking her for granted and making her think you didn't need her.

Wife: Okay, coming baby!

I got out of the car, and after standing out there against my Porsche for almost 10 minutes, my beautiful wife came out of the townhouse. She was wearing a tight burgundy dress that was nice and short, showing her sexy ass legs, with matching burgundy heels, the ones with her toes out; she knew those were my favorite kind. I didn't mind my lady looking sexy in public, because she was mine and I did enjoy bragging occasionally. Her hair was down, sweeping her waistline, and I could see the diamond necklace I bought her and her wedding ring all the way from here.

As she got closer to me, I inhaled her Marc Jacobs perfume, and admired the smile that burst through her face.

"You look beautiful as fuck, Khyle." I shook my head, looking her up and down.

Some of my homies would tell me about all the beautiful women they saw overseas and shit like that, but it didn't ever faze me because of what I had at home waiting for me. Khyle was a 20/10 just based off looks, and her personality looked even better.

"Thank you. You look so good. I love burgundy on you," she rubbed down my chest. I kissed her lips lightly so I wouldn't get her lipstick on me, and then I opened the door for her to slide in.

"Hey, munchkin!" I heard her coo to our son before I closed the door and jogged to my side. "He looks so freaking cute. I can't wait to get my hands on him," she beamed once I got in the car.

"My poor son," I joked, and she tapped my arm.

We made our way to Quarter Steakhouse on Fremont Street, and after parking, I let Khyle out before getting my son. She immediately took him from me to tear up his cheeks and hug him, before handing him back over.

When we walked into the restaurant, I saw Khyle frown at the fact that we were the only people here outside of the hostess, the cooks, and a waitress.

"Mr. and Mrs. Bishop, right this way," the hostess Zena grabbed some menus and led us through the upscale restaurant. "Your waiter, Sherry, will be with you in a few moments," she smiled and floated off.

"No one is here, Oden," Khyle looked to me as I adjusted my son in my lap.

"I know. I made sure no one was here for the night. I want it just be us, you know?"

"How much did this cost?"

"Doesn't matter. Nothing is too much when it comes to you, I told you that."

"Aww, baby," she poked her bottom lip out.

Laughing, I said, "They're willing to serve you champagne if you want."

She looked down at the menu, and after a few moments I heard her gasp. I already knew what it was.

"Your liquor is here as an option, Oden," she pointed.

"I know. Remember a long ass time ago I told you I was working on getting it in here? Well, it finally went through."

"Congrats, honey, we have to celebrate before I start school again."

"And, I own this location in particular. Well, we both do. This is a document explaining how much you own, and this one is the information on the bank account I opened for us. This is our joint business one, separate from our joint personal." I pulled the papers from my tuxedo pocket and slid them to her.

"I love how you do things, keeping your marriage in mind. Like, most guys would have just made this move for themselves, but you did something for us."

"Of course."

"I'm gonna suck your dick good tonight," she laughed as she eyed the documents.

"Girl, you better quit talking like that before I take you to the bathroom."

"Well, we do own the place," she winked. "But munchkin is here so we have to wait until we get home. It will be worth the wait though."

"Good evening, Mr. and Mrs. Bishop. Champagne?" Sherry our waitress came by, holding a bottle.

"Please," I replied as my son cooed softly.

She popped it open and filled both of our glasses.

"Can we have the lobster dip with pita bread as an appetizer, please," Khyle ordered.

"Of course, and I will give you a few minutes to order."

"Cheers to love, happiness, and being married forever," Khyle held up her flute with that psycho smile she loved to flash when being crazy. I just laughed.

"Forever? That's a long ass time. What you think about that, man?" I looked down at my son in my lap, and kissed his temple.

"Yes, forever, nigga. You know I'm crazy and I love you, so I'm never letting you go." She tossed her hair over her shoulder and grinned widely. I just stared, admiring what was mine for a little bit.

"To all that shit you just said, for forever."

We clinked our glasses and then took a few sips. I don't even think forever was long enough for me, but I would take it for now.

EPILOGUE

Khyle Bishop

Two and a half years later... Las Vegas, Nevada

I finished braiding my hair up in my bedroom, because I had to go out and finish setting the table. Today, Oden and I were having a little pool party with our friends, and I was beyond ready. Lately, all I'd been doing was being a mom to my son, Oden Jr., going to school for my Master's degree, and being a wife to my love. Trust me, I enjoyed my life and wouldn't trade it for the world, but I couldn't wait to have a few glasses of champagne and chat with my girls.

"Mommy, can you open this?" Oden Jr. rushed into my bedroom holding up a Snickers bar.

"Where did you get this from, baby?"

"Uncle Tony," he smiled up at me.

He looked just like his daddy, big curly hair and all. I loved my baby and he seemed to be growing up so fast. He was already turning three with his smart ass.

"Okay, well I will open it for you after you eat, okay, baby?" I scooped him up and kissed his cheek.

"Fair enough."

"Fair enough," I mocked him. He'd heard his dad say that and now he said it all the damn time, to every damn thing.

"Put his ass down," Oden said, frowning his sexy face up. "He's a big boy, he can walk, right man?"

"Yeah!" our son shouted.

"So, he's still my baby."

Although Oden Jr. had been perfectly fine with me carrying him, he was suddenly anxious to get down. As soon as I placed him to his feet, he ran off.

"You look nice," Oden pulled me close and kissed me. Holding my face, he sucked my lips and kissed me harder. "Mm," he grumbled, grabbing a handful of my ass.

"Stop before you start something." I nudged him and headed towards the kitchen to find Bella tasting one of the snack pastries I'd made.

"I'm sorry, I'm just so hungry," she said rubbing her pregnant belly.

"It's fine. Go sit down, and tell Tasmine to come help me bring out the dishes."

"K," she grabbed one more pastry and walked out.

She and Santino were now married like Oden and I, and they resided in both Los Angeles and Las Vegas since Bella was getting her next degree here. Her and Santino's relationship was for real something out of the movies. I loved them.

Bella was currently pregnant with their first child, while in medical school. She was determined to be a sports medicine doctor like she'd always dreamed of being. It felt good seeing her accomplish what she'd set out to do.

"I heard you needed me," Tasmine came into the kitchen, and she and Anton's daughter, Taniya, came running in behind her. She was two years old, and very advanced.

"You need my help, too?" Taniya asked in her little voice, with her small hand holding her Barbie doll tightly.

"Yes, baby. Take these napkins and don't drop them, okay?" I handed them down to her. She nodded before running out of the kitchen with them.

Tasmine and Anton had just gotten married a month ago, and I couldn't be happier for them. She'd agreed to move out to Nevada permanently, so I had her close, which I loved.

She'd gotten a few clients for her accounting business, so she, too, was living her dream, assisting the rich in budgeting. I'd never run across anyone that loved math, and almost didn't think it was possible until I met her.

"And you can take these plates." I handed them to her.

Tasmine and I started bringing the food and silverware out to the table, as everyone else sat situated. Once everything was on the tabletop, we all sat down and prayed over the food. The conversation began to flow as everyone began filling their plates.

"Is there chocolate cake?" Truman and Chiina's son Truman Jr. or just TJ asked. He was so cute and small, and he loved him some chocolate cake. Chiina said Truman did too.

"Yes, baby, I brought some just in case," Chiina chuckled. I smiled as I watched her interact with TJ.

"Chill, man, before you get fat. Being fat doesn't run in our family, but you may change that," Truman tickled him, making him giggle as he ate some macaroni.

Seeing Truman as a husband and father was still odd to me, but I guess people really could change. He'd been like a new man with Chiina, and I was happy for them both.

"Sister, you did a good job with this stuffing," Shayne complimented me as she adjusted her son and my adorable nephew, Landon in his booster seat. He looked exactly like her husband Lloyd, with his deep chocolate skin and curly hair.

"Thank you."

"You should get her recipe," Lloyd joked.

"Umm, excuse me, nigga, I know how to make stuffing. Wait until you taste mine and then talk," Shayne playfully rolled her eyes. He bit his lip and kissed her in response. He clearly got off on her having an attitude.

Shayne still danced in Las Vegas shows, but she had more prominent roles now. I loved being able to see free shows, and witness her do what she's always wanted to do. My mom and dad had even come out to watch her a couple of times, which meant a lot since they initially didn't approve.

"Let's open this champagne," Anton chimed in, holding the bottle up. We all agreed with head nods and mumbles. I know my ass was ready.

"I brought a couple bottles of Ace too." Santino lifted a bag and that got us all excited. Yeah, tonight was gonna be extra good.

Santino, as you know, signed with the Rams during his sophomore year. He didn't come back to UNLV obviously, but he and Bella made it work. He was always visiting when he could, since he had a place out here, and then she would always visit him in California. I liked that she had a home in both states because when I went home to L.A., a lot of times I got to see her.

We continued eating, drinking champagne, talking, joking, and just enjoying one another's time. Life had been crazy but good for us all, and I wouldn't change any of it.

If you're wondering where Perry is, all I know is that one night she went to Miami with her boyfriend Cash and never came back, transferring schools and everything. That was two years ago, and her damn parents didn't even know. I did see that she and Cash were having a baby on Instagram some months ago, so at least I know she's alive and happy. Still to this day, I'm surprised by the change in Perry, but I'm happy that we all found love.

"We're gonna make another baby tonight?" Oden whispered in my ear, making me chuckle like a little schoolgirl.

"Sounds like a plan," I pecked his sexy, full lips.

For the rest of the night, we enjoyed our guests. We drank, listened to music, joked, swam in the pool, and just had a really good time. I never imagined my life would be this good, and I never expected it to be filled with so many great new people. I just knew I would grow old with Emery and Brian, but that didn't happen and I was thankful.

As for those two, I had no idea what was going on with them and I didn't care to find out. I guess you stopped caring about bullshit and bullshit ass people when you fuck around and fall in love with a real one; and I had definitely done that.

FIN

Join our mailing list to get a notification when Shvonne Latrice has another release! Text **SHVONNE** to **66866** to join!

To submit a manuscript for publishing consideration, email us at fcpublishinggroup@gmail.com

www.ingramcontent.com/pod-product-compliance
Lightning Source LLC
Chambersburg PA
CBHW061337310726
48974CB00001B/80